The Case of Dr. Dude

Books by Judith Lucci

Michaela McPherson Mysteries
The Case of Dr. Dude
The Case of the Dead Dowager
The Case of the Man Overboard
The Case of the Very Dead Lawyer
The Case of the Missing Parts

Alex Destephano Novels
Chaos at Crescent City Medical Center
The Imposter
Viral Intent
Toxic New Year
Evil: Finding St. Germaine
RUN For Your Life

Artsy Chicks Mysteries
The Most Wonderful Crime of the Year: The Golden Rings of Christmas
The Most Awfullest Crime of the Year: Gawd Almighty and the Corn
The Most Glittery Crime of the Year: The Jewel Heist
The Most Slippery Crime of the Year: Death on the Slopes

Other Books
Beach Traffic: The Ocean Can Be Deadly
Ebola: What You Must Know to Stay Safe
Meandering, Musing & Inspiration for the Soul

Coming Soon: Sonia Amon, MD Medical Thriller Series by Judith Lucci

The Case of Dr. Dude

A Michaela McPherson Mystery

A NOVEL BY

JUDITH LUCCI

Bluestone Valley Publishing

Harrisonburg, Virginia

Judith Lucci

Acknowledgements

Thanks to all of you! Thanks to everyone who has listened to me dream aloud about Dr. Dude, the Michaela series or my Alex Destephano medical thrillers. Thanks to all of you who follow my work. I'd like to give a special shout out to my wonderful author friend, Eric J. Gates, a masterful thriller writer and author of The Cull Series and Outsourced, among others. Eric has been my technical expert in most things military, explosive, and gun-like. I'd also like to thank Mike Talbert, Richmond Police Department Detective (Retired) for his time in consulting with me about crime in my hometown. Kudos to my wonderful author friend, Sarah Mallery for her thoughtful review of Dr. Dude.

About the Author

Dr. Judith Lucci is a Wall Street Journal, USA Today and Amazon best-selling author. She is the award-winning author of the Alexandra Destephano Medical Thriller and the Michaela McPherson "Two Sleuth's and a Dog" Crime fiction series. Her newest series, Artzy Chicks Mysteries, features a group of eccentric and talented but zany artists in their Art Gallery at a Mountain Resort.

In 2017, 'Viral Intent' (Book 3) Alexandra Destephano Series) was awarded a Gold Medal by Readers' Favorites for 'Best Political Thriller' as was her crime thriller 'The Case of Dr. Dude' (Michaela McPherson #1) for a Gold Medal for 'Best Amateur Sleuth of 2017. 'The Most Wonderful Crime of the Year' won an additional gold medal for 'Best Holiday Read' of 2017.

Her favorite things are reading, writing, art and animals. In her spare time, she teaches painting, and raises money for needy causes. Judith lives with her family and her dogs in the Shenandoah Valley of Virginia. She loves to connect with her readers and is available at judithlucciwrites@gmail.com. Check out her website at judithlucci.com and sign-up to her newsletter for a free book.

DEDICATION

It's appalling but true. Every year millions of people, approximately twenty-seven million adults and thirteen million children, are bought, sold, and smuggled into modern-day slavery. People are trafficked in every state in America and in every country in the world. Eighty percent of persons trafficked are women and children. Victims are beaten, starved, sold for sex and forced to work as prostitutes or slaves. Oftentimes young people are trafficked for their organs that are sold on the black market for exorbitant prices. Children as young as seven years of age are captured by terrorist organizations and made to become suicide bombers. This novel is dedicated to the victims of human trafficking and the international agencies who are working to stop it. The toll on society, both personal and psychological, and the impact trafficking has on global health issues must be addressed.

Chapter 1

"Please don't do this to me. Why are you hurting me?" the young voice cried. "I don't know who you are!"

A large hand with dirty, stained fingernails grabbed her shoulder roughly. "Shut up," he growled as he shook her ferociously until her teeth chattered.

Her tattooed abductor terrified her as she focused on the snake tattoo on his hand. "Just let me go, and I promise I won't tell anyone," the young woman whimpered. "I promise."

"Shut up, or I'll really hurt you," the savage voice promised as he slapped her face and slammed her into the side of the vehicle. He shoved her again and bent her body like a pretzel. His body covered hers, making it impossible for anyone to see her from three sides.

The young woman's voice raised to feverish pitch as another person pushed her into the trunk of her car. The monster pinned her arms behind her head and shoved her elbow against the spare tire. She winced as an excruciating, burning pain sent stinging shocks into her head. She cried uncontrollably and could not stop shaking.

"Shut your yammer," the man hissed softly, his face so close to her blindfold she could smell his foul breath. "If you don't, it'll be much worse for you," he warned as he loomed over her, making her feel small and defenseless. She couldn't see him through her translucent blindfold but sensed he had dark hair.

"Please, please, please just let me go. My father will give you a reward. He has a lot of money." As she made the promise, her teeth chattered violently. Tears streamed down her face, making her cough. She was unable to brush them away.

The man laughed a slow, evil sound that caused chill bumps on her arms. "Your father doesn't have enough money to stop what we have planned for you, not nearly enough, so shut your pretty mouth and be quiet before I put your lights off."

A wave of fresh sobs exploded from the terrified woman as she lay in the trunk of the car. Her body shuddered from head to toe, and she couldn't control the tears streaming from her face.

The noise infuriated her assailant as he glowered at his helpless victim. A feeling of euphoria settled over him. He loved watching helpless women squirm. He shook her head and pounded it against the trunk of the car.

"I told you to shut up. Stop hitting your head, and if you don't stop screaming, I'm gonna cut your voice box out. Do you understand?"

Allison nodded and coughed.

"Be quiet." Allison heard a female voice speak for the first time. "I'd hate to mess up your pretty face," she said in a singsong voice that frightened the young woman more than the snarl and guttural voice of the man.

A wave of fresh sobs exploded from the scared woman, as she lay helpless in the trunk of the car. She thrashed around wildly. Where'd the woman come from? She tried to see her through her blindfold, but she couldn't. For some reason, she was more frightened of the woman. Her body shook, and her teeth chattered.

"I hope the bitch doesn't mess herself up," the man commented.

The woman stared at him. "You know what to do, so just do it."

The man hesitated for an instant, and the woman pushed him aside and glared at the helpless young captive.

That was when the lights went out for Allison Massie. The woman stepped back with an evil smile on her face and murmured, "Well, I guess I shut her up."

Despite the chokehold, the woman glared at him defiantly.

The tattooed man let her go and pushed her against the car. "Get back in the office and do damage control," he snarled, "and don't ever cross me again." He jumped in the car and headed west.

Chapter 2

Retired Richmond homicide detective Michaela McPherson tapped her pencil impatiently against her iPad as she peered over her reading glasses at her friend, Dorothy Borghese. Dorothy sat ramrod straight in an overstuffed brocade chair in Michaela's living room sipping tea, her pinkie finger raised elegantly she rattled on and on about a well-known Richmond dentist who was Richmond's claim to fame as the "dentist to the stars."

Mic yawned at the drone of Dottie's well-modulated chatter as she shared everything she knew about the not-so-mysterious Dr. Nicholas Smirkowitz, Richmond's premier cosmetic dentist. She tried to focus on the conversation as her eyes moved toward the double front windows in her living room where eight inches of freshly fallen snow dominated the small front yard of her Fan District home. It was a wet, heavy snow, and the massive pine tree in her front yard sagged under the weight.

"Boy, would you look at that snow. I thought we had our last storm on Valentine's Day," she said. "I was hoping so, anyway."

Dottie pursed her brightly colored lips. "Really, Michaela, are you even listening to me?" Mic could tell she had annoyed her by the impatience in her voice. "You were much more respectful when you were a real police officer, and I needed help."

Michaela rolled her eyes as Dottie continued. "This is important. I think something has happened to the poor girl."

Mic snapped back to attention when she heard the alarm in Dottie's voice. She did her best to look apologetic. "Sorry, Dottie, I have a bunch of stuff in my head, and I guess my mind wandered."

Dottie folded her hands tightly in her lap and sniffed her voice frosty as the outside air. "Well, perhaps I should come back when you're not so busy and can make some time for an old friend." She stood to leave, obviously peeved.

"No, Dottie, really. You've got my attention, I promise," she said, hoping her good friend would sit back down.

Dottie hesitated a moment. "Well, okay, since you insist."

Michaela smiled to herself and hoped Dottie didn't see her. After all, Dottie was an aristocrat. She was descended from an Italian count who traced their family roots back to Papal Rome in the 1700s. Dottie was, in fact, an Italian Countess by marriage and had her own line of royal blood flowing through her veins. She looked and acted every bit the part with her silver hair styled in a lovely updo and perfectly painted nails. Her outfit was impeccable and expensive. She sported a suede skirt, cashmere sweater, and expensive leather and wool-lined snow boots. A former Olympic swimmer, Dottie at age eighty-two was in great shape. She looked as though she belonged at someone's country estate outside of Rome or a country chateau in Provence.

Mic sighed and sucked it up, willing herself to listen. "Okay now, Dottie, what were you saying about the dentist? You're talking about Dr. Dude, right?"

Dottie gave her a broad smile and continued eagerly. "Yes. Dr. Dude, Nicholas Smirkowitz, the man who had the high profile divorce a couple of years ago."

Mic nodded. "Yeah, I know him. The one who is always on TV. I see his mug every night after the late news. I've never liked him, but go on."

"I admit it. I'm a nosey old lady. But you know I have enjoyed a pretty successful career as an armchair sleuth - not to mention our joint ventures in crime solving. Yesterday I was having lunch at the Jefferson with my good friend Margaret, and she mentioned her granddaughter, Allison, had finished dental hygienist school at VCU and had an appointment with Dr. Dude for a job. Margaret was worried that Allison would work for such a 'shyster' and tried to discourage her from going to the interview. In fact, Margaret was frightened and uncomfortable about the whole thing."

Michaela knew Margaret Massie, Dottie's old Virginia blueblood friend. "Frightened? Why would Margaret be frightened of a dentist?"

Dorothy raised her shoulders and sat up even straighter. "Allison had a friend who told her that young women disappear from Dr. Dude's office and never return."

Michaela laughed. "Disappear? People just don't disappear. There must be an explanation."

Dottie continued, nonplussed with Mic's matter-of-fact position. "I agree, but I told Margaret that every time I see Dr. Dude, he has an entirely new dental staff, and Margaret became more upset." She paused for a moment. "Have you noticed that he has quite a turnover in his staff?"

Mic shook her head. "I wouldn't know. I don't go to him anymore. I think he's a creep and a slime ball." She paused and noticed the concern on Dottie's face. "Um, so, he's your dentist?"

Dottie nodded. "He's everybody's dentist, or at least everybody who is anybody." She sniffed. "He's Richmond's number one dentist, and he's famous."

Michaela interrupted her. "Not everyone. I haven't seen him for five years. I quit going to him a while back. He's not my dentist."

Dottie ignored her and continued. "I've been seeing him forever. You know, I go there regularly, at least every six months, and every time I go, I hardly recognize a face in the office. Now, they all seem to come from foreign countries except for that mean, horrible bookkeeper and office manager. She's been there forever."

She paused, toyed with a strand of silver hair that had become loose and continued. "The rest of the staff are mostly Russian or South American, I think." Dottie wrinkled her forehead. "I'm not sure of the accents."

Mic pursed her lips but said nothing. "Oh, yeah, the bookkeeper. Is that the woman named Tilda? She's pretty awful. I had a bill insurance didn't cover and she called me and was quite rude. I said something to Dr. Smirkowitz, but I see she's still there."

"Yes, she's definitely still there. I think she's the one who runs everybody off." Dottie kept babbling away, her hands waving in the air, her startling blue eyes flashed with emotion. She was truly in a twitter about the changes in Dr. Dude's office.

"I see Dr. Dude's picture all over town and he's on TV too," Mic remarked. "Does he still think he's Jimmy Buffett and wear the parrot shirts in his office?"

Dottie nodded, "Yes, he does. He's on all of the billboards on Interstate 95 with his picture and the words "Dentist to the Stars."

Mic groaned and slammed down her coffee mug. "As I said, he's a loser. Margaret's probably right. Her granddaughter shouldn't work there."

Dottie ignored her and droned on, her hands waving excitedly. "Everybody calls him Dr. Dude because he's such a snappy dresser. Looks like GQ, even in his dental whites."

Mic shrugged and raised her eyebrows, "He's all over the place, slinking around with his patients. He gives me the

14

willies, the way he skulks around. That's why I don't go there anymore... that and his horrible bookkeeper."

Dottie's voice was indignant. "He's a good dentist. I've had hundreds of compliments on my veneers! He does great work, and he never gets in my face."

Mic laughed. "Dottie, you're hardly a sweet young thing anymore. In fact, were you ever sweet?"

Dottie ignored Mic's jab on her age and continued. "Dr. Dude has movie stars for patients. They come to Richmond, and he works on their teeth. Apparently, he doesn't give them the creeps." She shot Mic a dirty look. "And, as a matter of fact, he did bother me a few years ago, but now I'm pretty used to him. I think it's just his way."

Mic stared at her, as she remembered a story she'd heard about the dentist some years ago. Back when she'd worked vice, there'd been speculation that he'd crossed sexual boundaries with some of his staff. If she remembered correctly, the complaint was unfounded. Dr. Dude had been around for a long time, and his practice was booming.

"So you like him," Mic's voice was sharp.

Dottie nodded, her gold bracelets banging as she waved her enthusiasm, "Yes, I do. He's a good dentist. He does turn over a lot of staff, but he considers himself an artist, or at least that's what he told me one day."

Mic stared as her, "He told you he thinks he's an artist? What's that supposed to mean?"

Dottie nodded. "Yes, he said he changes the way people look and makes them more attractive, more beautiful. He considers himself an artist."

Mic shrugged her shoulders. "I rest my case. He's an idiot. He's a dentist for God's sake. A dentist and nothing else. In fact, he's kinda like a mechanic the way I see it. He fixes teeth."

Dottie gritted her teeth and gave her a stubborn glare. "I think he's more of an artist than a mechanic. Mechanics fix your car."

"Yeah, and Dr. Dude fixes your teeth. What's the difference?"

"I think he's an artist, so he's probably temperamental — you know like a surgeon — and that's why he keeps losing staff." She paused for a moment and looked out the window. "He probably throws things and has hissy fits, like a lot of surgeons do."

Mic smiled at her and shook her head. "Do you know his current staff?"

Dottie shook her head. "No, but I used to love his former dental hygienist, and she's the reason I kept going back, but now she's gone." She paused for a moment as her smart phone lying on Mic's glass-top coffee table vibrated and signaled a new text message.

"Are you gonna check that?" Mic asked, eyeing the phone.

Dorothy smoothed her updo and removed a pearl earring as she massaged her earlobe. "In a minute, hold your water; I'm in the middle of talking to you. I have a rule that a cell phone never interrupts a real conversation."

Mic shrugged her shoulders, and her eyes returned to the front window. She got up, walked across the living room, and looked outside. It was a winter wonderland. The snow contained fine particles of ice that pinged the window as it fell. It looked as though another inch had fallen.

"It's sleeting out there. The roads are gonna be a mess," she told Dottie.

Dottie turned and stared out of the window. "Yes, it's a mess. If I need to, I'll have Henry pick me up. Anyway, as I was saying, the old dental hygienist was great. She really knew her stuff, and I spent most of my appointment time with her."

"So what happened? Did she leave?" Mic didn't much care. She was becoming bored with the conversation.

Dottie ignored her question. "For me, it's generally a quick in and out with Dr. Dude. He comes in, peeks in my mouth and says stuff like, 'Hello, my dear, how are we today?'"

Michaela frowned. "How are we? What does that mean? Doesn't he know how he is? I hate stupid talk like that. It's like talking to a five-year-old kid. That's just crap."

Dottie continued, non-plussed. "Sometimes he says, 'Your x-rays look good for your age.' Now that angers me." Dottie raised her eyebrows in contempt.

Mic laughed. "I'm sure that did make you mad, Dottie. You still think you're forty."

Dottie shot her a dirty look and said, "I'm in better shape than most forty-year-olds. Most of the time Dr. Dude says something like, 'Hello Countess, you need this and that done, and it will cost somewhere around $10,000.'" Dottie sniffed with distain. "He is a bit more expensive than anyone else."

Mic nodded. "No kidding. Guy's a rip-off. Where'd your hygienist friend go? Did she leave or did you ever hear anything about her?"

Dottie shrugged her shoulders. "I've no idea. I asked everyone where she went last time I was there, and they said they didn't know — just that one day she didn't show up for work. I thought that was pretty strange because of all the staff in that practice, she was the oldest and seemed to be the most responsible, at least of the clinical people."

"Oldest? What does that mean? I've never seen anybody in there over thirty — the few times I've been there. I always thought that was pretty strange, particularly in view of his media profile and that scandalous divorce."

Dottie nodded and said, "That was a nasty bit of business. You know, Mic, I was concerned about my hygienist friend, so I called the state agency that manages her license and according to them, she still lives here in Chesterfield. The next time I went in, I asked Dr. Dude himself where she was and guess what he told me?"

"I can hardly wait to hear," Mic said, a touch of sarcasm in her voice. "But first of all, did he have on his parrot shirt and was Jimmy Buffett playing in the background?"

Dottie gave a quick laugh. "Of course, he had on his parrot shirt, and he sported a spray-on tan. I have never seen him without a parrot shirt or some island wear, rope bracelets, shell necklaces and stuff like that. Margaritaville radio was streaming through the speakers."

Mic shook her head in disgust. "I couldn't stand the guy. Isn't he a bigwig in that Holy Roller church in the west end?"

Dottie nodded. "He is. I think he paid for the new wing or something like that."

Mic was thoughtful. Dude was just plain gross and icky and suspicious. "So, what did he say about the dental hygienist?"

Dottie raised her eyebrows, "He said she called him up one day and told him she was in North Dakota and that she had gotten married. Said she wouldn't be back. I think that's nonsense. Do you believe it?" Dottie glared at Mic.

Mic considered the story for a moment. "So… she's supposedly in Chesterfield, but she lives in North Dakota. I guess she's not practicing as a dental hygienist."

"Probably not, but what do you think?"

Mic turned away from the window and returned to her chair. "Well, I don't know. I guess it's possible, but it sounds strange. Did you say anything about it to the other dental technicians or the office staff?"

"Yes, I did. None of them believed the story. None of them thought she went to North Dakota. One of them said she wouldn't have gotten married because she didn't like men. In fact, she had a girlfriend, and they were getting married in D.C. as soon as they could."

Michaela was quiet. Now that was a bit suspicious. "She was gay? Wow. That puts a new light on things."

Dottie nodded. "Yes, that's what they said. She was a beautiful girl, though."

Mic's detective instinct flared. "So, Dottie, you've got my attention. Let's go over this again.   You know Dr. Dude, and he's your dentist, right?" she questioned in a patient voice.

Dorothy arched her sculpted, patrician eyebrows and gave Mic the haughty look she'd honed to perfection. "Yes, Michaela, yes, I know Dr. Dude. His real name is Nicholas Smirkowitz. I just told you that, and by the way, now who's treating who like a five-year-old?" she asked in an icy voice.

Michaela smiled. "Come on, Dottie, you know I'm just getting my facts straight. Cut me a break."

Dottie glared at her. "You are apparently the only person in town who doesn't go to him. He has his office over on Monument, and he charges an arm and a leg for everything he does."

Mic shrugged her shoulders. "Yeah. We already established that. All dentists cost a fortune. He's not the only one, I promise you." She dismissed that as unimportant. "I need to go into the kitchen for a second. I'll be right back."

Mic rose from her chair and went into her kitchen where a beef stew simmered gently in a stainless steel Dutch oven.

The luscious smell permeated the dining room and living room. Dottie's stomach grumbled with hunger. "Mmm, that smells divine, Michaela. Whatever are you cooking?" Dottie hollered from the other room.

"What? Come in here," Mic called out.

Dottie made her way into Michaela's beautifully sedate, newly remodeled kitchen and commented, "I just love this kitchen, Michaela. The remodel is beautiful."

"What do you like best, Dottie?"

Dottie's eyes surveyed the kitchen. A fifteen-foot wall of wooden hand-rubbed cherry cabinets, lined the long wall in the kitchen. Black polished granite glistened on base counters, and a stained glass Tiffany fixture surrounded by polished copper and antique pots and pans hung from the ceiling.

"Well, I think I like everything the same, but particularly what's cooking on the stove," Dottie smiled.

Mic grinned at her. "Okay, enough about Dr. Dude and his disappearing dental technicians," Mic said, still stirring the pot. "This Irish stew is special, a new recipe I just tried. I want to try it out it at Biddy's this weekend, and I need a taste-tester."

Dottie peered into the stainless-steel Dutch oven and sniffed. "Wonderful. I'm your girl," she said and smiled happily. "It looks great. Irish stew, you say?"

Mic smiled broadly. "Yeah, but not just any Irish stew. This is an Irish stew made with Guinness. I am serving it at Biddy's on St. Patrick's Day, but first I'm testing it in a few weeks at Shamrock the Rock. It's a new recipe for me but an old one from my father's recipe books. He served it in his pub for eons in Dublin." She ladled a serving for Dottie, who accepted it graciously.

"So I'm the guinea pig, but that's okay. Smells divine. If it's as good as your other stews, it'll be a winner."

Michaela smiled and turned back to the stove and served herself a generous portion. "I also made some brown soda bread. It's great with the stew," she said, as she handed Dottie the ceramic basket full of piping hot bread.

Dottie carried her stew and the basket of bread toward the massive blond oak claw foot table adjacent to the bay window in Michaela's kitchen. "By the way, Michaela, how are things down at Biddy McPherson's? Did you get your problems with the waitstaff worked out?"

Dottie loved to hear Mic's restaurant stories and gossip about the array of young waiters and waitresses who provided great entertainment. Often Michaela was ready to pull out her Glock and shoot them a few times every day, which only added to the drama of the storytelling.

Mic groaned. "I'd rather chase, or be chased by two murderers and a mugger, than handle disputes between my waitresses. Honest to God, they make me crazy," she sighed as she joined Dottie at the kitchen table, a bowl of stew in one hand and a wooden bowl filled with a green salad. She sat the salad next to the homemade Irish soda bread.

Dottie laughed. "Yes, I'm sure, but I know you love mediating. You should give yourself a pat on the back. You haven't killed any of them yet."

"Yet. Yet is the important word in that sentence," Mic said as she poured a glass of Virginia Cabernet for them.

Chapter 3

The young woman woke, terrified, and blindfolded as the vehicle came to an abrupt stop. She could hear sleet and rain pattering on the body of the car. The trunk opened, and a blast of cold air chilled her. Strong arms grabbed her, dragged her through the snow into a building, and threw her on the floor. She lay here, sobbing uncontrollably as the man tied her feet and hands.

"Stay there, you little bitch. Don't try to get away. There are traps set all over this place, and if you step on one, you're dead," the man promised in an angry, yet convincing voice.

She heard the door shut and lay helpless on a pile of hay, covered by smelly blankets. Tears seeped from her eyes and froze on her face. She wished she were dead.

Chapter 4

Dottie chewed on her soda bread. "For a new restaurant, Biddy McPherson's is doing great. You had a good write up in the restaurant column last week and that restaurant critic can be a real pain."

In truth, Dottie had been jealous when Mic had decided to open the bar in memory of her parents. She'd been waiting for Mic to retire for years, so they could solve crimes together. They'd been like Thelma and Louise in years past, and Dottie wanted more of it.

Mic laughed. "Yeah, how well I know. And yeah, I'm happy with the way things are goin'. I'd been saving all of my life to open the place and have been lucky we've done so well. We've got a great manager in place, a fantastic cook who takes direction from me, a bunch of loyal customers, and we're the 'official home away from home' for the Richmond Police Department."

Dottie shook her head "The local watering hole for the RPD. Can't ask for more than that, Michaela. Now that Biddy's is up and running are you gonna do more of your private detective stuff?" she asked, hoping to hear a resounding yes.

Michaela munched her bread. She dipped her spoon into the succulent beef stew and sniffed the aroma before replying. "You know, I probably will. Kind of miss the excitement of police work. I just don't want to have too much work to do all of the time. After all, I am retired." She smiled broadly.

Dottie hid her smile behind a piece of bread. That was just what she'd been hoping to hear. Thelma and Louise would ride again.

Judith Lucci

"Umm, the stew needs more Guinness," Mic said. "I think I cooked it down too much." She pushed her chair back, walked to her refrigerator and reached for another bottle of the Irish stout.

Dottie's mouth dropped open. She couldn't believe what she heard. "The stew is great. You have more energy than anyone I know. I think you can handle both. You were complaining last week about having too much free time."

Dottie paused for a moment and glanced at Angel, Mic's seventy-eight pound retired German Shepherd police dog as he limped into the kitchen to his bed by the fireplace. "Is he okay, Michaela? He's limping pretty badly." Dottie scratched Angel's ears as he passed.

Michaela nodded as she rose from her chair. "Yeah, it's his leg where he took the bullet, but I think his Lyme disease is acting up, too. Dogs are just like us. In this kind of weather, they need their medicine. I need to give him his anti-inflammatory. It's so damp outside he's probably hurting worse than usual."

Dottie laughed. "Yes, my bones are hurting today, too and I haven't taken a bullet. It's the damp weather."

Mic moved towards the island, removed Angel's Meloxicam from the dog drawer, and drew up the dosage for an eighty-pound dog. She set it on the counter as she reached for his heartburn medicine. She called softly to Angel as he struggled off his dog bed by the kitchen hearth.

"Come on, baby, this'll make you feel so much better." Mic said. She sat on the kitchen rug next to Angel, her faithful friend and protector. Angel dutifully took his medicine and was rewarded with a beef jerky treat. She sat on the floor with Angel and rubbed the dog's ears as the dog struggled to hunker into his bed.

25

Dottie watched, mesmerized by the obvious attachment between the dog and his mistress. The love between the two was crystal-clear and the scene was poignant. Mic and Angel were inseparable, and truth be told, Angel had saved Mic's butt more than a few times.

Mic returned to the table and continued to eat until she heard Dottie's phone vibrating again in the living room. Another text.

She stood. "I'm getting your phone because someone wants to talk to you badly."

Dottie nodded, her mouth full of bread. She smiled as Angel's tail thudded on the floor as his mistress passed.

A few seconds later, Mic returned with Dottie's phone, her face serious. "It's a second text from Margaret, plus she's called three times. You need to pay more attention to your phone."

Dottie took the phone from Mic and read it. "Oh no," she wailed, "Allison never came home from her job interview at the dentist's office. Margaret's hysterical. Should we call the police?"

Michaela read the fear in Dottie's eyes and concern for Allison shot up her spine. "Tell Margaret to call the police immediately, and we'll check with them as well."

Dottie texted Margaret and pushed her plate aside. "I'm going over there. She sounds distraught, almost manic."

Mic nodded, "Call me and give me an update. I'm going downtown to the precinct to check things out, and see if anybody knows anything."

Chapter 5

Mic skillfully maneuvered her SUV into a parking space at her old precinct. Angel usually traveled with her everywhere she went, but she'd left him home today because of the weather. She groaned as a blast of frigid air smacked her in the face when she opened her door, and she immediately wished her butt were still firmly molded into her heated seat. The snow was still coming down quickly and fine particles of ice cut into her face. She pushed up the steps of the precinct. The double glass doors were hard to open in the wind. Finally, she pried the door wide enough so she could squeeze through and walked briskly toward the bullpen. Her old friends hollered, waved, and clapped her on the back as she made her way across the room.

Lt. Steve Stoddard, her old boss, was sitting behind his desk in his "corner office," better described as a wall of glass cinderblocks. Michaela hated glass cinderblocks. They screwed up her vision and made her dizzy. She carefully maneuvered her way around the block wall.

She knocked briskly, and Steve motioned her in grinning. "Hey, Mic, what's up?" He gave her an appraising look. "What are you doing here on a nasty, snowy day? If I were retired, I'd be at home drinking whiskey in front of the fireplace rather than show up here." He stood and kissed her on the cheek. "Coffee?"

Mic shook her head and extracted two large Starbucks' cups from a white bag. "Nope, here's a gift. You don't think I'm trashing my stomach with precinct swill anymore do you? It's taken me more than a year to get my heartburn under control from drinking that crap for twenty years."

Steve chortled, "Nah, guess not. Good decision, and by the way, thanks." He waved his cup in her direction.

Mic nodded and smiled sweetly, knowing full well he saw right through her fake demeanor and gift of coffee. You couldn't fool the boss. Stoddard knew she wanted something.

"What'd you want? Don't give me that smile crap. I know you're here for something. Otherwise you'd never come out on a snowy day with... wait a minute," he looked down on the floor beside her, "Where's Angel?"

"He's at home. His hip's bothering him, and it's such a wet, damp snow that I left him protesting in his bed by the fireplace in the kitchen."

Steve shook his head and grinned. "Dogs are just like us. They get the same diseases and everything."

Mic nodded at her old boss. He was a handsome man with salt and pepper hair and deep green eyes. More importantly, he was honorable and fair. She guessed he was approaching fifty. She loved the dimple on the left side of his face, and she remembered well his ears smoked when she pissed him off, which over the years had been often.

Stoddard picked up his coffee cup and savored the aroma. Michaela could tell he was done with the small talk, even if she was one of his favorite people. "What's up, Mic? Whaddaya want?"

She locked eyes with her old boss and smiled. "What makes you think I want anything? Maybe I just came down here to bring you coffee."

Stoddard shook his head. "Never. You be nice? Nah. In a snowstorm, never? Not gonna happen. Now, whaddaya want?"

"Dottie has a friend whose granddaughter went on a job interview yesterday and never came home." She searched his eyes and hoped he had heard something about a missing kid or something. His eyes were blank.

He waited for more. "And … is there anything else?"

"Her interview was over at that expensive dentist's office near Stuart Circle. You know, the one with all of the ads on TV and the palm trees in his office. The one who wears the parrot shirts and thinks he's a surfer stud?"

Michaela saw his pupils dilate ever so slightly. He cleared his throat "You mean that creep, Dr. Nicholas Smirkowitz? Better known by us as 'Dr. Dude' because he thinks he's so slick?"

Mic's stomach lurched. "Yeah, that's him. What do you have on him?"

Steve shook his head and threw his pen on the legal pad in disgust. His eyes blazed. "Nothing, not a damned thing. Just a lot of suspicion. He's smart, clever and hires a lot of — let me be politically correct here — non-traditional women or women from Central and South America. He hires most of his staff from the Richmond Education Center where a lot of immigrants go to learn a quick skill. You know the place, Mic, right?"

Mic nodded. "Yeah. Used to go do talks there all the time about police work to try to help the new American citizens understand the law enforcement system. I think they have a dental assistance program there, too."

Stoddard nodded. "They do. Smirkowitz is on their Advisory Board. He selects young women recently off the boat or recommended to him by local high schools and pays their tuition. In return, they have to work for him for two years."

Michaela frowned. She didn't like what she was hearing. "Sounds like he turns them into indentured servants."

Stoddard nodded, "Yeah, more or less. They either work their stint, or he socks them with a two-thousand dollar tuition bill. He pretty much owns them."

"Why's he on your radar?" she asked, as her mind exploded with possibilities.

Steve shrugged his shoulders. "Because he stinks and because I want to get him. He's been on our radar for years. We get complaints from people all the time who insist he's 'touched them inappropriately' or 'gotten in their space' or something along those lines. We had one case where a mother came in here in hysterics crying and accused Smirkowitz of kidnapping her daughter. This happened a couple of years ago, but nothing ever came of it."

Mic's brain clicked through potential possibilities. "You got the lady's name. I'd like to go see her. Did you ever find the girl?"

He shook his head. "Nah. We went out there a couple of times, but the mother clammed up. You can check with Slade McKane over in vice. He's got the mother's contact info." He paused at her straight in the eyes. "McKane hates Smirkowitz more'n me."

Mic nodded, "I'll talk to him. McKane's got a good nose for this stuff. What do you think? What's the gut sayin' to you?"

Lieutenant Stoddard laughed shortly. "Oh, I'm positive that stuff's goin' on. Probably has been for years. We've just never been able to get him. The guy's a snake and he's smart. I'd love to get him."

Mic nodded. "Yeah, me too. Let's do it."

"It'd make my day. Keep me in the loop, Mic." He thought for a moment and added, "This young woman could fit the MO for Smirkowitz. She's about the right age.

"Done." She started to leave, but turned around at the door. "By the way, we've got a great Irish stew with Guinness down at Biddy's this weekend. You should come and give it a taste test."

"I'll be there tomorrow night for sure—for happy hour. Save me a couple of pints and a bowl of stew."

Mic gave him a thumb's up, as he added, "Be careful, Mic, I think this guy's a sleaze, but he's smart and dangerous. I've always thought he was mixed up with a mob or syndicate, but we've never had the evidence. Keep your wits about you."

Michaela laughed. "Not to worry, Steve. Angel, Maggie, and me." She pointed to her back where she carried her Glock. "We'll be fine."

"I'm off to see Slade." She gave a small wave and beamed him a smile.

"Watch yourself, Mic! You know you like him." Stoddard smiled coyly.

Mic glared at him. "Down, boy, we're not going there again."

"Thanks for the coffee," Stoddard said and waved the cup at her again.

She flashed him a smile. "Yeah, next time you're buyin'." She shut his office door.

Chapter 6

Countess Dorothy Borghase gingerly picked her way through the mounting snow as she maneuvered around the snow-laden plants and shrubs outside Margaret's enormous, Windsor Farms home. Dottie had decided that since the roads seemed okay, she'd head out to Margaret's house and get the story directly from the horse's mouth. Dottie was like that. She didn't want any second-hand information. She supposed it was just part of her noble upbringing. She wanted to be in charge and know everything. She thought her friends should tell her everything first. Probably part of the competitiveness she learned as an Olympic silver medal winner as well. After all, I am an aristocrat. Well, maybe not royal like William, Kate, and the queen, but nevertheless an aristocrat.

Margaret Massie's neighborhood was the epitome of old Richmond. Designed in 1926, Windsor Farms was one of Richmond's first planned neighborhoods. It was designed like an English village, with curvy streets with English names like Dover, Canterbury, and Berkshire. The neighborhood was dotted with various architectural styles; but the most common by far were Colonial Revival and Cape Cods. Margaret's brick colonial mansion was located on an eighteen-acre parcel that extended down to the historic James River. Dorothy had attended dozens of parties, both inside and outside of the estate, always catered by the best Richmond had to offer and attended by local Bluebloods and moneyed people from D.C. and the first families of Virginia. Also included were Margaret's eccentric collection of artist and actor friends.

Margaret's husband, Beau, was wealthy. In truth, he was richer than most everyone and was arrogant and opinionated. Dottie wasn't sure she really liked him, and pretty much felt the feeling was mutual. She'd managed to tolerate him over the years since Margaret was her best friend. They'd been through thick and thin, and Margaret, even though she was pampered beyond belief, was a good soul, and spent a great deal of her time helping others less fortunate than herself. In the sixty years Dottie had known her, Margaret had managed charity balls, raised money for the homeless and unfortunate people, childcare centers, dog shelters, the Museum, and just about every charitable cause that had come her way.

Dottie and Margaret had lived their lives together. They'd ruled Richmond as ingénues, newlyweds, matrons, and now dowagers. The two had been docents at the Valentine Museum of Richmond that chronicled the life and history of Richmond. They organized and managed the Junior League of Richmond. They'd raised their children together, and essentially managed St. Christopher's and St. Catherine's private schools for about twenty years. Beau Massie, a University of Virginia alumni, along with his sons, had partied in box seats at Scott Stadium on Alumni field at 'the University.' They'd covered each other's asses too many times to tell and spent many an afternoon hunkered down either in the vodka or sherry bottle. They'd shared a lifetime of memories and were the best of friends.

Dottie carefully maneuvered her tall, elegant frame up the de-iced porch and rang the massive brass doorbell. Margaret's maid answered. "Good afternoon, Countess."

Dottie nodded stiffly and asked for Margaret.

The maid ushered her into the foyer and went to get Margaret who stumbled in shortly thereafter and fell into Dottie's arms, her eyes red from crying. Her maid followed her everywhere she went.

The two older women hugged for a moment, and the maid assisted Margaret into the parlor, helped her sit down, and left to get coffee.

Dottie stared at her friend. "Screw the coffee, Marge, we're hitting the bottle. It's five o'clock somewhere, right?"

Margaret started to protest, but Dottie was firm. "Just a small glass or two of sherry. We're not drinking the entire bottle today, I promise." She waved away Margaret's objections and smiled knowingly. "We've got to keep our wits about us and figure this out. Besides, I'm driving, so I'll just have a snort."

Margaret smiled weakly. "I'm sure a glass of sherry will certainly calm my nerves. What can it hurt?" she asked.

"We'll consider it 'medicine' for your nerves," Dottie suggested.

"I can get Frederick to take you home in the Town Car; it'd be a good idea anyway because when the roads freeze in a few hours we're going to have black ice."

"Perfect." Dottie poured two crystal glasses full of crème sherry from Margaret's cut glass decanter on the sideboard. She handed one to Margaret and said, "Now, catch me up. What's happened?"

Margaret drank deeply from her glass and the golden liquid slid smoothly down her throat and warmed her like gold fire in her veins and belly. She sighed and said, "That's good, Dottie. Just what the doctor would've ordered."

Dottie sat patiently as Margaret enjoyed her 'sherry moment,' as they chose to call them." Has Beau contacted anyone?" she prompted, knowing Margaret's husband could work the world from the top of his money tower downtown and that he would to find his beloved granddaughter.

Margaret shook her head.

34

Dottie looked at the strain on her friend's face as she remembered their lives together. Sixty years had flown by quickly. Now, they'd become a part of Richmond's dowager population where they spent most of their time conducting tours at the Virginia Museum of Fine Arts, having lunch at Bloomingdale's, and talking about people at the country club.

"He called the police chief, but they can't do anything officially until she's missing for twenty-four hours, which," she said as she looked her watch, "will be in just a few hours."

Dottie nodded. "Tell me everything. Everything you know, and I'll get the information to Michaela. Michaela left to go down to her old precinct to talk to the lieutenant in charge just as soon as I got your text."

Margaret smiled gratefully. "Michaela. God bless her. She's just the best. We'll be able to depend on her."

Dottie nodded firmly. "Yes, no question. She'll find Allison, and I'm going to help her." So tell me, what do you know?"

Margaret looked uncertain. "Not much. Allison was staying here. She has been for a few weeks. Her parents are still in Europe but should be home late tonight. As I told you the other day, she finished dental hygienist school at VCU and graduated in December. She traveled with her parents for a while and decided to get a job to put her degree to work."

Dottie nodded impatiently, "I know, I know. Why'd she go to Dr. Dude's place? We both know the rumors about him and young women."

Margaret gave Dottie a stern look. "I don't agree with all of those rumors. She chose Dr. Smirkowitz because of his prestige and his work. There's more than one story out

35

there. Nicholas Smirkowitz has the best, most lucrative practice of cosmetic dentistry in Richmond. She knew she could get the best experience. She's contemplating dental school, you know." Margaret paused for a moment as her eyes filled with tears.

Dottie sat impatiently and sipped her sherry. "Yes, yes, go on."

Margaret gave Dottie a peevish look. "Just be patient, Dottie, I'm talking as fast as I can. I'm a little stressed, you know."

Dottie nodded. "I'm sorry. I just want to help as best I can."

"She'd finished her travels and decided to get a job, and Dr. S. had an opening, so she applied. She called on Monday, the interview was two yesterday, Wednesday, and she never came home. She didn't call or text. I didn't get worried until about six last evening when she didn't show up for dinner." Margaret paused for a moment. "I thought she'd gone shopping or met a friend for dinner, but nevertheless, she'd have still called me."

Dottie nodded again.

"She's just so sweet and thoughtful. She's a perfect granddaughter," Margaret said as her face crumpled into tears. She pulled a tissue out of her pocket.

"Margaret, don't get so upset, at least until I can get all the information to tell Mic. Did you call Dr. Smirkowitz's office?"

Margaret nodded and gave Dottie a dirty look. "Of course, I did. The office staff said she'd left about three-thirty. I talked to Smirkowitz himself, who assured me she had the job and had left in the afternoon after a very delightful and fruitful interview."

Dottie rolled her eyes. "Was Smirkowitz there when you called to check on her?"

She shook her head. "No, or maybe I should say that I don't know. I called his service, and he called me about nine o'clock last night. He seemed surprised and concerned she wasn't home."

Dottie was quiet, waiting for more. Margaret remained silent. "Is there anything else?"

Margaret shook her head as tears streamed down her face. "No, not really. I called several of her friends, but they hadn't seen her. I don't know anything. Only that she is missing." Margaret brushed tears from her eyes, blew her nose and reached for her sherry glass.

Dottie stood up, paced the room, and returned with the decanter of sherry and a box of tissues. "I'm sure Mic will check the traffic cams and get back with us. At least we'll be able to track where she went in her car."

A flush spread across Margaret's face. "Good. If Michaela can find Allison, I'll buy her a new restaurant. In fact, I'll buy her anything she wants." She pushed her sherry glass towards Dottie, "Hit me again, friend. I'm feeling better." Margaret smiled and held her empty sherry glass out to Dottie. "Just one more."

Dottie smiled and complied. She rose and glanced out the window. It was still snowing furiously. Maybe she'd just spend the night with her old friend. After all, she did have her own room at Margaret's mansion, and the cook made great dinners. Yes, she'd stay she decided as she reached again for the sherry. She'd have to remember to call Cookie, her housekeeper so she wouldn't worry.

Chapter 7

Mic sat across the table from Slade McKane at the Starbucks near the fan. Slade was a little older than she was, in his late-forties, and attractive in the ways of the dark Irish. Slade was Cajun, and he'd been born on the Irish Bayou just east of New Orleans. He had dark hair and dark eyes and perfect white teeth. Slade was obsessed with his teeth. Mic knew from experience that he never missed a dental appointment and that he kept dental floss in his pocket, desk drawer, and in his wallet. She didn't know why he was obsessed with his teeth; she just knew he was.

She stared into the bottomless pools of brown liquid she'd allowed herself to melt into several times over the years. "So, Slade, how're things in vice?"

Slade smiled at her, and Mic felt a warm feeling in her stomach. "You're lookin' great, Mic. Whatcha here for?"

Mic gave him a bright smile but said nothing.

"To answer your question, same old, same old," Slade said when she didn't respond. "Stuff here is the same as always. Busy, not enough help, lousy budget, crappy leadership. Same old stuff …just the perps have gotten smarter, they have tech skills better than us and there're more of them."

Mic grinned at him. She knew he was right on track. That was one of the reasons she'd taken an early retirement. She had the years she needed, and had become frustrated with budget and safety concerns.

Slade had come to Richmond after fifteen very long years working vice at the NOPD. The man knew his stuff, no question. Besides, he was easy on the eyes, and they'd had a 'thing' a few years ago.

"Nicholas Smirkowitz. AKA Dr. Dude."

A look of disgust filtered across Slade's handsome face.

Mic studied him carefully, "What's your take on Smirkowitz? Do you have anything on him?"

Slade gave her a coy smile. "Now, Mic, those are two very different questions," he answered, flirting a bit as he played with his coffee cup, his Cajun accent different than any other she'd ever heard. His eyes roamed her face. "By the way, you're looking good. Retirement becomes you. He flashed her a white-toothed grin. His dark eyes smoldered with mischief and possibility.

Mic felt a blush creep up her neck and hoped her scarf covered it. She'd always been attracted to him, but was pretty sure she didn't want to go there again. "Uh huh, thanks, I guess," she said. The "thing" with Slade had ended badly, and there was no way she would let herself fall down that rabbit hole again. In fact, she'd hardly given it a thought in recent years. "So, what about Dr. S?"

She watched as Slade clenched and unclenched his fist …a sign of the black Irish anger he hid so well from others …or at least he thought he hid. Mic had his number, probably because she was Irish herself.

"He's a creep. A snake, a pervert, and he's getting away with all kinds of shit. That's what I think," he replied as disgust crossed his handsome features. His black eyes glinted with rage and became ever darker as Mic recognized loathing on his face.

"In what way? What's he getting away with?" Mic asked as she noted signs of anger in Slade's body movements and facial expressions.

Slade spoke through gritted teeth. "He's a sneaky bastard. He takes advantage of people who are less fortunate. I'm sure he offed a young Hispanic dental assistant several years ago. Her name was Maria. Of course, there's no body so I can't prove it."

Mic's heart rate increased, and her stomach moved precariously. "What makes you so sure? Do you think he actually killed her or had her killed?"

"My gut. Don't think he killed her. He's a coward. He probably had her killed."

"Tell me," Mic encouraged in a low voice as she moved her chair closer.

Slade lowered his voice, too. "My gut's not wrong often. I went out to see her after she called my office and complained about Dr. Dude. Maria lived in the trailer park off Chamberlayne Avenue with her mother, brothers, and sisters. Maria wasn't there. In fact, I never met her. Her mother said Maria was feisty and had a temper. Her mother told me Maria was gonna file a complaint against Dr. Dude with the State Board of Dentistry for sexual harassment."

"A complaint with the State Board against Smirkowitz. Wow, that's pretty brave," Mic commented.

Slade nodded. "Yeah, she was angry. More'n likely, young, angry and foolish," he finished, his voice low.

A dark feeling overcame Mic. "Gimme me the time line? How much time elapsed between the time Maria went missing and your talk with her mother?" she asked, taking out her notebook.

Slade scratched his head. "Not long, it was quick. Few days at the most. The girl complained, I went to see the good dentist, who denied everything and a couple of days later I went to see the mother. I talked to Maria on the phone, we were to meet, and then poof, she disappeared. Case closed."

"What happened?" Mic paused. "Tell me again," Mic murmured.

Slade shook his head. "She disappeared. It's as simple as that. I talked with her mother just after she disappeared. The mother was devastated and convinced Smirkowitz had hurt her daughter. The mother said her daughter was scared of him and that the prick had made sexual advances to her. When she refused, he'd told her she was fired and owed him two thousand dollars."

Mic nodded and repeated her question, "Owed him two thousand dollars? For what?"

"Smirkowitz had paid her tuition through the dental program. He holds that over them."

Mic shook her head. "Okay, then what?"

Slade stared at her, his dark eyes brooding.

Mic could feel the disgust building in her gut "Then what else happened?" She lowered her voice and leaned over the table, moving even closer to Slade.

Slade shrugged his shoulders and reached for his coffee. "Nothing happened. We were to meet that afternoon, and she disappeared. Gone! Just like that," he answered angrily. "Don't know if he killed her or what, but I do know he's responsible."

Mic was quiet for a moment. "Did you go back later to see Dr. Dude?"

Slade nodded. "Yeah, sure. He said he had no idea what happened to her. Said he heard from his office staff that she'd returned to Guatemala with her boyfriend."

"What'd her mother say? Did you ask her?"

Slade glared at her, and she could see the Irish anger working its way up, "Hell, yes. I went back that day, and she said the same thing. Of course, the first time I saw her she'd told me the girl didn't have a boyfriend."

Mic nodded, "What's your theory?" She smiled at him briefly. "I know you have one."

"Yeah," he snapped at her. "I've got one, and it's right. I think Dr. Dude killed her and did away with her body. My theory is he, or one of his associates, frightened her mother with the disappearance of her other two daughters. Probably paid her off, too. Hush money."

"Why you think that?" Mic asked.

'Cuz I went out there a few months later to check again to see if the mother remembered anything else, and she had a brand new doublewide trailer with a deck and all new plants. She also had a new above-the-ground swimming pool and a trampoline."

Reality set in, and Mic hated the possibilities it presented. She nodded and asked, "What about the complaint to the dentistry board?"

"Dismissed. No action taken. The accuser didn't show up." Slade gave her a lazy look as he reached for the non-existent pack of cigarettes in his breast pocket. Instead, he reached for his pack of dental floss and played with it. He noted the hate in Mic's eyes. She was a woman who hated pervs as much as he did.

Mic clicked her ballpoint pen shut, stood up and stared down at Slade, "I'm gonna get this bastard. Will you help me?"

Slade stood and smiled broadly. "I'm in. Whaddaya need?"

"Your help, and everything you know — as soon as you know it," she advised as she touched his arm.

Slade stood and took her arm. "Let's get out of here. The snow is even worse."

Judith Lucci

The couple exited the Starbucks with Mic feeling snug and comfortable clasping Slade's arm.

Chapter 8

Dottie yawned. She was tired as she sat in a large Queen Anne recliner next to Margaret's bed. The evening had lasted forever. Beau had returned home from work a little after six o'clock, and within a few minutes or so, two of Richmond's finest appeared at the door to take the missing person's report on Allison. Several hours of questions followed; from very personal questions about habits, drugs, boyfriends, and behaviors as well as mental stability. Margaret had dissolved into tears. Dottie and her maid had walked her to her bedroom where no amount of sherry, Xanax, or Valium could console Margaret.

Margaret wept constantly. "Something awful has happened to her, Dottie. I know it, I can feel it in my bones," she wailed over and over.

Dottie sat by her friend's bed and held her hand feeling about as useless as her royal title. Finally, they both dropped into a restless sleep.

Around midnight, Margaret's son, William Massie IV, and daughter-in-law, Helen, arrived home from Europe via Dulles. Dorothy gave William and Helen a huge hug and tried to offer them reassurance and hope about Allison but wasn't sure she was successful.

"Dottie, you look exhausted," Helen said, looking Dorothy over from head to toe. "I'll sit with Margaret a while. It might be better if you got some rest. You know she'll need you a lot in the next few days."

Dorothy nodded, her face gray with fatigue. "Thank you, Helen. I know you are tired and jet lagged, but I believe I will rest. I think Margaret's out for a while. She was doing pretty well until they filed the missing person report. I suppose it became very real to her then."

Helen's blue eyes filled with tears. "Dottie, what do you really think? I don't think any of this has truly registered with me. It seems like a bad dream. I can't believe that some dentist would in any way harm Allison. She's just a beautiful, young woman who needs a chance to live. She has her entire life ahead of her."

Dottie patted her hand. "Remember, my dear. We don't know anything at all. It's only been a real case for a few hours. I know Michaela is on top of it and checking in downtown. She'll find out what's going on, and as soon as she does, I'll let you know. I promise."

Helen's shoulders shook gently as she struggled to hold back her tears. She covered her face with her hands. "Thank you, Dottie. It's just that I'm so worried about her, particularly with her diabetes. If she doesn't get her insulin soon, it could be catastrophic."

Dottie's mouth fell open, "Allison has diabetes? I'd forgotten all about that. I don't think Margaret's put together her need for insulin. How long can she go without her insulin?"

Helen thought for a minute. "A while. Maybe eighteen hours or so. Her condition is a bit better now since she had that pituitary tumor removed several years ago."

"Yes, I remember."

"Now she's on insulin, and if she doesn't get it in a timely manner, her blood sugar goes up, and she can go into a coma, just like any other diabetic." A look of horror registered on Helen's face. "Oh my God, Dottie, she could go into a coma and die." Helen collapsed on the bed, tears streaming down her face.

Dottie's stomach dropped to her toes and alarm flashed through her body. "We need to let the police know this immediately. It's critical to the case. Be sure William tells

Beau so he can communicate it to the detectives in charge of her case."

Helen nodded and gave her a grateful smile. She answered in a shaky voice, "I will. Off to bed with you." She looked over at her sleeping mother-in-law and added, "It looks like she's out for a while. I'm going downstairs to talk with Beau and William. Do you need anything before I go down, Dottie?"

Dottie shook her head. "No, my dear, not a thing. Try to get some rest while you keep an eye out for Margaret." Dottie patted Helen's shoulder. "Things will turn out fine, I promise."

"I will, and I want you to as well. Do you promise?" Helen's eyes held those of the older woman for several seconds. Helen knew Dottie very well and was aware of Dottie's reputation as an armchair sleuth. She also was aware of how much Michaela valued Dottie's insights and opinion.

"I will." Dottie crossed her heart. "I promise."

"Seriously, Dottie. We need you to help us, so we need you to have a clear head. Get some rest," Helen begged as she reached up and hugged the older woman.

"Scout's honor," Dottie smiled as she left Margaret's room, her heart heavy with concern and her feet swollen from her long day. She felt a little short of breath as well and hated to admit it, but the doctor was probably right. She did have a problem with congestive heart failure and it bothered her sometimes, but she kept it under control most of the time

Dottie lay in the well-appointed bedroom on the second floor of Margaret's mansion. Sleep evaded her. What had she missed, what could she do to help Mic find Allison? She knew the first twenty-four hours were the most important, and those were over. She missed the comfort of her

Monument Avenue home. It reminded her of her old neighborhood in Vienna, where she'd lived part-time as a child. Dorothy closed her eyes and remembered her many trips to Vienna as a young girl. Vienna, the birthplace of music, art and romance. She'd met her husband there, the Count Umberto Borghase, and they'd spent many nights at the opera and at Chamber music concerts. They had walked hand-in-hand through the beautiful gardens of post-war Vienna. As she thought of her husband, her heart fluttered. She still missed him desperately, even though he had been dead for over forty years. They had had a magical life and a perfect, storybook marriage. The cont had made her feel like a princess, and in truth, she'd lived like one. Dottie closed her eyes and remembered her years with Rome's "Italian Stallion" as Umberto was known. Umbie had been proud of her and supported her career as a young Olympian in post-war Europe. He'd patiently followed her around the globe until she retired from competitive swimming, and they'd moved to Villa Borghase in Rome. She smiled to herself. Ah, yes, Vienna. The Austrian city was chiseled into her bones, and its memories locked in her heart forever. Vienna was the story of her youth and her love. She sighed contentedly and drifted off to sleep.

Chapter 9

Michaela was curled up in her bathrobe in a large green plaid chair in her office, coffee in hand, as she reviewed the files on Dr. Dude that Slade had sent over by courier an hour earlier. As Michaela read the files, her gut assured her something sinister was happening in the fancy dental practice over on Stuart Circle involving Richmond's premier cosmetic dentist. There were seven complaints filed in the past five years with the RPD against the wealthy dentist, and while each complaint had been dutifully and correctly investigated, the investigation always ended in a dead end.

Three facts smacked Mic in the face, and she pondered them. First, the complaints against Dr. Smirkowitz came from patients and staff suggesting the good doctor was confident or sinister enough to sexually harass both groups. Second, all complaints filed with the Board of Dentistry against Smirkowitz were never investigated, and third, the letter Smirkowitz had received censoring his practice because of turnover of staff was never made actionable. The commonwealth of Virginia was steadfast in its commitment to protect their citizens against unsafe practitioners. Michaela was deep in thought when the shrill ringing of her house phone shattered the quiet morning. Angel opened his eyes and growled softly. He rolled over and stared at her as she picked up the phone.

"Hi, Dottie, how are you today?" she asked, stifling a yawn. This was unusual. It was only a little after ten, and Dottie rarely called her before lunchtime. In reality, Dottie rarely rose before noon. Something was up.

"Tired," she snapped, resenting the peace and serenity she heard in Michaela's voice. "I was over at Margaret's most of yesterday afternoon and spent the night. Got no rest.

Anyway, I want to go home, get a shower and get over there to talk to you. Will you be around?"

Mic sighed. So much for her quiet morning at home. "Sure, I'll rustle us up some corned beef and cabbage for lunch. How's that sound?"

It sounded horrible to Dottie. She hated cabbage. After all, she was a countess and aristocrats didn't eat cabbage. "How about I just eat at home or pick something up for us. My stomach doesn't feel like cabbage today," Dottie offered.

Mic grinned. Dottie couldn't fool her. "That's okay. I have a Shepherd's pie in the freezer. I'll pop it in the oven, and it'll be ready by the time you get here."

"Oh, that sounds wonderful." Dottie was immediately happy and smiled as her mood improved rapidly. "I love your Shepherd's pie and that's perfect for my tummy." Her stomach rumbled in anticipation of her upcoming lunch. "I'll be there in a half hour or so. Need anything?"

"Nope. Not a thing. I do have an appointment downtown at two this afternoon though,' Mic reminded her. "So, I can't hang out all day."

"That's okay, neither can I. I'm quite busy," she sniffed. "I have an appointment I can't postpone. Just get out the bottle of Jamie Jameson. I've been frozen for two days and that stuff heats me up." Dottie hung up and her car audio returned to the Frank Sinatra station on XM radio.

Mic shook her head as she thought about Dottie driving slowly down the snow-covered streets in Richmond's Fan District in her big white Cadillac, taking over the road as she listened to Frank Sinatra. Dottie laid on the horn at every four-way stop. She knew that one day someone was going to kill her. She visualized Dottie looking both ways as she inched her huge car out in traffic. She probably had on those huge cataract black paper glasses she always wore in the

49

snow or when the sun was especially bright. She shook her head and laughed aloud as Angel stared up at her and thumped his tail happily on the wooden floor. Mic reached down and scratched his ears as he licked her hand greedily. There was nothing like the love of a dog, especially one who'd saved your life.

Mic looked into his eyes, "Come on, buddy, let's go out for a few minutes."

Chapter 10

Dottie knocked on Mic's front door about thirty minutes after the phone call. Well dressed as always, Dottie sported a different pair of expensive snow boots, skinny jeans, a flannel shirt and a hand painted silk infinity scarf tied around her neck. Since it was still cold and freezing outside, she had on a down vest and a warm hat.

"Wow," Michaela remarked. "You look like you're ready to go sleigh riding in the Alps. I thought it was supposed to warm up today."

Dottie gave her a doubtful look. "Supposed to is one thing, but I can assure you that it hasn't warmed up. The wind just blows through your bones."

Mic ushered Dottie through the long townhome back to the kitchen where she had set out her famous Shepherd's pie and a green salad. She handed Dorothy a cup of hot coffee laced with Jameson's Irish whiskey. "Here you go, this should heat you right up."

Dottie accepted the cup of coffee gratefully. "Love these cups, Mic. Who's that potter lady that makes these for you?"

"Her name is Susie. She's down at Artisans Galleries on Cary Street. Her stuff is the best. Everything she makes is freezer-to-oven and microwave safe. I wouldn't use anything else."

Dottie admired the handiwork on the cups. "Humph, think I may need a few of these. I'll get her number from you. Will she do special orders?"

"Yeah, and there's another gal down there as well who has great stuff, too. Her name is Jeanine. She made these for me," Mic said as she reached up and pulled down several beautiful clay bowls with a unique blue glaze.

Dottie rubbed her perfectly manicured hands over the glazed bowls. "These are beautiful. I want a few of these, too. Get me their numbers, will you?" she directed.

Mic pulled her address book out of the drawer and handed her their cards. "Here you go, enjoy."

Dottie slid the cards into her vest pocket. "How's he doing?" she asked, nodding at Angel lying in his bed by the fire.

"Better today, I think. We had a long walk this morning, and he had a good time playing in the snow. So tell me, what's going on? How's Margaret and her family?"

Dottie reached for a plate, spooned a generous serving of Shepherd's pie onto it, and said, "I guess they're okay, considering there's no news. And from what I understand, Beau is raising hell with the Richmond Police Department. He's had the commissioner on the phone a bunch of times. He's frantic with worry, and he's a man who's used to getting his own way so he's not patient at all." Dottie offered Mic an apologetic look.

51

"Why am I not surprised to hear this? I wouldn't have expected anything else. Don't worry. RPD can handle it."

"They want to officially hire you to handle the case. Margaret trusts you, and she asked me to come talk to you about it. What do you think? Do you know anything new?"

Michaela was thoughtful for moment and said, "I talked with vice and sexual crimes yesterday, and they think Dr. Dude is most likely guilty of many things, but they've never been able to pin anything on him."

Dottie smiled broadly, flashing Michaela her favorite, famous countess smile, the one that often showed up in *Town and Country* and *People* magazines and said, "My dear Michaela, that's exactly the kind of case that you love to get and sink your teeth into."

Mic gave her a sly smile and nodded. "My old friend, you know me so well. Yes, I will take the case. Have Beau let RPD know officially that I'm on the case so that I can access all the necessary files and documents. Can you do that for me?"

"Of course I can. You know I can," she assured her as she smiled smugly and continued, "But you've got to keep me as second chair. It'll be you and me working this case together, just like old times. Dottie and Mic ride again." Dottie's wrinkled face beamed and flushed with excitement. "You remember what they called us in *Style Weekly* a few years ago? 'Richmond's own Thelma & Louise!'"

Mic grimaced. She should have seen this coming. It was true that Dottie had been an invaluable resource to her in years past. Dottie had a keen, logical uncluttered way of thinking, and she processed information like a pro. Her gut and intuition missed nothing. No question she'd been good, but now Dottie was over eighty. She couldn't run fast, couldn't see well since her eye surgery, had a heart condition she didn't admit to, and still drove like a maniac.

She couldn't judge distances anymore, but then, she'd never been able to. She just bought the biggest cars she could find and hoped for the best.

Michaela glanced at her good friend, shaking her head. "Dottie, I love you dearly, but I'm not having you out and about in dangerous situations and gathering information at your age. You simply cannot drive the streets of Richmond in the snow and ice in that ginormous Cadillac of yours endangering your life and the lives of others. It's just not safe."

Dottie opened her perfectly painted lips and said in her uppity, countess voice, "I resent that, Michaela. I'm a good driver, and my vehicle protects me like an armored car. I only have one or two tiny digressions on my driving record." She stared Mic down. "What does your driving record look like?"

Dottie knew Mic had dozens of violations not done in the interest of public safety. She was an assigned risk for her insurance company and only God knew how many points she had against her license.

"That's just it." Mic retorted. "It protects you. What about the rest of us—the poor people traveling around Richmond? You drive your car like it's a yacht down the middle of the ocean."

Dottie sat stubbornly in her chair, cup in her hand and stared at Mic. Her look was icy, but Mic didn't flinch.

After a minute or so of silence, Dorothy finally said, "Okay, Mic, I promise I won't go off on a wild goose chase, I won't put myself in any situations that I cannot handle, and I won't get in your way. What I will do," with an emphasis on the word will, "is gather information safely, and I will let you know everything I plan to do. That is, if I have time. Is that fair enough?" she asked with a tone tinged in sarcasm.

Mic gave her a long, slow look before replying, giving herself time to think. "I guess it will have to be. But, if you get in any trouble, or if you get hurt, I'll hold myself responsible forever."

Dottie reached across the table, patted her hand. "Oh my dear, you won't have to. I promise, I'll behave myself, and I won't take any chances, and I'll carry my gun."

Mic's mouth formed a big letter "O". "Have you been to the range lately and practiced with your gun?"

Dottie sniffed. "Yes, I qualified once again last fall so don't worry. Henry takes me often, usually every couple of weeks. I have the proper permits, and I know how to shoot. Don't forget, I was brought up hunting quail in the Italian countryside."

The conversation ended with the shrill ring of Michaela's house phone. The digital display was Richmond Police Department. "Hello, this is Mic," she said as she answered the phone.

"Mic, its Slade. I just reviewed the CCTV information for the cams around Dude's office."

Mic smiled to herself. She loved the warm sound of his Southern accent. "Yeah. What'd you find? Anything?"

"Yeah," Slade growled. "Allison didn't drive her car very far. One or possibly two other people were in her car at the corner of Lombardy and Main. There's a shadow on the floor in the back we think may be the shadow of another person."

Mic's stomach lurched as she asked, "That's just a few blocks from Dr. Dude's office. Who was driving her car?"

"Now that's the question of the day," Slade said. "We can't identify whether it's a male or female. Whoever it was wore a hat, pretty much a non-gender hat. We lost the car when it turned off of State Route 33, headed west toward Montpelier." There was a long pause. "That's all I got."

Mic shook her head. "That's not good. How's the family?"

Slade groaned. "Not good, either. The grandfather's kicking ass and asking questions later, the grandmother's a basket case and all pilled-up, and the parents are beside themselves with anxiety. The fact that the kid's sick just escalates the problem."

Mic was surprised. "What, Allison's sick? Sick how?"

Slade's voice was surprised. "I thought you knew. She's diabetic, hard to manage and needs insulin. The docs say she could go in a coma if she doesn't get some soon. The insulin she had a couple of days ago was long-acting, but it's almost all out of her system by now. Her parents say she usually carried a syringe with her, so we're hopeful she'll self-inject."

"It just keeps getting worse," Mic shook her head. "I've decided to take this case on as a private investigator. I'm sure Beau will call you soon but take it from me, I'm their representative."

Slade nodded and smiled to himself, "Sounds good to me. Just lovin' working with you, Mic, you know just like old times."

Mic flushed and felt warm all over. She grinned and decided to ignore his implication. "Yeah, and I can probably settle the fireworks you're getting from above via Beau Massie. Anything else you can tell me before I start my own investigation?"

"Nah, not really. There's a news conference at two o'clock this afternoon. The family will be there talkin' about her illness and pleading for anyone with information to come forward to police or family. They'll also offer a hefty reward for information."

Mic was quiet for a moment, then asked, "Any chance this could be a kidnapping? Her parents and grandparents are filthy rich. Richmond Bluebloods and FFVs."

"Yeah, I know. They're pretty nice folks. Some of these rich folks are just... well...you know... not nice," he added in a sarcastic tone.

"Yeah, tell me about it, but these people are good folks," Mic said. "I know them pretty well."

"Anyway, we're not thinking it's a kidnapping, although we have considered the possibility. There's been no demand for ransom. There's been no communication at all between the family, police, and the perp."

Mic nodded. "Anybody been over to Richmond's premier cosmetic dentist's office today to ask him some more questions?" Mic knew her voice was sarcastic.

"I'm on my way over there as we speak. You wanna join me?"

Mic laughed aloud. "I wouldn't miss it for the world. I'll meet you outside his office in thirty minutes."

"It's a date, Mic. Don't be late."

Mic hung up the phone, looked over at Dottie and pointed to her Shepherd's pie. "Eat up, or if you'd rather stay and take your time, but I've gotta get dressed. I'm meeting Detective McKane over at Dr. Dude's office."

Dottie nodded and filled her fork with Shepherd's pie. "Call me when you get back. I want to know everything."

Mic nodded and headed upstairs to dress. Hmmm, I wonder why Dottie didn't fuss about coming along. Any other time she'd be badgering me to death. I hope she doesn't have anything up her sleeve.

Dottie smiled, scraped the last bit of her lunch onto her fork, and popped it into her mouth. She scratched Angel's ears, put the plates in the dishwasher, and closed the front door. She had things to do. No time to spare.

Chapter 11

Michaela strapped Angel in the passenger seat next to her and drove carefully over to Stuart Circle. She wheeled her SUV into a numbered parking spot behind Dr. Dude's stone and concrete building. The parking lot was cleared of snow and almost empty. She found that weird since it was early afternoon, and she'd assumed the good doctor would be extracting teeth and designing movie star mouths for most of Hollywood and anyone from Richmond who could afford his services. Oops, she'd forgotten he didn't extract teeth. It was "too barbaric," or at least that's what he'd told her a few years ago. He practiced cosmetic or "fashion" dentistry and was a "smile-maker."

Mic's attention was drawn to the side entrance where she spotted a young Hispanic girl, with long beautiful dark hair dressed in a short white faux fur-trimmed jacket hurrying to her car as tears streamed down her face. She wiped away the tears furiously with her hands. She sat in her car, an old Volkswagen Jetta, close to where Mic had parked. Mic watched as she frantically pushed numbers into her cell phone as she wiped tears away with her forearm. It was all Mic could do not to get out of her car, go over, and comfort the young woman. Instead, she grabbed her iPhone and snapped her picture. At the same time, she spotted Slade McKane in her peripheral vision. He slammed the door of his unmarked police cruiser and stretched his long legs as he walked toward her and opened her door.

"Ready?" he asked. "Let's go have some fun with the good dentist." His dark eyes twinkled and smoldered as he looked at her.

Mic put her finger to her lips to shush him and said quietly, "See the young woman over in the Jetta? She just left the office, and she's obviously very upset. I'm gonna check her out. You go start things with Dr. Dude, and I'll be along in a few moments. Then we'll ask the same questions twice."

Slade gave Mic an admiring look and sly smile, "I always thought you were pretty slick. Good plan." He headed around to the front of the building.

Michaela let Angel out of the car, grabbed his leash and walked over to the young woman in the Jetta. Mic could hear her talking rapidly in Spanish on her cell. Mic tapped on her window and the lovely young woman just about jumped out of the car. Her face showed terror.

"Sorry, sorry. I'm not going to hurt you," Mic said loudly through the car window. "And neither is my dog. I saw you crying, and I wondered if there was something I could do... someone I could call for you."

The young woman smiled through her tears and said, "Oh, thank you, but I think I'm okay. I'm talking to my mother."

Mic looked at her, and the two women locked eyes. She saw fear flicker in the young woman's brown eyes

"You look scared," Mic observed. "Here's my card." The Jetta window slid down. "I'm a private investigator, and if there's anything you're afraid of, call me, and I will help you figure it out ...no charge, I promise. By the way, what's your name?"

"Danielle," The young woman replied. She could easily be a movie star and flashed Mic a perfect smile. Her dark hair was piled on her head in a messy bun. Her white teeth gleamed in the sunlight, but her brown eyes glowed with pain.

"I'm a dental tech here at Dr. Smirkowitz's office, and I made a mistake, and the office supervisor told me to leave," she admitted in a shaky voice. As the tears rushed into Danielle's eyes again, Michaela touched her shoulder.

"We all make mistakes. It'll be better tomorrow, but if you need me I'm available."

Danielle gave her a grateful smile, thanked her, accepted her card and went back to her conversation with her mother."

Michaela and Angel walked to the door of Dr. Dude's office. Angel growled ferociously and strained at his lease.

"What's up, boy?" Mic asked as she placed her hand on his head and looked around. She saw a man dressed in scrubs and navy down vest move behind a tree. A bit later, he walked toward the alley behind Dr. Dude's office.

"I guess you don't like him, Angel," Mic said to her dog. "Let's move inside where it's a little warmer," she added as they moved closer to the door.

Angel turned his head and continued a low, deep growl until the man was out of sight. Then he followed his mistress into the office.

"Guess you didn't like him at all, buddy," Mic said as they entered the office. She scratched his ears and they moved to the reception desk.

Chapter 12

Dottie sat in her car over on Cary Street and stared at the traffic. She felt bored and useless, two feelings she didn't like at all. She'd just bought a new gourmet French coffee press from the kitchen store and had taken herself out for coffee and pastry at a nearby sandwich shop.

She stopped by Margaret's house after she'd left Mic's house, and her best friend was still inconsolable as the family prepared for the news conference that would beg the public for information about Allison's disappearance. Margaret looked horrible, tired, fatigued, with gray-colored skin and dark circles under her eyes. Dottie had suggested she skip the interview, but Margaret had refused. Dottie shook her head. She should never go on Channel 12 news looking like that. Margaret looked as though she had aged twenty years overnight. Beau was beside himself with fear and angst, and for the first time ever, Dottie had almost liked him in his current state of humility. Humility was an uncommon response for Beau Massie, one of the wealthiest movers and shakers in the Old Dominion.

Dottie considered the events surrounding Allison's disappearance and made a quick decision. Mic would probably kill her, but what the hell; you gotta do what you gotta do.

Dottie inched her mammoth vehicle out of the parking space on Cary Street and immediately rammed her wheels into a mound of snow left by a snowplow. She hit drive, and the wheels ground deeper into the snow, and then shot forward as her car jolted out onto Cary Street to a litany of honking horns and irate drivers. Dorothy flipped one of them off but fortunately, most drivers were more respectful of the road conditions than Dottie. After all, Cary Street was a main thoroughfare and one of Dottie's favorite shopping areas.

Dottie's heart jumped into her throat as she ran into another pile of snow left by the snowplows. The streets were so small with the banks of snow on either side, and she had a hard time steering her car and staying on her own side. For a moment, she considered that maybe she really should have stayed home and not driven in the snow. But that was what old people did and even though she was eighty-two, she really wasn't old. She stayed in shape, exercised, and pretty much had the same Olympic swimmer figure as she had sixty years ago. Besides, she'd needed that French coffee press. Now she was on a mission to rescue Allison.

As she pulled slowly in front of Dr. Smirkowitz's office on the corner of Lombardy and Monument, she spied Mic's Land Cruiser and the unmarked police vehicle in the parking lot in the back. There were only four other cars there, and she knew Mic would recognize her car and fuss at her. Dorothy decided to park across the street and wait for Mic to leave. She looked at her watch. It was three thirty. She doubted they'd be much longer. She figured Dr. Dude would be furious after they left, and she knew just where to hide in his office and eavesdrop. Yes, she told herself this was what she needed to be doing. Her heart was beating with more excitement than she'd felt in five years. I'm going out in a blaze, one way or the other.

Chapter 13

Mic pushed the shiny brass knocker on the door of Dr. Smirkowitz's office and entered Richmond's Premier Dental office inner sanctum. Angel, well-mannered and quiet, was on his leash. She noted the perfectly polished brass kick plate and the handsome brass-etched sign with the good doctor's name. She could see her face in the shiny polished floors as she shut the door and unconsciously fluffed her hair.

Directly in front of her was the reception and billing desk and two women working behind the counter. The older woman, probably about Mic's age, wore the traditional garb of a local religious order... a sprigged shirtwaist dress covered by a heavy woolen sweater. Mic knew the woman had on converse tennis shoes under her dress. Her nametag identified her as Tilda. The younger woman shuffled paper charts nervously and avoided eye contract with Michaela, but both women stared open-mouthed at Angel who stood politely at Mic's side.

Mic handed her card to Tilda, who motioned her toward the waiting area and said, "Ah ...your dog isn't allowed in here. This is a dental practice and a sterile environment." She gave Michaela a smirk and pointed toward the door. Mic swore she could see a glint of malice in the woman's eyes.

Michaela laughed. "Sterile, are you serious? It's debatable as to whether an operating room is even sterile, so I know this place isn't." She pointed at the brass doorknob. "Look at all the germs on the door knob. It's smeared with fingerprints."

Tilda tried to interrupt, but Mic continued to talk, waving her hands around the office. "Check out the handle on the coffee pot. Have you sterilized that recently?"

Tilda moved from behind the counter, came out the side door, and faced Mic in the waiting room. Her voice was icy, "Your dog is not allowed," she hissed. "Take him out of here now." Tilda's eyes blazed with anger.

Mic ignored her. "Most of the areas in this waiting room have more bacteria than my dog's mouth. I'm sure you know how dirty someone's mouth is."

Tilda stared at her, but said nothing as rage suffused her face.

"Besides," Mic added as she patted Angel on the scruff of his neck, "he's a therapy dog."

The woman opened her mouth to protest, but Michaela's voice was firm as she stared the woman down. "He stays."

Tilda's eyes flashed with anger as she pointed toward the upholstered sofa. "Wait there," she ordered with a snarl.

Mic avoided the sofa and sat instead in a chair where she could view the front office. Tilda disappeared, but the other clerk looked like a scared rabbit. She decided to press her for information. "How are you today? Are you busy?" she asked the younger woman who tried to disappear into herself. Her nametag read "Janie."

Finally, she spoke. "Um, well, yes, we've been busy all day, but it is a bit slow right now. Although we did have some cancellations because of the weather." Her voice was soft and timid.

Mic gave her a warm smile. "Good! Time for an afternoon tea break. By the way, my friend's granddaughter was here yesterday afternoon for a job interview and ..."

The younger clerk's eye darted quickly toward the front door like she wanted to bolt, but Tilda, who'd returned, gave Michaela a defiant look and said, "Yes, that would be Allison. She met with Dr. Smirkowitz for about an hour or so yesterday."

Mic smiled and nodded. "Yes, that's her. Did you see her leave? A pretty blond-headed young woman."

Both woman shook their heads quickly and replied "no" in unison.

Mic laughed aloud. "Ladies, that sounded rehearsed. Now, let me ask again. Did either of see Allison leave yesterday afternoon?" Mic's voice had a sharp edge to it.

The younger woman met her eyes for the first time and said, "I left early because my baby was sick so I didn't see her."

Mic turned to Tilda, who gave her a cheeky look, but she finally replied. "No. I must have been busy or in the bathroom when she left." Mic knew she was lying.

Mic studied both women and decided they knew a few things more about Allison's disappearance that they weren't saying. She decided to move the conversation along.

"Well, she never returned home last night, and she's missing. Her parents are worried to death about her. She's a very serious diabetic, and they're afraid she could be in a coma. Her doctor says finding her quickly is a matter of life and death."

Janie's hand flew to her mouth, and she gasped. "Oh, I'm so sorry. I didn't know she was sick." Tilda shot Janie a dirty look but said nothing.

Mic nodded. "Yeah, she is. She could die, so anything you can remember might help us find her. Maybe you heard her say something to someone."

The young woman shook her head while Tilda stared at Mic, anger seething from her pores. "I remember you. You're that cop that doesn't pay your bill. You had an outstanding debt with us for months," she accused Mic, with an ugly look.

"Not really," Mic said sweetly. "It was an insurance error."

"Sure it was," Tilda said harshly.

Mic ignored her and handed Janie her card and left one for Tilda on the counter. "Call me anytime ...day or night if you hear or remember anything about Allison," Mic directed them as she observed Tilda's angry body language. "By the way," she address both women, "I noticed a man in blue scrubs leaving here a few minutes ago. He went down the alley. Do either of you know him."

Tilda shook her head defiantly and Janie said, "Oh, yeah...him. I don't know. He stops by sometimes. I think he may work for Dr. Smirkowitz sometimes."

Mic's ears picked up, "Really, what does he do?"

Janie shook her head. "No idea. Maybe he works in his yard. I'm clueless."

Tilda said nothing and returned to her work. She stared at the screen on her computer as anger surged through her.

"Tilda, do you know the man?" Michaela asked in a sharp tone.

Tilda looked up from her computer. "No, never saw him in here," she muttered as her eyes returned to her keyboard.

Michaela nodded, moved towards the waiting area, and sat in an expensive chair covered in blue silk. *She's lying and I know it.* As her eyes perused the waiting room. The word "opulent" crossed her mind several times. Custom window treatments adorned the decorative wrought iron windows that coordinated beautifully with the thick Persian rugs on the highly polished oak floors. Beautiful paintings and photographs, many signed by Dr. Dude, adorned the walls. What is it about dentists who painted watercolor and became photographers? I suppose if I spent my life in someone's mouth, I'd do something with the rest of my time too. A Keurig coffee maker beckoned from a sideboard opposite her, resplendent with fresh flowers that hinted spring was around the corner. A gleaming silver tray offered every possible hot beverage available in a K-cup. The office was eerily quiet except for the occasional sound of a suction hose and a slurping drain that interrupted Michaela's thoughts. Christian rock music played softly through piped speakers in the background. A large cross adorned one end of the room. The place was an interior designer's masterpiece. Too bad it was the office of a creep and pervert.

Mic studied her surroundings for a couple more minutes, before she became bored and started to fidget. She detested sitting still and wondered what Slade and Dr. Dude were discussing.

As she rose to complain, Tilda, her green eyes darkened by hate, beckoned Michaela with her index finger. She had put on a white lab coat with "office manager" embroidered in red. Tilda ushered her into Dr. S.'s office where the atmosphere was hushed and strained.

Chapter 14

Allison Massie opened her eyes to the sound of low voices. She was quiet and still as a mouse as she focused on the words of her captors. Her head thudded dangerously, as her brain vibrated in her head. Her mouth was cotton, and her throat so dry she could hardly swallow.

"I'm gonna meet up with someone soon and get the others here in a few hours," a heavily accented male voice announced. "I have to travel part-way to Virginia Beach to pick them up." He stared down at Allison and admired her beauty. Her blond hair, covered in straw was beautiful and she looked like a princess. "Be sure this one is okay. She's a prize."

"You're traveling in this weather?" a voice asked. Allison couldn't identify whether it was a man or woman. It was just a voice.

"Yeah, but it won't be bad once I get to the interstate. It never snows on the coast where I'm headed," the accented voice said.

Allison could feel movement as the man moved closer and stood directly over her. She closed her eyes in pretend sleep and tried to suppress the shiver that raced over her body. Her ears strained to hear the other voice. She thought one of them sounded Russian.

"She'll be okay. No one knows where we are. I've gotta get outta here for a while. Got to make an appearance, you know. Keep everybody's suspicions down."

The man with the accent grunted and laughed. "Yeah, yeah, I know. What a game. How about medicine for this one?" he gestured as he kicked Allison's knee sharply. "Do you have insulin? I hear she has diabetes. She needs to be beautiful and in top form later."

A sharp, piercing pain flew up Allison leg to her groin and settled into her intestines. She moved slightly, unable to ignore the discomfort.

"Looks like she's waking up some, don't it?" the man observed. It was the man with the snake tattoo on his hand. He still had on blue scrubs. Her abductor. Allison could see the tattoo through her half-closed eyes. "That's good. She's been out of it for hours." The man appeared satisfied.

Hours, how long have I been here? Why hasn't someone found me? Fear raced through the young woman as she tried to piece together what had happened to her.

"Looks like her eyes are twitchin'. Maybe she's awake and playing cat and mouse with us," the accented voice muttered angrily. The man kicked her sharply again, this time near her kidneys. Allison's blue eyes popped open with pain.

"Ah ha, you're right," the man said with a short laugh. It was the man with the tattoo. "No worry, we'll fix her right up." He reached in his shoulder bag for a syringe.

Allison looked at him. He had on scrubs, like someone would wear in the operating room. The man jerked her face to the left, and pressed the side of her face to the cold ground. "Don't look at me," he ordered as he injected her in her right arm. "This will make you sleep," he said harshly.

"Yeah, shut the bitch up. She's seen enough already," the accented voice said angrily. He glared at the man next to him and grabbed him by the shoulder. "I thought you were better at this. You should've known she was half awake," he ranted as he shot him a murderous look.

The tattooed man grabbed the Russian's hand and slung it away from his shoulder. "Don't you touch me, don't you ever touch me again," he threatened, a look of revulsion and hatred on his face. "If you do, you'll be sorry," he said quietly through half-veiled eyes.

The big Russian stared into eyes that glinted like steel. "Just take care of her; I'm getting out of here."

Allison, semi-conscious from the insulin strained to listen to the men. She felt fear pulse through her body.

The man knelt next to Allison and injected her again with the same syringe. Allison watched the needle slide into her thigh. She was helpless.

"And don't you screw any of this up," the Russian threatened on the way out. "If you do, no one will help you. Remember, you work for me, get it?"

The man said nothing but watched Allison's pupils dilate and close. Then he got up, brushed off his clothes and left.

Allison's eyes followed him as he left the barn, then she lost consciousness.

Chapter 15

Dottie turned the heat up in her Cadillac to eighty-four degrees and turned her seat heater as high as it would go. She loved what she often referred to as her "butt cooker." Sometimes, if her back hurt, she'd go out and sit in the car. The butt cooker was much better than a heating pad, although the doctor told her that was absurd, and it was the same thing. Dottie just stared at him with her frosty countess look and said nothing else.

The pale afternoon sun was fading, and it was cold again, really cold. She was worried about sliding on black ice on her way home. Admittedly, her eyes weren't 20/20 but were better since her cataract surgery and her lens implant, no matter what Mic said. She closed her eyes to rest for a moment and about jumped out of her skin when someone knocked loudly on her driver's window. Her eyes flew open.

It was a blue uniformed Richmond police officer. Dottie jammed her hand on the electric window button, but her window wouldn't move. She pushed all of the buttons trying to make something happen, but nothing did. She started to yell at the cop as she tried to explain, but he only stood quietly and gave her a stony look. Finally, she pushed the right button and the errant window rolled down slowly.

"Yes, sir?" Dottie inquired as she gave him her best smile. She was so glad Dr. Dude had done a great job on her veneers. She hoped her dental bridge didn't click as it often did when she smiled sweetly. "Am I doing something wrong?"

"Driver's license and registration, please," the officer said solemnly. He didn't return her smile.

Dorothy fumbled around in her glove compartment and console and searched for her registration. She could never find the thing. "I'm searching, Officer. Here's my license." She poured everything out of her designer purse and emptied it on the seat next to her. Nothing. She looked at him. "Suppose I can't find my registration?"

He just stared at her and said nothing.

Dottie fumbled a little longer and said, "Well, I just can't seem to put my fingers on it, but I think you need to tell me why you have stopped me."

The officer pointed with his nightstick to the "No Parking" sign right beside her car.

Dottie's eyebrows arched in surprise.

"Yes, ma'am. You are in a no parking zone." He took her license and added, "I'll be right back."

"I didn't know. I'll move," she said quickly before he left.

"You've been parked here for over twenty minutes."

Dottie opened her mouth to protest, but he didn't give her time.

"I've watched you. You've been here," he said as he checked his watch, "actually closer to thirty minutes."

Dottie smiled as demurely as any member of noble family could. "I'm so sorry. I'll move right away."

"Yes, you will, but not until I write your citations, one for the parking violation and the other for no registration. I'll be back in a few minutes." His voice was firm, his eyes unsmiling.

Dottie stared at him as her blue eyes narrowed into slits. She couldn't believe it. He was giving her a ticket. Her, the Countess Borghase. An aristocrat. A noblewoman. She started to say something smart but decided she didn't want to spend the afternoon in Richmond police lock up. And this guy would lock up an old lady. No question.

Damn. She'd never gotten a parking ticket before. Maybe Mic can fix it. Dottie railed against all of the injustices in the world while she waited for the officer to return.

The officer came back to Dottie's car and stood outside the window. Dottie grabbed the tickets, frowned at him and gave him her iciest blue-eyed, haughty stare.

"Have a great day," she snapped as she stabbed at the button to raise her window. He was disgusting. He couldn't have a girlfriend, a cold fish like him. No way. Dottie waited for him to turn the corner before she left her parking place.

Chapter 16

The tension was thick in Dr. Smirkowitz's office. So thick, it stifled Mic when she entered with Angel. Dr. Dude rose and greeted her respectfully, keeping as far away from the dog as possible. He offered her a seat on the couch opposite his desk. Angel sat next to Mic fully alert as he listened to the conversation.

"Would you like some coffee or a beverage, Ms. McPherson? I am sure my office manager would be happy to bring in anything you'd like. Mic shook her head. She seriously doubted the office staff would bring her anything that wasn't laced with poison. "No, thank you, Dr. Smirkowitz. I'm fine, but you do have a wonderful assortment of beverages out there on the table."

Dr. Dude beamed as Michaela studied him. He was probably in his early fifties, hair cut in the style of the 1970s, parted and combed to one side. Yuppie and clean cut. He had one of those coffin bed suntans, or he got sprayed a few times a week. Mic wasn't sure. He had on his trademark island shirt with a parrot embroidered on the back. He had taken off his white dental coat. She noticed it hanging on a hook behind his door. All in all, Dr. Dude looked the picture of success as he smiled at them from behind his magnificent walnut desk. His thick gold wedding ring gleamed in the lamplight. A pair of khaki pants and a pair of New Balance tennis shoes completed his outfit. Mic wondered if he knew it was the twenty-first century and that 9/11 had occurred. He seemed stuck in the 1980s.

Slade had adopted his usual interrogation posture, which fluctuated between boredom, arrogance, and apathy. He glanced at Mic with hooded eyes.

Dr. Dude smiled graciously at Mic. "Ah, I don't believe I've seen you in the office for a while, Ms. McPherson. Aren't you a patient of mine?"

Mic smiled, "Was a patient. I stopped coming when your office manager, Tilda, called and harassed me about an overdue bill a few years ago. So, I now get my dental care elsewhere."

Dr. Dude remained silent.

"Perhaps I'll change back to you and make an appointment soon."

An uncomfortable silence followed. Dr. Dude broke it by saying, "I was telling Officer McKane how sorry I was to hear that Allison didn't return home last night. She was here in the afternoon yesterday."

"Detective McKane," Slade corrected, a snarl on his handsome face.

"Oh, duh, excuse me, Detective. I didn't know," Dr. Dude said officiously.

Mic watched the flicker of anger dance across Slade's face followed by the resolve to nail Dr. Dude's skinny, affluent ass. She smiled pleasantly at Smirkowitz and said, "Yes, her parents are very worried. It's not like Allison to disappear like this. Particularly without her medicine."

Smirkowitz nodded and offered her a sympathetic look. "Yes, I'd be very worried if she were my daughter. I don't possibly know what else I can do or say to help you." He paused for a second. "I had planned to hire her... just so you know. She was very qualified."

Slade's phone signaled a text. He checked the display and passed it to Mic.

"Dr. Smirkowitz, did you walk Allison to the door?" Mic asked as she noted the pained look on Dude's face as she passed the phone to Slade.

He nodded. "Yeah, I walked her to the side door and shook her hand. Told her I'd be in touch and she left. That's it. That's all I know," he said, a touch of defiance in his voice. Angel growled softly. Mic reached down and scratched his ears. He stared at Dr. Dude, his eyes never leaving his face.

"Did you see her get into her car?" Mic asked.

He shook his head. "No. I went back to my office."

Slade gestured toward the back window in Dr. Dude's office and repeated the question. "You sure you didn't see her get in her car? You have a perfect view of the parking lot."

Smirkowitz hesitated. "Uh, no. I was working."

"We have her car on a traffic cam two blocks away from here on Main Street, and she's not driving." Slade's dark eyes locked with Dude's eyes.

"How could that be?" Smirkowitz asked with a look of surprise that Mic thought he faked. She wanted to strangle him but kept her cool.

"You tell me, Smirkowitz, I've no idea," Slade challenged, his voice abrasive and sharp with accusation.

Dr. Dude shrugged his shoulders. "No idea, Detective, but I don't like your tone or the implication." Smirkowitz's voice was haughty and angry. "Do I need a lawyer?"

"Do you?" Slade challenged him.

Mic intervened. She smiled to herself. She and Slade had fallen right back into their good cop, bad cop routine. "Dr. Smirkowitz, anything you can tell us about Allison's behavior while she was here? Did she appear uneasy, frightened, anything at all that could help us?"

Dude scratched his perfectly coiffed head. "No, nothing. She was a lovely young lady."

Slade jumped to his feet, his voice loud and angry. "What the hell do you mean, 'was' a lovely young lady? Did you kill her?"

Angel growled loudly and barked. Mic thought Dude was more frightened of Angel than Slade.

Dude's pupils dilated. "No, of course not. Allison was well qualified for the job and I planned to check her references and hire her. That's all I know." He finished with a half-smile. "That's what I know, regardless of what your colleague thinks," he snarled as he looked at Slade. Dr. Dude stood as his hand swept through the air towards the door. "Is there anything else?"

Mic had never seen such a blatant dismissal.

"I'm sorry, but I must cut this short. I have a patient," Smirkowitz said as he walked to the door and opened it.

"Really, I don't see any cars in the parking lot," Michaela noted as she looked out the window.

Dude was silent for an instant. "It's a staff member. Free veneers are a job benefit here." He grinned broadly.

Slade was seething as he stood, asking again, his voice angry and accusatory. "What did you mean 'was' a lovely young lady. Is she dead? Did you kill her?"

Dr. Dude paled under his fake tan. He stuttered as he looked at Angel out of the corner of his eye. "I simply meant she was lovely. She 'is' a lovely young woman. I noticed that when she was here yesterday. That's all I meant."

Michaela watched him carefully as she checked his body language. He was upset and frightened.

Slade pushed his business card at Dr. Dude. "We'll probably need to talk with you again since you were one of the last people to see her. Are you planning to be in town for the next week or so, Smirkowitz?"

Dr. Dude nodded, and Mic could swear she saw smoke pouring out of Smirkowitz's pointy, elf-like ears.

Mic interjected, "By the way, Dr. Smirkowitz, I saw a man with dark hair and scrubs in your parking lot behind the office. Do you know him?"

Dr. Dude looked out the window and said, "No, I don't think so."

"Um, that's strange," Michaela lamented. "Your staff seems to think he works for you." She paused for a moment and added, "Are you sure?"

Mic saw a flicker of fear dance across Dr. Dude's face but he answered, "Of course not. There are nurses around here who provide special duty for the elderly residents in the apartments. He was probably from over across the street."

Mic nodded, tossed her short dark curls and left the office without offering her hand. *This guy's bad news. He's up to his eyeballs in deep poop on this one.* Mic knew he didn't stand a chance with Dottie, Slade, Angel, and her on the case.

Chapter 17

Dottie was shaking with anger as she parked her car across the street from Dr. Dude's office. She gripped the steering wheel with white-knuckled hands and counted to ten to settle her temper and lower her blood pressure, which she was sure, had skyrocketed. Dr. Smirkowitz's office was near the old Stuart Circle Hospital that had been renovated into ritzy, luxury apartments. She carefully maneuvered around the puddles of ice and snow.

Last damned thing I need is a broken hip. That would just finish me.

She waited to cross the street with the light so she wouldn't get her jeans splashed with dirty snow and water. She gingerly maneuvered the walkway opposite Dr. Dude's office and ducked behind a bush, cursing to herself as the snow and pine needles pricked her face. She quietly slipped into the side door of the office and closed the door with a soft click. Seeing no one, she ducked into a storage area located between Dr. Dude's private office and the staff break room. This was precisely the place where she'd overheard gossip among the employees about Maria several years ago. She sat on a gray tote filled with dental supplies.

She didn't have to wait long. Within a couple of minutes, she heard Dr. Smirkowitz enter his office, slam the door and yank his rolling desk chair out. He must have turned on the TV. She heard a rerun of the news conference about Allison from the morning. She heard Margaret's weeping, Helen's soft crying, and Beau's loud angry voice followed by the placating, reasonableness of Allison's dad. They'd offered a $250,000 reward for information. Her heart twisted with their pain.

Smirkowitz cursed, clicked off the TV. It sounded as if he slammed the remote on the desk. He began to talk to himself and curse Michaela and Slade. Dottie's ears burned with anger at the obscene words he used to describe Michaela. Finally, he quieted down, and Dottie could smell the scent of a cigar. It smelled good.

I like that brand. I should get some of those for me.

Only a few select people knew The Countess Dorothy Borghase smoked cigars, a habit that irked Mic to the point of murder. After all, she did have a smoking room in her home. Someone has to use it, but she hadn't had a good smoke in forever. Dottie had offered the very same rationalization to Michaela and thought Mic would have a stroke she turned so red. Mic just doesn't get it that my body is my body. I'm in great shape and if I want a cigar now and then, I'm going to have one. Period.

Dr. Dude's cell phone rang with the default ring used by millions of Americans. His voice was angry as picked it up and hissed. "I told you never to call me on this phone. This is my personal number."

He must have the phone on the speaker because Dottie could hear someone replying to his angry greeting. She strained to hear the voice on the other end, but she couldn't. She could tell it was a male voice, but it was garbled. She couldn't make out any words, and she had the hearing of a twenty-five-year-old, according to her doctor. She wondered if the voice was foreign since it sounded so garbled.

Smirkowitz snarled at the man. "Do you realize how much trouble this has caused me? I got cops crawling up my ass 24/7. They've been here twice, and I expect they'll come again. And the girl's family is rich, powerful, and connected. I told you not to take her. And, they've offered a $250,000 reward." He ended his tirade, his voice in the high range.

Dottie couldn't hear the response, but she was convinced the speaker was foreign.

She heard a loud noise. It sounded like Smirkowitz had banged his fist on his desk. He continued in an angry voice. "No, absolutely not. She's gonna die if she doesn't get insulin. She can't leave until we get some." Dottie wondered if Richmond's premier cosmetic dentist would ever be able to fashion veneers again. That fist had to hurt.

Dr. Dude must have somehow pressed the volume on his phone because she could hear the voice better. The man answered in Russian. She heard it loud and clear. The male voice was angry, hostile. Dottie knew a little Russian, not a lot, but she did understand the words, which translated as "tomorrow, seven o'clock" along with a string of expletives.

Smirkowitz cursed in Russian. Now, Dorothy understood curse words. She knew lots of curse words in every language. Dottie's imagination went wild. What? Is this jackass dentist a spy or something? She had no idea he was Russian. She had to get to Mic and let her know.

"She must look good and be fit for travel," the Russian's voice continued in an angry tone. "The bidding is tonight. She must be beautiful tonight."

Smirkowitz scowled, his voice was biting. "I'm telling you this is a bad idea. The girl is missed. She's not some refugee or immigrant you plucked off the street or out of the barrio. They won't let this go like the others. It could be our downfall."

"You must make it happen, Nikolay. It must happen tonight," the voice insisted quietly. "We're counting on you."

"But, suppose she's in a coma. I had trouble waking her this morning. I didn't know she was diabetic until the news conference. She needs insulin or she'll die," Smirkowitz pleaded. Dottie could picture the anxiety on Dr. Dude's normally composed, handsome face.

"The medicine is taken care of. We handled it a short while ago," the voice informed him in a cold tone.

Dottie shivered when she heard the harsh laugh on the other end of the phone. It was pure evil. "No, Nikolay, this will be your downfall. And the downfall of your family... those beautiful children of yours."

Dude's heart hammered in his chest. They were threatening him. He remained quiet.

After a few moments of silence, the voice continued, with an implied threat, "And, what is your new trophy wife's name?" The voice continued in English, soft and threatening.

Dottie could barely breathe. She could hear everything. The walls were paper-thin. She wasn't sure whether it was anger or fear, but as the moments passed, she recognized fear and was deeply disturbed by the man's threat. If they'd hurt Dr. Smirkowitz's wife, what would they do to Allison?"

The voice persisted, louder and threatening, "I asked you her name, Nikolay, your new, young trophy wife ...the one with the ...what, fourth little Smirkowitz on the way?"

"Deidre, her name is Deidre." The threat was clear. He was terrified. The voice loomed in his conscious, over and over, the threats jetting through his brain like nails shot into a board with a nail gun.

"Ah, yes, sweet Deidre. That pretty, young college student you corrupted and married after ridding yourself of your faithful wife of eighteen years. The wife from the homeland, the beautiful Constance, the one we selected for you." The Russian's voice was soft and loomed in the room, the threats implied. Dorothy shivered from the icy tone.

Smirkowitz said nothing as he struggled for breath. His brain flashed a dozen fears in color. He knew what they were capable of doing and he knew they'd do it. He was unable to speak. Worse of all, the silence terrorized him.

Finally, the voice spoke again. "Do you want details, Nikolay? Details of what we will do to your children and your new, young wife?"

"No, no. I don't. I will do it," Smirkowitz gasped, his voice hoarse with fear.

"See that you do. Immediately. And get her the insulin now. The bidding is tonight, and she will bring a pretty penny. Much more than her grandfather is offering for a reward. Our buyers love blond American woman. It's their way of getting back at the West."

Smirkowitz was silent and wondered if the loud breathing was his. He ran his fingers back and forth through his hair until all semblance of style was gone.

After a silence, the voice rasped again. "Or you know what will happen to your family while you watch."

Dr. Dude was drenched in sweat and shaking as he stared at his cell phone. He had no choice. He'd have to do it. He remained silent as he tried to cover his breathing.

"Oh, and the young girl from today, the one named Danielle? We'll get her, too, I promise. She's on the list, too." The Russian's voice was matter-of-fact.

Smirkowitz's voice quavered with fear. "Danielle knows nothing. You should leave her alone. You are moving too fast," Smirkowitz added, hoping to dissuade the bloodthirsty maniac. "You'll be the downfall of all of us."

"Danielle, yes, we know about Danielle. She will either come with us, or she will die like the others."

The phone went dead. Dottie could hear nothing. She also heard what she thought was a sob escape from Dr. Dude's throat. After several minutes, she heard his office door close quietly. Rushed steps passed by the supply closet door.

Dottie sat quietly in her hiding place, paralyzed with fear. She hadn't heard all of the conversation, but she was petrified. These were very bad people. They had to find Allison. She had to tell Mic. Allison's life depended on it.

Chapter 18

Michaela was annoyed, bored, and started to fidget for the second time that day. She crossed and uncrossed her legs for the fifth time in three minutes and felt the slow creep of her temper working its way out into the open. She looked around at the cubicles in the Virginia State Board of Dentistry offices. She decided she would hate to work there.

She took a deep breath and tried again, her voice patient and her smile professional. She stared across the refinished oak desk at the attorney for the Virginia Board of Dentistry.

Her dark eyes bored into those of the smug man across from her. "Now, Mr. Burton, I have in my hand five complaints against Dr. Nicholas Smirkowitz, and as you know, complaints are a matter of public record. Tell me, once again, why none of these complaints have ever been investigated." Mic knew her voice was biting, but she didn't care.

Tony Burton, the attorney for the Board, was a youngish-looking thirty-something with a hawk-like nose, black glasses, and a receding hairline. He looked just like any young lawyer who worked for the Virginia Attorney General's office. He pasted on his bland smile, furrowed his brow, and said, "Ms. McPherson, I've told you several times already. What is it that you don't understand?" He glared at her as though she was a moron.

"What I don't understand, Mr. Burton, is why Dr. Smirkowitz hasn't been investigated," Mic snapped, her voice peevish. "He's had multiple complaints lodged against him."

"They were not investigated because the intake officer, the person who takes the complaint initially, didn't feel they had merit."

Mic could feel the blood rush to her head. She worked to control her temper and her body language. "What are the credentials of these intake officers?" Michaela demanded in an angry voice. "Are they qualified to make these decisions, such as who's a questionable practitioner and who isn't?" She hoped her smirk wasn't too obvious.

Michaela saw a flicker of anger jump across Burton's face. He clearly didn't like his authority challenged. He glared at her over his black, horn-rimmed frames. When he spoke, his voice was condescending.

"Yes, of course they are. They've met the requirements for the job position and been hired by the state personnel system."

"Well, that convinced me," Mic retorted, in an equally sarcastic voice. "What I mean is how have they acquired the skill set or the assessment skills, to determine whether a case has merit and whether it should be handed over to a Board of Dentistry investigator? Are they dental school flunkies or something?"

Burton scowled at her. "They have continuing education and on-the-job training. I assure you, they are more than qualified."

"I'm not assured," Mic stated flatly and stared him down, her dark eyes locked with his.

Burton shook his head and continued to drone, like he was talking to an idiot. "There are specific criteria, based on Virginia law that a complaint must reach in order to be sent forward. Frankly, none of those complaints rose to that level."

Mic was livid. It was hard to keep her temper. "Okay, so you're telling me that five women, a combination of patients and staff members, who've filed similar, and in some cases, the same complaints against Smirkowitz, don't suggest a problem."

"Apparently not," Burton said as he moved papers around his immaculate desk.

Michaela shook her head. "That's impossible. I don't accept your conclusion."

Burton smiled tightly. "No one has asked you to accept it." The sarcasm level rose in his voice.

"It's not plausible to me that no one has seen fit to send a Board of Dentistry investigator to his office or had an investigator interview any of the complaints? Is that correct?"

Burton cleared his throat and reformed his bland smile. He stared at her over his half glasses, "Yes, that's absolutely correct."

Michaela's laugh was sarcastic. "Really, Mr. Burton, that sounds ...well ...at best, ludicrous and derelict to me. Generally, where there's that much smoke, there is a fire, and you and I both know it."

Burton doodled on his legal pad for a few seconds, shuffled a few more papers, looked up, furrowed his brow again and asked, "Will there be anything else, Ms. McPherson?"

Mic wasn't finished yet. "Yes, what about the complaints of staff turnover and lack of experienced staff in the practice."

Burton consulted his files again and took several moments to think. "The charges were not substantiated, and the complaints were made from several staff members who'd been dismissed due to insubordination."

Michaela shook her head. "This is just too much to overlook, Mr. Burton. Why won't you help us? Another young woman is missing …this is the second we know about in less than eighteen months."

Burton stood and extended his hand. His voice was curt. "I believe we're done here, Ms. McPherson."

Mic stood, all five feet three inches of her, plus another two inches, thanks to her boot heels. "I am a citizen of the Commonwealth of Virginia, and your job is to protect me against unsafe practitioners, and you're not doing that. I'll be going down to see the Attorney General. Be advised."

Burton remained standing. "That's your right. Have a good evening."

Michaela nodded, held her head high and quickly left the Board of Dentistry offices, angry to the core. What kind of control does Smirkowitz have over these people? Whoever is steering this boat has some pull. A woman followed her out of the suite.

Mic pushed the button for the elevator and got on with another woman. Lost in her thoughts and anger, she was stunned when the woman called her by name.

"Ms. McPherson, I work for the Board of Dentistry as an investigator, and you are correct, Dr. Smirkowitz should be investigated."

"Then why hasn't he been? What's he got over these people or who does he have in his corner?" She paused for a second before adding, "Where's his power?"

Mic surveyed the woman, who was attractive and professionally dressed, maybe in her late forties. She appeared anxious but intent on doing the right thing.

The woman gave her a sad smile. "I wish I knew, but I don't. I can tell you this, though. Smirkowitz has connections at the highest levels of state government because absolutely nothing, and no one, can touch Nicholas Smirkowitz."

Michaela's brow furrowed. The elevator doors opened into the main lobby and Mic turned to the woman.

"How do you know this? What's your name?" Mic couldn't let her go without more information.

"My husband is a state trooper, and my name is Claire Daniels. I was so concerned about Dr. Smirkowitz's behavior and the complaints against him, I asked my husband to use his resources to check him out."

Mic stayed put, keeping her finger on the button to keep the elevator door open. "What did your husband find out?"

"Nothing. Nada. Zip. He was told to leave it alone," she said as her face reddened in anger.

Mic frowned but said nothing.

Claire continued, "I can tell you this. I'll lose my job if anyone knows I've spoken with you." She looked nervously over her shoulder.

Mic placed her hand on the frightened woman's shoulder. "I will do everything I can to keep your confidence. Here's my card, call me if you hear of anything."

Claire accepted the card but remained silent. She looked uncertain.

"You did the right thing, Claire," Michaela assured her. "We are afraid Allison Massie, the young woman taken yesterday after leaving Smirkowitz's office, will die if we don't find her soon."

Claire said nothing and stared at Mic's card.

Claire raised her head to look at Mic, her eyes huge with fear. She gave Mic an uncertain smile and pressed the elevator button for her floor. "Good luck. I hope you get him," she whispered.

Mic gave her a bright smile. "We will. Never fear. We'll get him." She waved goodbye as the elevator door closed. "Keep in touch, Claire," she pleaded again as the elevator closed. She thought she saw Claire nod briefly as the door closed.

Chapter 19

Allison woke again but couldn't keep her eyes open. She was barely conscious. She desperately wanted to stay awake, but she was so cold, she just wanted to sleep. She'd curled her body up into a little ball when a loud noise jarred her awake. She strained her neck to see if someone had entered her jail, but she couldn't see anything. She could only smell the dark, dank earth and the blankets and quilts the man had hurriedly thrown over her. They smelled like old blood. They had that metallic scent she associated with the blood lab she'd taken in dental hygienist school.

She heard the noise again and realized it was a tree branch brushing against a metal roof. She forced herself to look around and realized she was in a barn. Allison tried to stay calm and focus on her surroundings, but it was hard and big tears oozed from her eyes. As she struggled to maintain consciousness, several terrifying thoughts nagged at her. *What are they going to do to me? What did I do for this to happen to me? I'm going to die soon if I don't get some insulin.*

Allison shut her eyes as more hot tears squeezed through her eyelids. She lay there and prayed for help as she tried to reconstruct what had happened after she'd left Dr. Smirkowitz's office. Who had jumped into her car at the stoplight at Monument and Stuart Circle? Had someone already been in the car? Who pushed her to the ground in the parking lot at Dr. Smirkowitz's office? Why had Dr. Smirkowitz been mean to her? She was perfectly qualified for the job, and he'd known it. One of the people who had jumped her had worn a hat and she still didn't know if it had been a man or a woman. She did remember the person had been big and strong. She remembered thick-pursed lips that could have belonged to a man or woman. She sifted through numerous images that flashed through her mind but nothing was clear. Everything seemed unclear and she couldn't focus. She really needed her insulin.

She had been terrified and couldn't remember anything.

I wonder if there's something else I could have done to stop this? If I had my insulin, I would think better.

She felt the night closing in on her brain again as she lost consciousness.

Chapter 20

Dottie stayed in the closet, petrified with indecision as she thought about what she'd heard. She was sick with fear, and her legs felt paralyzed and too heavy to move. Her mind replayed the conversation and fear for Allison and her family mounted. Finally, Dottie stood, her legs shaking as she hoisted her body up and grabbed a wall shelf for support. She felt dizzy and giddy all over. She was getting old, but she refused to acknowledge that her eighty-third birthday was just a few short months away.

Dottie reached for the doorknob and snuck out of the supply closet. As she passed the staff kitchen, she heard female voices. It was the two front desk women. Tilda and the younger lady, the one with the baby whose name she couldn't remember. She strained her ears to listen.

"Why haven't you cleaned these dishes? It's not like we've got a bunch of patients. What have you been doing?" Tilda asked in a low angry voice.

"Working. And where did you go?" the younger voice asked defensively.

Dottie could hear the anger in Tilda's voice. She's one mean woman.

"Were you out shopping again? I'm sick of all the perks you get and the rest of us don't. It's not fair," the younger woman hissed. "We're all thinking of talking to Dr. S. about it."

"I had to go to Staples to get a few printer cartridges," Tilda's voice remained calm, but Dottie imagined she'd like to strangle the younger woman. "I've got to print the end of month reports next week."

"Where were you? You weren't at the office supply store," Janie accused.

Tilda ignored her. "And, I suggest you talk to no one. Don't forget, you all work for me first, then the doctor. You wouldn't want to be fired now, would you?"

The young woman's mouth fell open and then she clamped it shut.

"We could fire two of you in one day, no problem." Tilda continued as Dottie stayed transfixed just outside the door.

"Is that what you did to Danielle? Did you fire her? What's gonna happen to her now? Is she gonna disappear too? Or never be heard of again?"

"Shhh, be quiet, someone might heard you," Tilda's low voice commanded hoarsely.

The young woman continued as if she didn't hear Tilda. "That lady cop, or whatever she is, I know she knows something." The young woman's voice had reached a feverish pitch. "Could you believe she bought that monster dog into the office? I just about died."

"Hush," the older woman cautioned sharply. "Lower your voice. These walls are paper thin," and I don't know who is still here." Her voice was low and serious.

Dottie listened carefully. Tilda presented herself as very pious and religious. She was supposedly a super religious lady in the quilting guild. Dottie had purchased a hand-sewn quilt from her a few years ago, but she'd never liked her much. She thought the woman had an ugly streak. Tilda had mean eyes and a cruel smile.

"Dr. Smirkowitz is gone," the young woman said as her voice rose as she challenged Tilda. "I saw him drive by the front window in his gold Porsche. The dental techs are cleaning supplies. It's okay for us to talk."

Dottie knew Tilda hated defiance, especially from someone she supervised. "I told you to quiet down, Janie.

Now." Tilda grabbed the younger woman's upper arm and squeezed it hard.

Janie screamed at her, "Don't you touch me and don't you ever push me again."

Dottie could imagine Tilda's face suffused with anger.

"Shut up, you little fool. I'm not gonna ask again. You're going to get us in trouble."

"Suppose something happens to me? I resisted him when he came on to me. He's a letch."

"He was just teasing you, making you feel good and pretty," she said.

"No, he wasn't teasing me," Janie said, her voice cracking. "He would have raped me, if you hadn't come in, and you know it."

Tilda laughed. "You have quite an imagination. It was nothing like that. Besides, if you don't shut up, something will happen to you," Tilda threatened.

"What? Who's gonna take care of my baby? Nothing can happen to me." Janie's voice was frightened and hysterical. "And, you shut up. You're not my boss."

"Lower your voice. You'll get in trouble for sure if someone hears you and tells Dr. S. Then you will disappear for sure, and to be honest, I'd help him do it." Tilda's voice was rough and abrasive.

"Let go of me, Tilda. That hurts," Janie whined. "You're mean and crazy. I believe what the techs say about you now."

Oh my God. Tilda really is mean, much meaner than I thought. I've gotta get Mic to check on her. She could be part of Allison's disappearance. Dorothy remained silent, sick with fear as she listened.

"And just what do they say?" Tilda mimicked

"That you're crazy …crazy and cruel. You hurt me, Tilda. It's gonna be a bad bruise, and besides, it's bleeding."

"Shut up, you little wimp, and tell those stupid techs to be quiet if they value their jobs and life." Her voice reeked of malice.

Dottie's heart beat quickly as she heard the water faucet and the clanking of dishes. She leaned her good ear against the wall but couldn't hear anything else. She could picture the two women washing and drying cups, saucers, and glasses and placing them in the cabinet for the next day. Finally, someone cut off the water, and she could hear again. It was Janie.

"Well, I just don't know. I'm gonna tell my husband about all of this tonight. He's good friends with some Richmond police officers, and they can look into what's happening' here," she said, her voice now a whimper.

"NO. Absolutely no," Tilda hollered, her voice raspy and hoarse. "Keep your mouth shut, if you know what's good for you."

Dottie could imagine Tilda waving her arms, her face beet red with disapproval, and her face scrunched up in a scowl. Tilda was a tall, strong, formidable woman.

Tilda wasn't done. "If you do say anything, I can guarantee that you'll disappear and go the same route of Maria, Danielle, and most likely Allison."

Janie was quiet for a moment and Dottie heard her choke back a sob. "So, what do we do? Aren't we contributing to this if we do nothing?"

Tilda's voice softened. "Not really, we truly don't know anything. We just have our suspicions."

Janie said nothing.

Tilda's voice changed back to anger. "Did you hear me? We just have suspicions. That's all. Besides, no one is hurting us or threatening us, are they?"

"That's not true, Tilda, and you know it. We know Dr. S. tried to force himself on Danielle, and we know the Allison girl ran out of here crying yesterday. We know something is happening here, and it's bad."

Tilda said firmly. "We don't really know about Danielle. We only know what she told us. For all we know, Allison could have run out crying because she didn't get the job."

"I don't know how much longer I'm gonna be able to be a party to this. It's keeping me up at night and I can't sleep." Janie voice was firm.

"You'll be quiet for as long as it takes. That is, if you want to see your baby grow up," Tilda snarled.

Dorothy's heart almost stopped beating in the hall. She's threatening her!

"Are you threatening me, Tilda? Are you involved in this nasty business with Smirkowitz?"

"I'm simply telling you what will happen, that's all," Tilda said, her tone superior and self-righteous.

Janie gaped at her, turned and left the room with tears in her eyes.

Tilda watched her from the window as she walked wearily to her old beat-up car in the parking lot. *I'm gonna tell Dr. Smirkowitz, and he's not gonna be happy.* She smiled in anticipation of the conversation. Janie was a little pathetic baby and she was sick of her anyway.

Dottie stayed hidden outside as she processed the information. They'd have to investigate Tilda. She was looking more and more like a problem. I've got to call Michaela. I've got to call her now.

Chapter 21

Dottie sat in the blissful solitude of her Cadillac as thoughts raced through her mind as quickly as blood coursed through her body. She laid her head against the plush leather cushions and waited for her heart to quiet down. Her mind was overloaded with the possibilities. Dr. Dude sounded worse than a pervert. He sounded like some kind of sexual pervert and murderer, and he wasn't acting alone. It was Tilda too. And there was some other man, a Russian — at least she thought he sounded Russian — involved. Dottie's mind was reeling with possibilities.

She reached for her car phone and dialed Michaela, but there was no answer on her cell and home phones.

I'll call her again when I get home and tell her everything but let me get out of this parking lot before someone sees me.

Dottie started her car and backed out of her parking place. It had started to snow again, and she drove carefully through the piles of plowed snow near the curbs. She jumped out of her skin when her phone rang. It was Cookie, her housekeeper.

"Hello, Cookie," she answered, her voice quite unlike her own. It sounded shaky.

"Countess, are you okay? I was worried. I've been calling, and I couldn't reach you. Where've you been?"

Cookie's matter-of-fact questions irritated Dottie. Everyone treated her like a baby, or at least a babbling old lady, and she was neither of these things. Older maybe, but not senile, demented or babbling.

"Just shopping. I'm on my way home now, though," Dottie lied as she tried to keep the anger out of her voice.

"Would you like for Henry to pick you up in the Jeep? It's supposed to sleet later and the warnings of black ice are all over the TV."

"No, no, no. I'm on my way. I should be there within thirty or so minutes," Dottie said sharply. "Now, leave me alone and let me drive. You know the world's in danger when I talk and drive."

"Yes, the world is in danger. Good bye, Countess," Cookie said. "See you shortly."

Dottie slammed down her cell phone, rolled her eyes and wished everyone would leave her the hell alone. First Michaela, then the cop, and now Cookie. She tried to remember her thoughts before the phone call, and it all came rushing back to her. And what about that conversation between the two front desk clerks? Should she worry about that? Dottie pulled her vehicle off the road into a parking space to answer her mobile. It was Michaela.

Chapter 22

Smirkowitz gritted his teeth and glanced in the rear-view mirror of his Porsche GT2RS as he backed out of his driveway. Life had been good to him, at least, so far. He stared at his face in the rearview mirror and hardly recognized himself. The face that looked back was scared, white, and uncertain. Smirkowitz brushed his fears away. No one could touch him. He had money, prestige, and a beautiful, young wife. Even though he paid alimony and child support, he could easily afford it. He drove a two hundred and fifty-thousand-dollar automobile that was arguably one of the finest in the world. His imposing Tudor-style home located in Richmond's elite west end was the most expensive in the neighborhood and was larger than any other of the McMansions in the area.   As he considered his accomplishments, his spirits rose. He'd made it. He had it all. Money, fame, cars, women, a thriving dental practice, great kids. There was nothing he didn't have. He smiled at himself in the mirror, and his confidence returned briefly before fading.

Is my life ever going to be the same or are the good times over? Dude could feel his anxiety ratchet up as he headed down Cary Street, a vial of long-acting insulin tucked into a cold backpack on the seat next to him.

He cursed as his cell phone rang and the digital display on his dash announced the familiar number of his ex-wife. The last person in the world he wanted to talk to, but he grudgingly clicked the button.

"Hello, Constance. What's up?" he barked in his gruffest voice. He wasn't up for a bunch of whining from his ex. There was enough stress in his life without having to talk with her. The divorce had been painful enough, and their relationship had only worsened with his new marriage and new baby. They were barely civil.

There wasn't an answer, and then he thought he heard a stifled sob. "Constance, what's wrong? Are you crying?"

Another stifled sob escaped. He could picture her sitting in the sunroom of their former home in her favorite chintz chair, her dark hair pulled up in a chignon with tendrils framing her face. She'd be dressed in a silk blouse and dark pants thumbing through a magazine. Now in her mid-forties, Constance remained a beautiful woman.

"Nicholas, I'm scared," she finally managed. "Someone tried to kidnap Nicholas, Jr. this afternoon. After school." Her voice ended in a high-pitched screech.

Smirkowitz's blood turned to ice, and he could feel his heart jump violently in his chest.

"What do you mean? Did they snatch him from school? Who took him from school?" Dude's voice was sharp. He was short of breath. He took his hand off the gear control to rub the chill bumps from his arms.

Constance's voice was hesitant. "I ...I don't know. I don't know what to say. A little while ago, a police officer came here and brought Nicholas home. The officer told me a tall thin man in a black sedan tried to pull Nicholas off the school bus as he climbed the steps. Nicholas's friend kicked the guy in the groin, and another boy kicked the man in the behind, and Nicholas managed to get on the bus. The bus driver called 911, and the officer assigned to the school tried to follow the assailant, but the man escaped in his car."

Dr. Dude's fear was palpable. He was silent for a moment and then asked, "What kind of black car? Did they get a license number? Have they chased the car down or do they know who it is?"

A sob escaped from Constance before she spoke. "I don't think they got a license plate, and I don't think they know who it was. I didn't really ask. I was just happy that our son was safe."

Smirkowitz was quiet.

After a moment Constance asked in an accusing tone, "Don't you want to know if he is safe? Don't you want to know if your son is okay?" Her voice was loud and angry.

"Of course I do," Dude snapped. "What the hell do you think? Of course, I'm worried about him. How is he?"

Constance was silent for a moment and said in a low voice, "What have you done, Nicholas Smirkowitz? Are you in trouble with those people again? Are these the same guys that threatened you a few years ago back?"

Dr. Dude was silent for a moment. "Of course not, Constance," he assured her.

The silence was deafening. She didn't believe him.

"You know I haven't gambled in years," he said wearily. "There is nothing that I've done to cause this. Maybe it was an attempted kidnapping."

"I wish I could believe you, Nicholas," she said sadly.

Dude could hear the question and uncertainty in her voice. For some reason he felt the need to reassure her and said,

"I promise, Con Con," he said, reverting to a nickname he'd used for her in the old days when things were good between them. "I've done nothing to cause anyone to want to kidnap our son. I promise. You know how much I love him."

Constance was silent. She could hear the inflection in his voice that she could always hear whenever he lied. "I don't believe you, Nicholas. You're a liar and always have been. I am going to call the Richmond Police and ask them to look at everything you've been doing lately. I think you're involved in this somehow, and I think you're involved in something up to your eyeballs... something that involves our son's safety."

"What are you talking about? Constance, Constance, please let's talk about this."

But it was too late. His elegant ex-wife had hung up. With a huge sigh of anxiety, Dr. Dude speed-dialed his best and only friend.

"Hello, handsome," the voice was sensual and musical. "Do you want me? Do you need me?" she asked hopefully.

"It's Constance," he said hoarsely. "You've got to do what we discussed last week, scare Constance to keep her from talking. Do it now. Right now."

"Okay, with pleasure." the voice said before clicking off.

Dr. Dude accelerated his powerful car and flew down Route 33 as he pushed his car as fast as the streets allowed. He sighed deeply as fear for his children became a permanent reality in his mind. All because he hadn't paid his due to the devil. Dude reviewed and rationalized his life. There'd always been so much expected of him, and he'd done his best. Everything and everyone had been so unfair.

Chapter 23

It was almost dusk when Dottie pulled her Cadillac onto Monument Avenue and crawled down Richmond's famous Avenue, oblivious to the honks, beeps, and curses of other drivers. She was headed home. The roads were freezing, and she didn't want to wreck her new car or slip and fall. Mic would just have to come to her house. She called Michaela.

Mic answered immediately. "Dorothy Borghase, where are you? I've been worried to death. I've called and called your cell phone, left messages, and you never responded," she said, relieved Dottie was safe.

Dottie felt short of breath, most likely from anxiety. Her words came in small gasps. "Michaela, I have to talk to you. It's critical."

"You sound short of breath. Are you okay? Where are you, Dottie?" Mic spoke hurriedly, picturing the worst.

"Yes, yes, yes," Dorothy panted. "I'm okay, and I'm in my car and almost home. You come to my house. I need to get home before the roads freeze again. It's already dark, and you know I don't drive much after dark."

"Are you sure you shouldn't be going to the hospital? I can call your heart doctor and have him waiting for you." Mic was concerned over Dottie's shortness of breath.

Dottie tossed her head in anger and part of her silver hair fell out of her bun. "I'm fine. I've been spying over at Dr. Dude's office, and I want you to check out Tilda, the woman who works at Dude's office. I just overheard her threaten one of the other staff. I think she's involved in this, in fact I'm positive she is."

"Involved how?"

"I think she knows about the missing women... and Allison. I heard her mention names and now she's gone and threatened Janie, the young lady that makes appointments."

Mic was quiet. She didn't like Tilda either. "I'll check her out and I'll have Slade look into her too. She's a pretty angry person, no question. Now, do you need Henry to pick you up?"

"No, I am driving home now. I'm fine. Just excited, and I need a glass of sherry. Now, get over here," she demanded using her haughty countess voice. I'll have Cookie make us some snacks."

Michaela sighed. "All right. Give me about forty-five minutes. I'll go to Biddy's after I see you but first, I have to do a few things on Allison's case and I'm calling Slade to check out Tilda."

"You can have happy hour at my house," Dottie snapped as she pulled into her circular drive in front of her mansion. "It's not such a bad place," she reminded her friend sharply.

Mic ignored her. "See you shortly," Mic added as she placed her home phone on the cradle and shook her head. There was no one, absolutely no one, like the Countess Dorothy-plus-three-more-names Borghase. She loved her dearly and worried about her constantly.

Dottie laid on her horn and waited for her male servant and chauffeur, Henry, to come help her from the car. He always pulled her car into the garage ever since she'd run into the side of the garage last year. Damned wall. If she hadn't known better, she'd swear someone moved it.

Chapter 24

It was just past dusk when Dr. Dude swung his old pickup behind the weathered barn near Barboursville, not too far from the home of General Barbour and the excellent Barboursville Vineyard. He had stashed his Porsche and good clothes on a farm he owned several miles away. Dude had a love affair with Barboursville wine. He'd even managed to stop in on his way and pick up a case of Barboursville's dry, sparking wine, a great rival for any French champagne. He noticed the looks he'd gotten from a few customers as he'd loaded his eight-hundred-dollar case of wine into the bed of his old beat-up pickup he used as a decoy whenever he traveled to his other "property."

Dude smiled happily to himself as he sped down Route 33 towards the next remote farm he owned, one of three he'd purchased as storage areas for his "other business." He was feeling better. He'd taken care of the "Constance" problem, secured his bubbly for later in the evening, and arranged for roses to be delivered to his wife. He'd even changed into dirty old jeans and a red flannel shirt that he kept in the backseat of his pickup so he'd look like he belonged in the old vehicle. He had done everything possible not to attract attention to himself, and he knew he'd been successful... nobody would remember the wine. They'd all been tipsy from the tasting room. He nodded to strangers and waved at them as he backed his old Chevy pickup out of the parking lot of Barboursville Winery.

Smirkowitz parked the pickup behind the barn where it was usually hidden from the road by a grove of hardwood trees. The winter trees offered little protection from peering eyes. He hoped the old pickup looked as abandoned as the barn he used to hold his "transports." Fortunately, there was some protection offered by a line of cedar trees that stretched along the perimeter of the property. Dude had purchased the farm about seven years ago with the original intention of building a grand manor home and starting a Virginia farm winery, but the easy success of his trafficking business had become so lucrative that he hadn't had time to get the vineyard planted and the home designed. Good thing, since he had a different wife now. Besides the cost of his divorce took a large chunk of his time and money, and for several years his practice revenues had dipped.

Smirkowitz thought about Constance as he walked towards the barn. They'd had a lot of good years, but she'd always been suspicious of his activities, his bad habits that had always included gambling, women, and cocaine. Over the years, he'd managed to give up the gambling and the cocaine, but he still needed that extra "edge" in life to keep him engaged and entertained. Constance had made him see a psychiatrist when they were still married, and he'd been diagnosed as a sex addict, a disease he chose to do nothing about. At the same time, he'd been diagnosed with a borderline personality and addictive disorder. When an old family friend from the homeland approached him about "storing" some women for a few nights and promised him thousands of dollars in return, Smirkowitz could hardly wait to get involved. Six years after he'd stored his first "transport," the returns had been considerably lucrative. He loved the money, selecting the girls, and all the benefits his "extra" business offered him.

Dude smiled to himself as he slammed the door of his pickup and rounded the corner of the barn. He yanked opened the old wooden doors and entered the freezing, gloomy building and went over to the stall where he saw Allison bundled up in a small heap. She was as white as a ghost and as cold as a corpse. He knelt next to her and shook her, but she didn't wake up.

He fervently hoped she wasn't dead. They'd kill him if she were. His partners had anticipated her worth at several million dollars. A feeling of dread permeated him. He reached out and touched her carotid artery. He could feel a faint heartbeat. He smiled thinly and breathed easier as he opened his leather pouch and searched for the syringe of insulin he'd received from one of his physician friends after a racket ball game the evening before. He uncovered the young woman and admired her beauty. Her pale face had a sheen of perspiration that gave it a glow, and even in the dark light, he could see the shining highlights of her long blond hair. She looked like a beautiful wax doll, even in a coma. He lifted her navy blue dress she had worn with such high hopes to her job interview yesterday. He pulled out his pocketknife and cut a hole in her tights, and injected the entire syringe of insulin into her thigh.

He watched her carefully, but she didn't move. Her breathing was slow and labored, and he could smell a fruity odor on her breath, one common in diabetes when their blood sugar was low. He checked his watch. Two minutes had passed since he injected the insulin. He knew a person unconscious from hypoglycemia was pale, had a rapid heartbeat, and was often soaked in sweat, but he wondered if she needed more.

He fingered the second syringe in his leather pouch as he pulled up Web MD on his smartphone. He'd forgotten everything he'd ever known about diabetes mellitus and diabetic coma. You didn't need any diabetes info when you made several million a year designing teeth for the rich and famous. He smiled to himself and laughed aloud. He couldn't believe his dumb neurosurgeon friends took calls and operated for ten hours a day for the same amount of money he earned. His liability costs were almost nonexistent, while their malpractice insurance had skyrocketed.

Web MD was not helpful, but he remembered if he gave her too much insulin, he could give her a cookie or orange juice or something with sugar in it, and she'd calm right down. Wouldn't she? Dude really wasn't sure, but knew he didn't want to kill her. He'd been told she would bring an easy few mil at the bidding tonight ...maybe more if they could get her looking good ...and in his opinion, she looked great in a coma. Middle Eastern men loved blond American women and would pay millions to own them. They were transfixed by the color of their hair and their pale skin. He'd seen men reach out in the streets just to touch an American woman enthralled by cascading blond hair. The men were awestruck and captivated by the differences. The women were special to them and stood out. Fair and blond, well ... that was at the top of the prize list. If anything happened to this prize, they'd kill him and his family for sure. Dude stared at her a bit longer and thought she looked like a sleeping beauty. Then he shook her roughly to wake her up.

Allison's eyes fluttered open and widened in fear when she saw Dr. Smirkowitz leering over her. "What are you doing here? Someone kidnapped me outside your office."

Smirkowitz smiled at her but said nothing. She truly was beautiful. He watched her critically as her lovely blue eyes stared at him and oozed large tears. Sad and crying, she was more tragically beautiful. He felt a wave of excitement pass over him. He didn't speak to her at all or offer any comfort. Why should he? Her fate was set. He checked his watch impatiently and pulled his coat closer around his shoulders. Damn, it was cold in that barn, and it was getting dark. He wanted to go home and curl up with his wife and a bottle of wine.

Allison continued to stare at the dentist until it began to dawn on her that he was her captor. Her face crinkled as she started to cry, her tears accompanied by mournful sobs. "Why are you doing this to me, Dr. Smirkowitz? You know my father will pay you a lot of money to get me back?" She kept her arms down by her sides so he wouldn't realize she'd managed to untie herself.

Dude laughed aloud, loudly. "Now, really my dear. Do you think I need any money?"

Allison hesitated and gulped. "But...why, why then would you have me kidnapped and put in this freezing place?"

Smirkowitz smiled slowly and said as he brushed blond curls off her forehead, "Because, it's the sport of the game. I am playing a game, and the stakes are high. It's sort of my second business. Your number came up, that's all. Nothing personal against you or your family. He smiled slyly at her.

She reached up and slapped Dr. Dude. "Don't touch me, you pervert. What are you, some kind of sociopathic monster?" she screamed as she attempted to sit up, smacking his hands away. "What do you mean 'my number came up'? What's that supposed to mean?"

Dr. Dude looked at her and smiled. "You're even more beautiful when you are angry. I just love a feisty woman." His eyes roamed over her.

She sat up on her elbow and was only inches from Dude's face. She could smell his cologne and remember she'd detested it at her interview. It made her nauseous. "You're a monster, a psycho," Allison assured him as her blue eyes locked with his. "You'll never get away with this."

Dude laughed shortly. "Not true, my dear. I've been getting away with it for years and that's not going to change. It's a game I play, and the stakes are high," he added proudly.

111

Allison continued to glare at him but said nothing.

Dude continued. "Your number. Your attributes. Your looks. My friends, or the men who play this game, love young beautiful women with blond hair. You possess all of these characteristics. So, you're the winner."

"Winner of what?" Allison asked, fear evident in her voice.

Dude gave her a strange look. "Why the game of course, you silly girl. Haven't you been listening to me? You are the winner. We picked you over many others. The game I have been playing for years. You'll bring the most money of any woman I've ever entered."

Fear froze her blood. "What are you talking about, Dr. Smirkowitz? Just call my dad and drop me off at my grandparents' house. I promise I won't tell him any of this, and we'll forget this ever happened." Her hand reached for her jacket pocket.

Dude shook his head and gave her a strange look. "Call your father? I couldn't possibly do that." He grinned at her. "That'd be cheating, and they'd never understand." He shook his head. "Besides, I like this game, especially when I win, which I will tonight, thanks to you." He patted her shoulder softly.

Allison shook off his hand and demanded in a strong voice. "Who are 'they'? What are you talking about and what is this game about?"

Dr. Smirkowitz was silent and stared into Allison's eyes.

Allison stared back, but he could see her shaking.

"Really," she said in a voice dripping in sarcasm. "Don't you think I deserve to know about the game since I am the 'winner' of the game for you?"

Dude stared at her and felt pleasure flow through him as he considered how exciting it would be to confide her fate. He could only imagine her dread and terror, and for some reason, he liked causing people pain. At least most people. Of course, he'd never caused pain to the people he truly loved, like his children. But Allison? She was nothing to him except a commodity. His body shuddered in anticipation.

He gave her a malicious smile. "Are you sure you want to know?" he asked as he changed position and sat cross-legged by her body.

"Yes, yes, I do," Allison insisted in a clear voice as she dug deeper and deeper into her pocket for her cell phone. The dose of insulin that had awakened her now worked against her and she felt sleepy and confused. She had to get her hands on her phone and dial for help.

Dude thought for a moment. "I have a commitment, a very old commitment." Then he added for some reason. "A commitment to some men who are different than anyone you have ever known. It's a family commitment. These men make lots of money selling women — beautiful young women — to men in different countries. I've turned this commitment into a game because it's fun and..."

He watched as Allison's mouth dropped open. "Selling women is a game? Are you telling me that you plan to sell me to some man somewhere?" The angst in her voice was palpable.

Dude nodded. "Yes, yes, yes," he answered as he stroked her shoulder, "but to a very rich man who will buy you for a lot of money, maybe several million dollars," he said in a soothing voice. "He'll pay more for you than anyone has ever paid for a woman we've sold. That's why I'll win the game."

Allison stared at him, terror displayed in every aspect of her face. "You're selling me?"

Dude ignored her and continued to tell his story. He enjoyed her attention and shock.

"I picked you as a winner over two years ago when I visited your first class at the dental school." He reached out and stroked her face. "You should feel proud that I was so compelled by your looks and beauty that I—"

Allison sat up and flung Dude's hand off her with all the force she could muster. His shoulder popped from the force, and Dr. Dude screamed in pain.

Allison screamed at him. "You're crazy. You'll never sell me. You're a sick psycho, a lunatic." She struggled to stand, but she couldn't. "What have you done to me, you pervert? I can't move!"

Dude whimpered as he grabbed and massaged his shoulder. His arm hung uselessly at his side. He stared at her. "You've hurt me; my shoulder is killing me. I think it's out of the socket." He groaned as he tried to move his arm.

Allison reached for the leg on an old farm table and tried to pull herself up, but she fell back down. Smirkowitz stared at her and rubbed his shoulder in confusion as she frantically wiggled her toes and massaged her thighs in an attempt to warm them up so she could move.

Dude watched her from the sidelines, obsessed with the pain in his shoulder.

Finally, she pulled herself to her knees and knelt for a moment as she looked up at the apron of the table.

I can do this, I can do this, she told herself repeatedly, as she slowly and methodically pulled herself up from the floor.

She held tightly to the table leg while the table supported her weight as she inched her way up. Dizziness and nausea washed over her. She stood unsteadily as she clung to the table edge and looked down at Smirkowitz, who was pale with pain. He had lifted his right arm with his left hand and was trying to stand as well.

When Dude saw Allison almost standing, he started yelling at her. "Don't you move, don't you go any further, you're gonna pay for this. I'm delivering you in a few hours."

The pair locked eyes just as Allison finally managed to stand upright on both feet. Excruciating pain shot up her legs from her feet and calves and it felt as though a trillion pins were sticking her extremities. Dude grabbed for her but missed as she scooted around the old table, grasping the sides to keep her balance.

Allison moved around the table out of his reach, but the pain in her legs was fierce, and she fell again. Once again, she righted herself, but the pain increased until it felt like long needles pricked her skin and muscles constantly. She was in agony but surged forward, praying for help as she saw daylight through the crack in the door. She struggled and grabbed everything she could to keep from falling. She looked back at Smirkowitz as he attempted to stand. She heard him cursing and yelling into his phone, obviously calling for help.

She knew she had to hurry. The door was right in front of her. She clawed at the old barn door latch when she heard a growl behind her. She turned her head as Dude reached for her with his good arm and pulled her down. The two tumbled to the floor. Smirkowitz screeched in pain as his leg pierced the pitchfork lying nearby. Allison had fallen on top of him. Blood spurted from his upper leg and pooled around them. Allison covered her ears to silence Smirkowitz's screams as she struggled to get off of his body. His warm blood flowed over her jacket.

Allison ignored the blood and the screams as she scratched her way along the barn door. She felt the prick of a needle enter the back of her leg as she noticed Dr. Dude had managed to crawl behind her. Allison kicked him again and slid out of the door before the insulin raced through her veins and sucked her speed and strength. She felt the cold patch of snow against her cheek as lay in there, half in and half out of the barn door. She spied a patch of blue in the sky before her world went dark.

Chapter 25

Tilda stirred her butter beans, mixed her dumplings and dumped them in the chicken stock. She reached for the stove dial and cut the burner down to low so her chicken would boil. She sat down at the kitchen table and contemplated the task before her. She smiled as she considered the duality of her life. She ran Dr. Smirkowitz's dental practice and met his every need during the day, and at night, she was the dutiful, religious wife to Wilbur. She was brilliant. She knew that because the voices told her so. In a little while, she would show Nicholas that she would do anything he ever asked her, and do it happily and without remorse.

Why does this man have so much power over her? She let him push her around for just a little bit of money every year when she knew he made millions in his dental practice not to mention his other "work" she helped him with. In truth, Tilda knew exactly why she did it. She loved Nicholas Smirkowitz and had loved him for more than twenty years.

Of course, he'd rejected her for the beautiful Constance, but Constance was only the first in a line of "other" women. Tilda shook her head and smiled as she removed her apron and hung it on a hook on the back of the kitchen door. She walked into her bedroom and freshened her makeup, except for her lipstick. She'd had her lips tattooed on years ago, not dark, just a pale pink. As she stared at herself in the mirror, she couldn't understand why Nicholas would want someone else. She was beautiful, many would say gorgeous, and her hourglass figure hadn't changed in twenty years. She knew she was a knockout and talked about it all the time. She smiled to herself as she remembered how girls in the office rolled their eyes and smiled. They know I'm the prettiest there. She'd been livid when an old high school friend had compared their figures a few months ago. Her old friend looked awful, every bit her age, and she'd gained more than thirty pounds since high school, had saggy boobs, wrinkles, stringy brown hair, and yellow teeth. She looked nothing like Tilda who'd remained a stunner at forty-three, especially with her perfect Smirkowitz smile. When the friend had commented the two of them "looked their age," Tilda had told her friend she was wrong and that she looked exactly the same as she'd looked twenty-five years ago. Her friend had smiled benevolently, refilled their wine glasses and told Tilda her eyes were "pasted on" and that she needed a new mirror. If the wine hadn't been so good, Tilda would have smacked her in the restaurant. Later she had decided her friend was just jealous of her, as were most women. She was smokin' hot, and she knew it. She just covered it up most of the time because of her religious convictions.

Tilda sauntered over to her husband's wood shop where Wilbur, tall and thin at fifty-one, knelt as he repaired a tractor motor. He'd been a good husband, but not too good in the sack, which was why she, a beautiful, sensual woman, had needed to go elsewhere to have her needs satisfied.

She touched Wilbur's shoulder and said softly, "Honey, I've got to go to Walmart for a little while and pick up a few things. I shouldn't be long."

Wilbur gave her a long look as he wiped grease off his hands. "You're right dressed up for Walmart. You goin' anywhere else?" His voice was suspicious.

Tilda gave him a demure smile, ran her index finger up his face and said, "No, of course not, honey, I got your favorite dinner cookin'. Chicken and Dumplins'. I'm fresh out of carrots, and I wanted to have them, too. We'll eat by the fire and watch the new religious flick on the DVR when I get back," she promised and winked at him.

Judith Lucci

Wilbur's dark eyes remained doubtful. "I got a meetin' at the church. The Vestry is meetin' tonight," he reminded her. "I won't be home until after nine o'clock. We're workin' on the budget."

Tilda smiled, she hoped not too brightly, "That's right, sugar, I'd forgotten. I'll wait up with your plate in the oven. Tomorrow's my late day, so we'll watch the movie when you get home, and who knows . . ." she said slyly and gave him a suggestive smile.

Wilbur kissed her cheek, "Take the truck, the roads will be slick as glass. Be careful."

"Do you need anything?" she asked coyly as she offered him her most sensual and inviting smile.

Wilbur shook his head, and Tilda hopped up in the truck and started the engine. She spotted a speck of blue in the sky as she checked the rearview mirror. This is going to be fun and some trip to Walmart. She chuckled, her heart pumping happily. She turned up the country station and sang along with the music as she headed out of her gravel drive.

Chapter 26

Michaela slammed her landline down in frustration as she contemplated what to do next. She'd called an old friend, a retired state trooper who'd been head of the investigations division and asked him about an investigation into Dr. Nicholas Smirkowitz. With his permission, she'd taped the phone call. He'd told her the Virginia State Police had received complaints on and off for years about Smirkowitz but said they'd had never really been allowed to fully examine the case because roadblocks were constantly put up in their way. He'd told her evidence tapes had gone missing, potential complaints and witnesses had changed their minds and that once, a judge had blocked their search warrant.

She clicked on the tape recorder and listened... "I just don't know how to explain it, Mic, or what to make of it. Our investigation always stopped at the attorney general's office or evidence kept disappearing. I was never part of the 'inner sanctum' that was permitted to know why Smirkowitz was untouchable."

The next part of the conversation had chilled her to the bone. "What I think is that somehow, this is tied to some powerful international group... maybe some sort of organized crime group. I just don't know any more than that."

Mic clicked off the recorder and texted Slade.

Chapter 27

Oleg Branislava, a bald, mid-level Bratva soldier in his mid-fifties sat with his feet propped up on a deeply scarred oak table at the unofficial, makeshift office of "the brotherhood" located in a rundown tobacco warehouse just south of the James River. He finished his report to Dimitri and tried to avoid the look of rage on his boss's face. Oleg chewed his pencil anxiously, put it down for a moment, picked up his heavy glass of vodka and drank greedily.

Dimitri Kazimir, a forty-some-year-old leader in the Bratva Russian mob raised his thick, black eyebrows in disapproval. His face was suffused with anger. Dimitri was powerfully built, a tree trunk of a man. His upper arms were the size of a Gwaltney holiday ham, and his thighs were even larger in proportion. His face had a long, thick scar that ran down the right side, adding to his sinister appearance. He grunted in disgust and rose from his seat, moving near the windows. He blew smoke rings toward the grimy warehouse windowpanes. The numerous windows, designed more than a hundred years ago to offer sunlight to cure tobacco, were grimy with a hundred years' worth of dirt. Even on a bright, sunny day, the light in the room was dull and dismal.

Oleg sat uncomfortably as Dimitri paced back and forth in front of the windows.

"How're things at home?" Oleg finally asked. "How's business?"

Dimitri returned to the table, sat down and reached for a smoke. "Good. Business is good. We've about recovered from the Soviet days when our businesses ran on the black markets. Even though we didn't thrive in those days, we managed to persevere and wait out Communism."

121

Oleg smiled and nodded. "Thank God for that. I've been away from the homeland a long time and didn't know." He reflected for a moment and said, "Those were bad times for Bratva, particularly for the family business since so much of our work back then was taken over by the gangs in Stalin's Gulags."

Dimitri frowned as angry emotions flickered over his heavy face as he remembered the past twenty-five years. He'd been a young man in Bratva then, a street soldier, but he remembered what had happened. "Yes, back when the "official" bastards in the Soviet Union cooperated with us during the day and cheated and murdered us by night," he growled as he slammed his fist on the table. He cursed in Russian.

"I remember," Oleg responded, his face sullen. "Bastards, indeed. Murderers, thieves, kidnappers. You name it, they did it."

Dimitri coughed and gave him a half smile. "But those days are gone, my friend. We're in power with our enemies dead or dying. It's been a heroic revival to have planned and been a part of." He toasted air with his heavy goblet.

"Yes." Oleg reached again for the vodka bottle and refilled their tumblers. "Now we control the government instead of them controlling us. I hear we control more than ten percent of Russia—particularly Moscow, St. Petersburg, Siberia, and the land to the south. Is this true?"

Dimitri smiled his wicked smile as the pair clinked glasses. "Oh yes, and more now. We control the richest and most productive areas of the largest country in the world. We've come a long way baby, eh." He downed his vodka.

Oleg slid the bottle toward his boss. "How big is the slave trade for us? I've not heard for a while."

Dimitri's smile widened. "It's huge and profitable. Second only to drugs and much safer. We're projecting over ten billion in women alone this year. We're getting them by the thousands from South and Central America and selling them as sex slaves all over the world." Dimitri looked happier than a kid on Christmas morning. "It's easy. Like taking candy from a baby."

Oleg nodded, pleased his boss was in a better mood. "Ten billion is a lot of revenue. Any problems getting them transported?"

Dimitri shook his head. "Nah, not much. No one cares about these people. They are poor, come from poor countries. It's so easy, low risk, very safe," he added as he rubbed his huge hands together in glee.

Oleg smiled broadly. "So, you're pleased to be heading up this profit center? Running the Bratva trafficking syndicate?"

Dimitri shrugged his shoulders and gave him an ambiguous look. "It's fine, I guess, but boring. I like more exciting assignments where you encounter danger ...you know, like running arms, even drugs. Running women and children is dull for me. It is an old man's job, and I am not yet old," he scowled as he considered his position.

Oleg said nothing but sipped his vodka. It was almost dark outside. He wondered where Smirkowitz was but didn't want to raise Dimitri's anger again. He'd heard stories that the man's temper was horrific, and he'd lash out cruelly at most anyone, even if they were his closest friend.

Dimitri continued to talk. "There is one thing though ...there is a growing market for white, blond American women, so we need to plan a way to capture more of them for the slave trade. They are a highly desirable commodity in the Middle East. Each woman is worth easily one mil. Let's think about that, eh, Oleg?"

"Of course, I've some ideas as does another comrade you haven't met yet."

Dimitri nodded, "Good. Things are set for tonight, Oleg, correct?"

The men drank in silence for a few seconds, and Dimitri stared at Oleg and repeated his question. "Things are set for tonight, yes?"

Oleg wiped his dry lips with a soiled handkerchief. He stared at the short, stocky, man across from him and said, "I don't know. I saw one woman yesterday. She's a prize."

"What do you mean you don't know? Things must be set for this evening," he said harshly.

Oleg groaned inwardly. "I hope so, but Smirkowitz isn't always reliable, at least like I'd like."

Dimitri waited patiently to hear more.

"I talked to Nicholas earlier, and he assured me things were set and on schedule."

"Do you think they are fine?" Dimitri glared at him, his face angry.

Oleg swallowed, "I hope so. But, I'm not sure. I've found him to be more and more unreliable lately." Oleg sighed deeply. "Nikolay has been slipping lately. He's difficult to reach and hard to read."

Dimitri turned and focused his non-expressive, beady eyes on Oleg. "That's not acceptable, Oleg. He must deliver or be expended." He paused for a moment and studied Oleg's face to be sure he understood and then continued, "Tell him he must deliver or else."

Oleg shrugged his shoulders and nodded. "I've done that. I threatened the lives of his children today as well as the life of his new wife and baby."

Dimitri's scarred face darkened in anger as he reached for the vodka bottle and threw it against the wall. "Unacceptable," he hissed as the smell of vodka permeated the senses and clear liquid spread across the scarred, wooden floor.

Oleg ignored the outburst. "Nikolay thinks he's untouchable."

Dimitri stared out the windows and said nothing.

"His wealth and power have gotten in the way of his commitment to Mafiya."

Dimitri slammed his huge hand on the table and roared, "That arrogant little prick. This is offensive. Get him in here, so I can talk with him and show him just how 'touchable' he is." He jumped from his chair, picked up a large piece of glass from the vodka bottle and hurled it at the brick wall. The glass broke into smithereens and fell to the floor. Fear crawled up Oleg's back.

"I have tried to reach him," Oleg began and stared at Dimitri's knotted fist. It was enormous and covered with long, black hair. The hand resembled the paw of a wild animal, perhaps a bear, with short, stubby, powerful fingers. He wondered how many people Dimitri had killed with his bare hands. Dimitri hadn't risen to his power in the Bratva by being a choirboy. "I've called him. There's no answer."

Dimitri hurled another piece of glass against the wall and walked over to the window, lit a cigarette and stared down at the James River. "Can you track his phone?"

Oleg shook his head. "No, he has a private cell. He doesn't check in like the rest of the comrades," he mumbled softly.

Dimitri turned quickly and glared at him, his beady eyes blazing. "And why is that? Why doesn't he have a GPS in his cell like the others? Why is he treated differently?" His voice was accusing, and the red scar on his face glowed dark with anger.

Oleg shrugged his shoulders in defeat. "His handler was Sarkanov, and he allowed him special privileges. He's never been treated like the others. He's well connected and has been given concessions."

Dimitri snorted in disapproval. "He is rich and connected but only because of us." He turned from the window and faced Oleg. "That changes today. Keep calling him and tell him if he doesn't deliver the women tonight, he is a dead man, but first, he will watch his family die, one by one by one." Dimitri's eyes were cold as he stared at Oleg.

"I will tell him. I will keep calling," Oleg promised as he reached for his phone. In truth, Oleg had his cell programmed to redial Smirkowitz every five minutes, and as he checked the display, it was clear the phone had indeed dialed him more than fifty times."

"What's the plan? We do have a plan, don't we, Oleg?" Dimitri prodded sarcastically, his face dark and furrowed.

Oleg felt fear shoot through him. It took his breath away, and his gut constricted as he nodded. "Yes, Smirkowitz will bring the two women, one an American and the other from South America to the port of Richmond at about one in the morning. The American is a real prize. I was there when we abducted her."

Dimitri looked pleased. "A prize? She will fetch a lot of money," he said happily. "Does she have sisters?" he joked as his smiled widened

Oleg gave a short laugh. "I don't know, but we'll find out. She's a real looker, and American women with pale skin and blond hair are a dime a dozen. They're all over Virginia Beach and the beaches in North and South Carolina. All of the southern beaches, in fact," he added cheerfully. "There'll be no problem finding them."

Dimitri nodded, "Ah ha! A dime a dozen? I like that price." A smile flickered across his face. His beady eyes danced in anticipation.

Oleg nodded. "Yes, they're everywhere, I promise," he said as raised his glass in a mock salute and drank from his glass of vodka.

Dimitri was pensive for a moment, caught up in thought. For once, his broad arms looked less fearful to Oleg. "Eh, um, what do you say? Perhaps we should take a road trip tomorrow after we conclude our business. Consider it a scouting expedition?" Anticipation brightened his face, and his angry red scar paled in color.

Oleg raised his glass in a toast. "To a road trip. Tomorrow. A new plan and more money for Bratva." The pair clanked glasses again.

"Now, tell me the plan for tonight," Dimitri demanded, once again all business.

"Yes, the women. We'll put them on a trawler and take them down toward the North Carolina coast. I hear they picked up several blond beach bunnies over near the Outer Banks. And some others as well. All in all, six or seven women. It's easy, and all should go well."

Dimitri smiled and nodded. "I hear Richmond's an empty port? No people? No police, eh? You know we've had trouble in Baltimore," he cautioned as he filed his stubby fingernails.

Oleg wagged his head in agreement. "Yes, Richmond's port hasn't been used much for years. Mostly barges travel up and down the James River carrying supplies," he assured Dimitri. "We should have no trouble. Don't even think there's a guard there overnight."

Dimitri smiled happily. "Good, one more drink, and then a nap before we work tonight."

Oleg nodded.

"Find your boy, Smirkowitz, and make sure we're on track. If he screws up, he and his family are dead." Dimitri barked as he downed his double shot of vodka.

Oleg studied the clear liquid in his glass, and his anxiety increased. "Done, now get some rest."

He redialed Smirkowitz's private cell and got no answer. What the hell would Dimitri do if they couldn't find Smirkowitz? A bad feeling nagged at him.

Chapter 28

Tilda ground the pedal to the metal in her husband's old Chevy truck. It was his pride and joy. She felt great and more lighthearted than she'd been in ages. She turned the radio up loud to hear Miranda Lambert sing about her man. She loved Miranda Lambert, and for the life of her, she couldn't understand why she'd run around on Blake Shelton. Why, they'd been the king and queen of country music for years! And, hadn't Miranda given all of that up for a roll in the hay with somebody else? She shook her head as resentment charged through her. Miranda had had it all; she'd just thrown it away. What an idiot she was. To show her anger, Tilda clicked off the radio and slammed her fist into the dashboard before she found another country music station.

She sped down the highway and paid no attention to the snow and ice on the road. She knew God would take care of her. She wondered if God would forgive Miranda Lambert for screwing around on Blake. Somehow, she doubted it because Blake had loved Miranda dearly and still did, but the hot little wench just couldn't keep her thong on. She shook her head as she considered heathen women like Miranda. Women like that pissed her off. 'Course, Blake had gone and knocked up Gwen Stephani so he couldn't be so heartbroken now.

Tilda was a religious woman, and she rarely acted outside of the Ten Commandments, or at least her interpretation of them. She knew God had forgiven her for her indiscretions with Dr. Nicholas Smirkowitz. After all, Nicholas had been her first love, and they'd been perfect together. They were soulmates born to love each other. She loved him as much now as she had the first time they'd met more than nineteen years ago. She'd applied for the job of bookkeeper in his new dental practice. After she was hired, she spent the late afternoons doing sexual gymnastics with Smirkowitz in his dental chair. She'd stood by Smirkowitz, managed his money and his practice, and always made herself available to him whenever he needed her. She knew God had forgiven her because after all, Wilbur really had not been able to attend to his manly duties. That gave her all the excuse that she needed. After all, she was a beautiful woman in her prime. Her body heated up as she reminisced about her years with Nicholas.

Life with Wilbur crossed her mind a few times, as she flew down the snow-covered highway. He was a good man, and he'd tried to help her, especially with the voices that plagued her so often. He'd always been so patient and kind to her that she'd lost respect. And Constance. That bitch Constance. Anger exploded in her brain when she remembered the day Nicholas had met Constance. Her body felt hot all over, even on the inside where she could visualize her blood boiling as it plunged through her arteries and veins. She remembered, in great detail, the very day that Constance had come to the small practice to have her tooth capped. She'd seen the way the young bitch had ogled Nicholas Smirkowitz, the love of Tilda's life. Constance had driven a wedge between them on that very day. Nicholas had spoken to her sharply for interrupting him during his first appointment with Constance. Things had never been quite the same since that fateful day. She remembered crying her eyes out in the ladies room, and hot tears streaked her face now as she was consumed with fury.

The brakes screeched on the old Chevy as Tilda swerved around a sharp curve and skidded on the ice. She didn't even notice. Constance--her blood raged just hearing her name. Constance in her pretty pink dress with perfect white pearls around her long thin neck, perfect pearls that matched her perfectly white teeth. Tilda could feel her

Judith Lucci

breath coming in short spurts as her blood stewed with thoughts of her nemesis. She hated the woman as much today as she had twenty years ago. An image of Constance flashed through her mind. Constance, with her long dark hair flowing softly down her back and soft tendrils that framed her face. Constance's large, thick curls had immediately captured Nicholas's attention. Nicholas loved to play with hair—he loved to wind and unwind her hair when they were together. He would remove her hairpins and shake her hair loose in his office as a prelude to their lovemaking. He'd told her just a few months ago that curls were sensuous. Tilda reached up and felt her long hair.

I should've curled it before I left.

She smiled and a thrill went through her as she imagined how wonderful things would be later in the evening.

An orange light popped on and illuminated her dashboard. She could smell something burning. Her brakes. Her thoughts returned to Constance. It had taken Nicholas four appointments to finish capping Constance's tooth. Four very long appointments where she'd had to watch the bloom of love take over the soul of her beloved man. She'd watched the two love birds exchange long glances as she'd patiently stood by and assisted the good dentist, and then retreated to the bathroom to bawl her eyes out.

Tilda slammed on the brakes in the Chevy and skidded to a stop in the turn lane that led into a convenience store. Screw the brake light. She needed some energy, and a caffeine energy drink would help. She decided to splurge for a Red Bull. After all, she had a lot of work to do. She hesitated when she saw the price of the Red Bull, but the voices screamed in her head and told her to get it. She rubbed her fingers through her hair to stop the noise, picked up the drink and headed for the checkout.

131

Tilda grunted at the clerk as she grabbed her drink and change and raced for the heavy glass door, her boots squeaking and trailing water as she moved.

I've gotta calm down, I've gotta settle down, she told herself over and over again as she took deep breaths and backed out of the parking lot. I don't want anyone to notice me, no one at all. I have a lot of work to do ...for Nicholas and me.

Chapter 29

Mic pushed her chair away from her computer. She put down her magnifying glass, rubbed her eyes, and stared out the window at the falling snow. She'd spent the last two hours searching all of her informational databases on Tilda and had come up with several things that bothered her. She phoned Slade.

"Hey, have you found anything on Tilda?" she asked.

"Nah, not too much, nothing we can really use. Just what you'd expect. She's been married to the same man for over twenty years, no kids, no criminal record, and a few traffic tickets. She's a member of some sort of religious group that I don't really understand, but they're not in trouble with any federal agencies, at least not the IRS. Her husband, Wilbur, is one of the deacons in the church. I've sent a couple of uniforms to talk with her neighbors. Nothing on any of the major criminal databases."

Mic listened carefully and said, "Well, I think there's more there than we're seeing. Dottie did some eavesdropping today and said it sounded to her like Tilda was in some sort of cahoots with Dude about the missing women."

"Dottie, eavesdropping? I'm appalled," Slade chuckled.

"Yeah," Mic chortled. "Imagine that," she said with a smile. "Anyway, she indicated that Tilda threatened the younger woman, Janie, we saw in the office."

"Threatened her. Threatened her how?"

"Not sure. I'm going by Dottie's before I head down to Biddy's for happy hour. But I did learn one thing about her," Mic added slowly.

"What?"

Mic smiled. Slade was gonna like this. "I saw in some court documents I reviewed that Wilbur and Tilda had a right-of-way dispute with the property owners of the farm located in front of them. So, I pretended to be from the highway department and I called about posting a road sign. I asked the woman about Tilda and would they object to the sign? She said, and I quote, 'Tilda was a mean, nasty woman with a horrible temper and that she's crazy to boot.' She said Tilda runs up and down the roads past her farm at all hours of the night, often coming home at two or three in the morning. "

Slade whistled. "That's some late hours for an office manager at a dental practice."

Mic nodded, "Yeah, I'd say so. Anyway, this lady wishes Tilda nothing but ill will. She said her husband's pretty nice and that he deserves better than Tilda. In her mind, Tilda's an awful person."

"Yeah. I wonder if this lady is just mad at her over the court thing or if this is just a cat fight?"

"Hard to say," Mic admitted, "but it's worth checking out. She told me Tilda even got thrown out of the local 'Ladies Crafting Club' because she played a dirty trick on another member. If nothing else, she sounds like a persona non grata in her local area."

Slade was silent for a moment. "I wonder if she has something going on with Dude. Suppose they are having an affair? Maybe she's in love with him and does anything he says."

Mic was quiet for a moment and added. "Well, if she is, then it's highly likely she's involved. Can you bring her in for questioning?"

"Let me keep digging, and I'll see what I can come up with. If I can get enough on her, I'll get her in here."

"Okay, I'm gonna try to get into some of my medical databases and see if she has any type of a medical history. I wish I could get some information on her family. From what I can tell, she's from a small town in Arkansas."

"Sounds good, Mic. I'll see you later this evening at Biddy's and we'll catch up. In the meantime, I'm gonna see if I can pull enough together to get Tilda picked up."

"Okay, talk later," Mic said, hung up and returned to her medical databases. She typed in Tilda's full name and date of birth and was surprised when she was able to access her medical records in a children's psychiatric hospital in a small town in Arkansas.

Tilda had been diagnosed with an "undefined personality disorder" that could mean just about anything, particularly since Tilda was now an adult.

What Mic did know, was that time was running out to rescue Allison alive. Even though her insulin needs could be decreased if she were somewhere cold, her stress level could increase her need for insulin and she could go into a diabetic coma.

She prayed silently that something would break soon on the case... before it was too late.

Chapter 30

Today was the day. Today was the day she'd get her revenge on Constance. Even though Nicholas and Constance had divorced years ago, Tilda still harbored hostility, jealousy, and rage against the now middle-aged ex-wife who had so dramatically ruined her life.

Tilda drank her Red Bull and played with her curls as she continued down the highway. She fiddled with the radio dials until she found a heavy metal station. She smiled in satisfaction and turned the sound up as loud as she could, her anger matching that of the metal music fueled by the energy drink. The drums and electric guitars raged and screeched in her head, drowning out the voices and filling her with more hate and anger. She closed her eyes and imagined killing Constance, swiping a guardrail on the side of the highway in the process. Her eyes jerked open as she slammed on the brakes and left the vehicle to assess the damage. It was just a small dent, but Wilbur would have a fit. He loved his old Chevy truck. It had been his friend through thick and thin. She shook her head and got back into the truck, and drove at a slower, more respectable speed. The last thing she needed to do was attract the attention of the police. That'd really be bad.

Five minutes later, Tilda slowed down and turned off the highway as she carefully maneuvered her truck down a secondary road that approached the expensive west end subdivision where Constance still lived with her two children, Nicholas Jr. and Sarah. Nicholas Jr. was the apple of his dad's eye, "the fruit of his loins," as Nicholas would say. Sarah, well she really didn't think Nicholas liked his daughter because he considered her to be plain and frumpy. Unfortunately, the twelve-year-old hadn't inherited either of her parents' good looks, but she had inherited her father's intelligence. Of course, Nicholas never looked for intelligence in a woman, except in her of course. Just look at this new wife, she was dumb as a doorknob, but all the men ogled her. Once again, a wave of hatred surged through Tilda's body, but she reminded herself her hate was only with Constance. She was the woman who had ruined her life.

Tilda turned her radio down as she entered the sedate, gated community and drove down the familiar tree-lined boulevard toward Nicholas's old home. She smiled to herself as she remembered the few times she and Nicholas had made love in the beautifully appointed guest room on the second floor. She had wanted to make love in the bed he shared with Constance, but Nicholas would never allow it. In some ways, he seemed to consider his bedroom with Constance as some sort of holy place or sacred temple when all Tilda had wanted to do was desecrate it. Nicholas always laughed at Tilda because he wanted to "have sex," a phrase Tilda abhorred. She and Nicholas never just "had" sex, rather they created beautiful music, a symphony when they were together. When she'd told this to Nicholas, he'd laughed at her and shook his head. For him, she was nothing but a sex object, a sex toy who still looked good. Tilda admitted this to herself because the Red Bull and metal music had made her brave. She knew he didn't love her, but she knew he needed her. Just look who he had called this afternoon to "take care of things." She was addicted to him. *Nicholas has it made with me*, she thought as she cut down the radio.

The old Chevy with the freshly dented right bumper crept quietly along the streets filled with ivy-covered brick and stone two-story homes with snowmen in the yards, beautiful wreaths on the doors and late-model cars in all the driveways. Tilda had always scoped out the neighborhood and wondered what was happening behind all of the shuttered doors and draped windows. She pictured the life she'd always wanted – dinner in the dining room wearing her perfect string of pearls, beautiful children, and a beautiful home with a husband who loved her and not the impotent, religious fanatic with whom she lived. *Wilbur, the man who watched her all the time and was unable to fulfill his manly duty*, she thought in disgust.

Once again, she was crazed with jealousy and anger but steadied herself. She reached for her Glock in the console and stroked it fondly as she drove down the beautiful, high-end neighborhood.

I have work to do, she reminded herself as she parked several houses down and behind a garage at Dr. Dude's old home.

Chapter 31

Oleg pulled the final Camel from the pack, crumpled the package and threw it on the floor. He picked up his butane lighter, lit the cigarette, and inhaled deeply. He sat quietly and blew smoke rings at the windows as he redialed Smirkowitz's cell. Each unanswered ring heightened his anxiety. As the minutes ticked by, he considered his options. He glanced over at Dimitri who slept, dead to the world on a ratty, smelly sofa in the corner. The man snored loudly, as loud as he'd ever heard anyone snore, most likely attributable to the combination of vodka and jet lag. He'd felt his blood pressure drop as soon as Dimitri had plopped his enormous frame onto the sofa. Even in sleep, the Bratva boss had a sinister scowl on his face and looked like a monster. A shudder ran through his body when he considered what Dimitri would do to him if Smirkowitz didn't pull through in a few short hours.

Oleg propped his legs up on the old wooden desk, but the much-needed sleep wouldn't come. He grabbed his cell and dialed again. Dude was stressing him to death. He knew Dimitri would kill him, or at least have him killed, if Smirkowitz didn't deliver. He got up, and as he moved from the chair, he cringed as its legs scrapped the floor. He sighed with relief when Dimitri didn't stir in his sleep. He moved quickly and quietly out the door, pulling it closed with a soft click. He wound his way down ten flights and opened the recessed door of the old tobacco warehouse inhaling the cold air that stung his lungs and cleared his vodka-addled brain.

The walk to his rental car energized him and by the time he started the rental, he had a plan. He pulled around a pile of snow and headed away from the river toward I-95 and points beyond. Perhaps Nicholas's new wife knew where her rich husband was. He'd decided the new Mrs. Smirkowitz was going to lead him to her husband or die in the attempt. The new Mrs. Smirkowitz kept Dr. Dude under her thumb and massaged him like putty. Oleg had decided he would do whatever needed to be done in order to survive.

Chapter 32

Tilda pulled her nondescript, beige jacket around her, hugging the walls of the neighbors' garages as she snuck through their yards. She doubted she'd been spotted as the sky remained gray, and it was almost dark.

When she got to Dude's yard, she reached above the doorframe for the garage key that had been hidden there, in the same place, for more than fifteen years and easily unlocked the door. The garage was dark and shuttered against the light. She saw Constance's car, a pale silver Buick Regal and noticed a new bright red sports car Nicholas must have gotten for Mike Jr. She continued to gaze around the garage. She hadn't been there for a few years but little had changed. The work benches were just as she remembered, and the tools as organized as Dr. Smirkowitz's dental surgery area. She smiled at the tool belt on the bench and remembered, her heart racing, the night she and Dr. Dude had cooked dinner in Constance's perfect kitchen, and he'd worn only his tool belt. Now, that was a night to remember. Her mind enjoyed a surge of endorphins that soothed her stress.

Tilda moved quietly toward the stoop and door that led into the utility room. She turned the knob, and the door opened easily. The washer and dryer were brand new and the room smelled fresh, like laundry detergent and fabric softener. She moved to the laundry room door and listened. She didn't hear any noise at all in the kitchen, so she entered quietly. A half-full bottle of merlot and an assortment of cheeses were on the counter along with an unused wine glass. Tilda picked up the bottle of wine and sniffed the bouquet. She detected the scent of black cherries and tannin. For a moment, she considered pouring herself a glass but decided against it. She didn't want to leave any DNA evidence. She smiled to herself. Nicholas had taught her everything she knew about wine, and now she loved vino dearly. But only good red wine. No Boone's Farm or sweet swill for her, like those bumpkin friends of Wilbur's drank.

Tilda continued to hold the bottle and admire it. She traced the beautifully designed black and gold label with her fingertip. She memorized the Virginia Estate Vineyard and the vintage year. Sometimes at the office, after everyone had left for the day, she and Nicholas would share a bottle of merlot or a cabernet. Then they would huff a little nitrous oxide from the tank and laugh for at least an hour before making incredible love on the expensive Aubusson carpet in his office Constance had purchased for him years ago. Sex on the floor of his office was always hot and passionate. Oftentimes, they would "do the dirty" under his expansive walnut desk. Tilda shivered in delight as she remembered the day one of the dental technicians had almost caught them. It had been sensual and heady. Sex in his office had been the best days of her life. But Nicholas seemed busy lately, so preoccupied that there'd not been a day like that for months. At first, she'd thought it was his new wife who would be her rival, but that fear was short-lived. Within a month or so of his second marriage, Nicholas was hers again. It was as if they were made for each other and that they lived in their own world.

He's my Adonis, I'm his Venus. We complete each other.

Nothing and no one would ever keep them apart because they were made to be together. Tilda's heartbeat increased and her blood warmed as she thought of her lover.

She was jerked out of her daydream by the scraping of a chair against the floor. They're in the dining room. *How stupid am I not to have figured as much.* She quickly moved behind the wall that jutted out from the refrigerator as a tall, attractive dark-haired man entered the kitchen and grabbed the bottle of red wine on the counter and left. She heard the sound of Constance's voice and her tinkling laughter as the man reentered the dining room with the bottle of wine. Hate and fury grabbed her at the sound of Constance's laugh. Where did she find a boyfriend? Maybe she'd marry him and give up her alimony. Fat chance. She knew exactly how much of Nicholas's income the bitch got every month. For some reason, the knowledge of Constance's boyfriend enraged and consumed her, and her eyes darted over to the block of knives on the counter next to the stove. She selected an eight-inch deboning knife and admired the sharpness of the stainless-steel blade. She rubbed the wooden handle with her index finger and ran her fingers up and down the cool metal in a strange caress. She pricked her finger with the point.

It looks like I have more than one person to take care of. Nicholas would be upset if I left a witness.

Tilda placed her handbag on the island and smiled at the glint of steel in her purse. She reached in and touched her gun - for luck - then snuck around the side of the refrigerator and passed through the butler's pantry. She flattened her body against the wall shelves to peer into the dining room. Under the Baccarat crystal chandelier and beautifully reflected in the antique gold mirror, was Constance. Her image was exquisite. Her opera-length, fifteen-millimeter creamy white pearls adorned her neck, and she wore a white silk blouse with a deep V that showed just enough cleavage to make her enticing. A gold watch and several gold and pearl bracelets adorned her wrists. Her diamond — her five-karat solitaire diamond — surrounded with platinum and smaller diamonds, reflected prisms of light from the chandelier. Tilda's blood boiled as she remembered when Nicholas had shown her the diamond years before, and then told her it was for Constance. She'd never gotten over it. Twelve-year-old daughter Sarah, unattractive and frumpy in her St. Catherine's school uniform, sat across from her.

Constance's boyfriend was at the head of the table in Nicholas's seat. Mike Jr. was not present. Tilda was crazed at the sight, and the voices were biting at her brain and causing a frenzy in her head. She covered her head with her arm in an attempt to silence them.

Tilda took several moments to devise a quick plan. She returned to the kitchen where she pulled her Glock out of her handbag, screwed the silencer on the barrel and grabbed the carving knife from the counter. Then she grabbed a stainless and copper metal pan and threw it on the ceramic floor as hard as she could.

Within seconds, the tall man rushed into the kitchen frantically looking for the source of the noise. Tilda darted from behind her hiding place by the refrigerator and shot him directly in the chest. Red spread across his white shirt, and blood spurted all over the kitchen as he fell to the floor.

I must have nicked his aorta. Cool.

The man lay bleeding profusely on the kitchen floor as Tilda watched his pupils widen and glaze in death. A thrill raced through her, and she laughed happily. The entire scene had taken less than a minute. Then, the voices urged her forward. She picked up her eight-inch knife and walked into the dining room, the gun in her right hand and the knife in her left. Constance rose from her seat, standing by the table and staring at her, unable to speak or move. Sarah sat still, a fork full of food halfway to her mouth. They looked paralyzed in place.

"Tilda, what are you doing here?" Constance cried, panic in her eyes. "Where's my friend? Where's John? Have you hurt him?" Her voice rose to a screech. "Did I hear a gunshot? Where's John?"

Tilda laughed loudly and pushed her hair out of her face. "Oh, John. So that's his name. I didn't know you had a boyfriend."

144

Judith Lucci

Constance stared at her but remained silent, her eyes wide with fear.

"Of course I've hurt him, Constance. He's dead," she replied, her face in a snarl as she mimicked Constance's hysterical voice.

"He's dead?" Constance screamed. "Are you crazy?" she asked as she rushed toward her daughter.

Tilda gestured her forward. "Come on, come on closer," she whispered as she brandished the knife that reflected dancing shadows onto the dining room ceiling.

Constance stood still, her mouth open in horror as her eyes searched Sarah's eyes attempting to offer reassurance.

"Look at me, bitch." Tilda's crazed eyes locked with Constance's ice green ones. "Nicholas sent me here to hurt you, too. He can't have you making trouble for him." She hissed the words as she moved closer to the paralyzed woman and the voices exploded in her head.

"What are you talking about?" Constance asked, her face confused and streaked with fear. She moved to the end of the massive dining room table.

"That's all you've ever been—a burden and trouble for Nicholas. And besides, you got in the way of the love that Nicholas and I have for each other," she hissed as she waved the knife around in the light of the chandelier with the stainless-steel glinting on the tray ceiling.

Constance shook her head, "You're crazy. Nicholas would never have anything to do with someone like you. He has better taste than that." Constance spat as Tilda approached her with the knife."

145

Sarah jumped on Tilda's back and swatted at her with her hands, screaming, "Don't you touch my mother. I'm gonna call the police."

"I don't think so, little Sarah, you ugly duckling," Tilda hissed as she jerked the girl off her back and body-slammed her on the marble dining room floor. "Just so you know, your father hates you and thinks you're ugly, and so do I." Tilda looked like a monster in the candlelight.

Sarah lay on the floor, blood oozing from the back of her head, with her dark hair, so much like her mother's hair, spread around her head.

The young girl cried out in agony, "My mother is right. You're crazy. My father loves me."

Tilda shook her head again and a large smile spreading across her face. "No, he doesn't. He thinks you're fat and ugly and that's why I'm gonna kill you. And your dad won't even care."

Sarah stared up at Tilda as tears gushed from her eyes and the pool of blood from her head wound widened and sprawled across the white-veined marble floor. Sarah struggled to get up, her mouth open in disbelief.

Tilda kicked her down on to the floor and struck the child in the side of her head with her muddy boot.

"Stop it, stop it," Constance screamed. "I'm coming, baby, Momma's coming."

Tilda gave her an evil smile. "Come on around and join the party, Constance. It'll be fun," Tilda goaded, as the helpless woman slid around the banquet table holding on to the sides for support.

Tilda watched Constance move closer to Sarah as she placed her bloodied boot on Sarah's abdomen. "Stay down, you little bitch," she jeered. "And don't try to sit up again."

Sarah's enormous eyes stared at Tilda as she tried to speak. The words wouldn't come and she reverted to her childhood stutter. "Why... why are you doing this to us? My, my, my fa... fa... father is your friend, your boss."

Tilda stared down at the child. "Your father loves me and has since before you were born, and he'll be my husband someday, so shut up." To prove her point, Tilda kicked Sarah violently in the head again.

Nicholas loves you, Nicholas loves you, the voices rattled over and over in her brain. Kill her, Kill her, Kill, the voices demanded.

Sarah lay on the floor, gasping for air. She shook violently. "Please, please . . ." she pleaded quietly as she looked up at Tilda looming over her.

"Shut up, Sarah, and don't beg," Tilda hissed. "I hate people who beg." Her voice was loud and harsh as the stared down at the helpless child. A moment later, Constance lunged at her with a steak knife, her eyes wide with fury and disbelief.

Tilda grabbed Constance by her long dark hair and knocked the steak knife from her hand. She set her Glock on the table and yanked Constance's face close to her own.

"Oh, Constance, how long I've waited for this day," she purred. "I've wanted to hurt you for a very long time, forever, actually." She spoke softly as she locked eyes with her arch rival.

The two women stared at each other for several seconds before Tilda, enraged more than ever by the screaming voices in her head, ripped a handful of hair from her

Constance's head and tossed it to the floor. Blood seeped from Constance's scalp.

Constance gasped but remained silent, her eyes locked with Tilda's. "You're insane, you're totally insane," she whispered, her green eyes wide with realization and fury.

"Oh, aren't we the brave one," Tilda said. "Let's see how well you handle this."

Constance stared dully as Tilda held her by her hair. She moved her right arm up slowly, the gunmetal shining in the light of the chandelier, raised the weapon slowly and targeted her prey.

Constance jerked forward and grabbed her arm, but Tilda easily overpowered her, took aim and shot Sarah between the eyes, destroying the countenance that was so much like the man she loved. Sarah's face, a mass of blood and tissue, was unrecognizable.

Tilda looked at what was left of twelve-year-old Sarah's face and laughed, snorting with glee. "She ain't looking too good now is she, Constance? Guess we won't ever know if she'll have your looks, you know, to see if the ugly duckling turns into a swan." Tilda continued to laugh at her own jokes as the voices in her head laughed with her.

Nicholas will be so happy that I've done this. I need to hurry up and call him.

Constance howled and kicked Tilda in the shins trying to push herself toward her daughter's lifeless body.

Tilda's legs bowed over, but she righted herself and with a quick arm sweep, clutched Constance's hair again and pulled her forward as she grabbed her throat with her other hand and squeezed.

Constance's deep green eyes become larger and larger as Tilda squeezed the life out of her. Constance clawed and scraped, but her movements were useless and made Tilda angrier.

Squeeze, squeeze, squeeze, harder, harder, harder, the voices instructed as Tilda hefted the knife and plunged it under Constance's left breast. She saw Constance's eyes widen with pain, but only for a moment. Tilda was orgasmic with joy, but it was short lived.

The voices again urged her forward. Tilda was so angry, the strength of her fingers broke Constance's neck and robbed her of the pleasure she'd had long dreamed of — the pleasure of watching her nemesis die a slow death. She tossed Constance's body on the long walnut dining table and overturned a glass of wine in the process. Tilda watched, mesmerized as the merlot spread over the dead woman's silk blouse and mingled with the thick blood that was spurting over the table from her chest wound. She snatched the coveted pearls from her neck, the pearls that had long symbolized the life she couldn't have. Tilda wanted to take Constance's enormous diamond ring, but she was disrupted by the sound of an alarm. She saw blue lights reflected in the snow from the side of the house. Constance must have set off the alarm system.

I've gotta get out of here. Now!

She took one more look at the bodies and the beautiful dining room and smiled to herself as she briefly watched the light reflect from the crystal chandelier onto the blood-covered floor. It was a beautiful sight. She grabbed her gun from the table, rushed through the kitchen and jumped over the body of the tall stranger, leaving the house the same way she'd entered.

Images and memories flooded her brain as she made her escape through the garage and the back alley to her car. It had been a good day's work. She darted through the snow to her truck and drove quietly along the back roads of the subdivision as she headed home. That was some trip to Walmart, as she pulled the Walmart bag from her purse and filled it with the dish detergent she'd left in the truck earlier in the week. Wilbur must never know where she'd been.

She turned up her radio and took a final sip of her energy drink. Damn, life was good.

Chapter 33

Mic was in the kitchen making a cup of coffee when she heard her fax machine ding in the office. She grabbed her cup of coffee, left the kitchen, patted Angel who was sleeping in his kennel and returned to the office. She removed the fax from the tray and her heart rate increased as she scanned the report. It was from her retired friend over at state police headquarters. It was a copy of an investigative report on Dr. Smirkowitz from five years before. The report was directed to the attorney general of the commonwealth of Virginia, and in the conclusion, the investigator asked for a grand jury investigation of the well-known dentist on the charge on international felony conspiracy.

Mic read the report carefully and dialed her friend again. He picked up the phone immediately. "Thought I'd be hearing from you, Michaela. What do you make of these apples?"

Mic was surprised at the anger in her voice. "What I make of this is that it's a good solid report and Dr. Smirkowitz needs to be questioned by a grand jury. Where is the breakdown?"

"Damned if I know, Michaela, but there is one hell of a disconnect. The State of Virginia spent thousands of dollars investigating Nicholas Smirkowitz and we never got anywhere near a courthouse. Or close to bringing actual charges. Man has friends in high places. No question," he finished angrily.

Mic thought for a moment and said, "But who? This implies someone at a top level of government."

"Yeah, like the governor."

Michaela was quiet. "The governor of Virginia... Wow."

"Yup, that's what we thought five years ago. Now, at least there's a new governor. If you can generate enough noise with this abduction, maybe they'll pick the ball back up and we can put him away for good."

"That's exactly what we're gonna do. We're gonna break this case wide open," Mic promised as she seethed with rage.

"I'm waiting to hear about it, keep me in the loop, Michaela."

"I will, don't worry."

Damn, I've got to talk with Slade and Stoddard. We're gonna bust this thing wide open.

Chapter 34

Dr. Dude woke to the ringing of his cell phone as pain cascaded through his body. He was cold, wet, and confused. He lay on his side and studied the barn roof as he tried to remember what had happened. He spied a pitchfork near the open barn door that was damp with congealed blood, and more bloodstains were on the floor next to him. Smirkowitz tried to sit up but a stabbing pain seared through his groin, stopping him. He looked down as blood poured from his wound onto the dirt floor. He lay there helpless as he compressed the wound with his good arm. He rubbed his forehead and tried to remember what had happened. His right arm was numb and useless as though it didn't belong to him. He tried to move it with his good hand, but as soon as he took the pressure off his groin, blood spurted anew.

What happened to me?

For the life of him, he couldn't remember.

A tourniquet, I need to make a tourniquet. If I don't stop the bleeding, I can't get out of here.

He looked around him, but there was nothing nearby except for a dirty, old tarp. He turned his body as best he could and grabbed for it, but it was too far. He grasped at an old table leg, used it for leverage, and painfully inched his body forward until he could grab the tarp with his good arm. Part of the tarp disintegrated at his touch and fell to pieces. Smirkowitz dropped his head to the ground and inhaled moldy straw and dirt as tears dripped on the cold, dirt floor.

The persistent ring of his phone helped him focus. He tried to locate it in the dim light. Finally, he saw it, the light blinking each time it rang. It was about ten or twelve feet away where it had been tossed. Dude took a deep breath, and used his good arm to drag himself painfully, inch-by-inch toward the ringing sound. He was covered in sticky blood and sweat from the pain and exertion by the time he reached the cell. His heart quickened in excitement as he pushed his embattled body another foot and reached for the phone, as a gasp of pain and a sigh of relief simultaneously escaped from his mouth.

A harsh voice startled him as the phone was kicked half way across the barn. He looked up, but his vision was dim from blood loss, dizziness, and pain.

"Looking for this, Dr. Smirkowitz?"

The voice floated above and taunted him. Dude tried to visualize the shape and identify the voice, but he couldn't. His throat was dry, and the only sound that escaped his mouth was a wheeze of pain.

"I asked, are you looking for this?" the female voice continued harshly. She moved closer to him and mocked him with the cell phone, placing it four or five feet above his head, just out of his reach. He grabbed frantically for the phone with his good hand.

"Please. Yes." His voice was a hollow squeak.

The woman bent down, and Dr. Dude recognized the swollen face of Allison Massie, the girl he'd captured just a few days before. Her long blond hair matted with dirt and straw, hung loosely around her shoulders. Her clothes were ripped and torn. She was covered with blood and had a half-crazed look in her eyes. He tried to remember what had happened, but he was so weak and dizzy, he couldn't focus. As his brain began to float, he felt a sharp kick in the stomach. His eyes fluttered open.

Allison held the phone a few inches from his face, taunting him. "Wake up, Dr. Dude," she said, a smirk on her face. "Is this what you're crawling after?" Allison kicked him sharply as the phone began to ring again.

Dude was frightened. The woman had a crazed look in her eyes as she stared at the ringing phone. She looked at him, a sneer on her face. "Whose number is this? Who keeps calling you?"

Smirkowitz stared at the digital display. The number was familiar, but he couldn't place it. He gave her a bewildered look and shook his head.

Allison shoved the phone right in front of his eyes and kicked him again. He grimaced in pain.

She screamed at him. "WHO THE HELL IS CALLING YOU? Answer me. NOW."

Dude shook his head, shrugged his shoulders and gasped in pain as the movement sent a shot of blinding pain through his right shoulder. He could feel bile rise from his belly and enter the back of his mouth. He turned his head and vomited into the straw and dirt.

Allison watched the famous Dr. Nicholas Smirkowitz writhe in pain, his normally dapper appearance obscured by the old jeans, flannel shirt, blood, and vomit. No one would recognize him. No one would believe her story.

Dude turned his head back, and whispered, "Please, please, help me. I think I am dying. Please call an ambulance. Please, I beg you." His pleas went unanswered as he stared into the angry, smoldering eyes of his captor.

Allison laughed hysterically. "Why would I help you? You've tried to kill me for two days. I will never help you. I may just stand here and…"

Dude had tears pouring down his face. "They...they made me take you. They said they would kill my ..."

The phone rang shrilly again. It was the same number. Allison pushed the green button, "Who the hell is this?" she snarled into the phone.

Oleg was shocked. Who'd answered Nicholas's phone? Where was Smirkowitz, but most importantly, who was on his phone?

Allison hollered into the phone again, "Who is this. Tell me or I'm hanging up."

Oleg said quietly, "Is Nicholas there? This is his friend, Oleg."

Allison was furious, and anger overcame judgment. "Nicholas can't come to the phone right now," she said softly, "because he's almost dead."

"What, what's wrong with him?" Oleg asked, as fear thudded in his chest. "Let me speak to him."

"Nope, too late. He's going to sleep now," Allison said. "Don't call back. We're not gonna answer." She turned off the phone.

"Who ...who was that?" Nicholas asked in a frightened tone.

"I don't know, some guy with an accent. Don't worry about it. You're going to go to sleep now," Allison promised as she walked over near the door and picked up a shovel.

"Please, don't" Dude pleaded, his voice trembling as she returned to his side and held the shovel over his head.

"Putting you to sleep, just like I said," she replied as the shovel crashed over Dr. Dude's skull with all the force Allison could muster.

I've got to get out of here. Whoever was on the phone may know where we are. Allison briefly searched the barn for her cell but couldn't find it and shoved Dr. Dude's cell in her coat pocket.

Chapter 35

Michaela checked herself in her full-length mirror in her dressing room. She had on a black wool dress and three-inch black boots, a beautiful Eisenberg Ice rhinestone brooch she'd inherited from her grandmother and matching earrings. She rearranged her short dark curls and applied a bit more mascara to make her vivid green eyes pop. She moved back and surveyed herself critically in the mirror. She looked pretty good for a forty-four-year-old retired homicide detective, she decided. Not bad for an old girl. She moved closer to the mirror and tried to press out the wrinkles around her eyes and the permanently-etched frown mark on her forehead. It didn't work. The rest of her face was unlined, and all in all, she looked okay. She reached for her Avon facelift-in-a-bottle and smeared it over her makeup. The stuff really worked, firmed up the face for about two hours, and then all was back to normal. Anyway, she liked it, and it smelled good. Besides, she was meeting Slade later at Biddy's to talk about Allison's case, and she was warming to him again. *Do I really want to go there?* The two of them had enjoyed a torrid affair several years ago that had ended after about three months when Mic had decided it was more about sex than substance, and she really wanted to know her lovers and be able to connect with them.

Mic called Angel, and the two left the house and hopped into Michaela's SUV. The truck had ample room for Angel who loved riding shotgun in his seat belt. The pair headed over to Dottie's house, driving a bit slower than usual because of the snow and ice. Dottie's house was a short drive, usually only five minutes, ten or twelve minutes in traffic or if she caught the lights. Tonight, it was even longer because of the snow and ice.

Michaela pulled into Dottie's circular drive and looked up at the mansion. It was impressive to say the least. The
158

7,600-square-foot Mediterranean residence had been designed and built by noted Richmond architect William Lawrence Bottomly. The property was custom built and designed for the Borghase family for "vacations" when they visited their tobacco holdings in Virginia. The three-story stucco mansion, complete with two elevators, had twenty-four rooms with seven bedrooms and seven baths.

Michaela opened the car door for Angel, rang the bell and was greeted at the door by Cookie Vagglia, Dorothy's long-time housekeeper, who at sixty-something had her hands full taking care of, or perhaps keeping up with Dottie and the enormous house.

"Mic, how're you doin?" Cookie greeted her warmly. She ruffled Angel's ears, and he looked at her with adoration in his eyes. Angel loved Cookie, and he knew he was about to get a huge plate of treats.

Michaela watched the pair and laughed. "I guess you know what Angel is expecting."

"Indeed I do, and he'll be getting them shortly," she promised as she squatted on the dog's level, and he gave her a quick lick on the face.

Mic laughed and asked, "How's Dottie?"

Cookie gave her an exasperated look, as she shook her head, "Angel's not a problem. It's the countess. She is in the library, and she's on her third glass of sherry." She rolled her eyes. "She seemed to have had a very bad day. I guess Henry and I'll be up all night." She gave Mic a tired smile.

Mic shook her head. "I'll talk to her. I' gather she had a rather upsetting afternoon?"

"Yeah, she did," Cookie agreed "but I'm not too sure what happened. And by the way, Michaela, you look exceptionally beautiful tonight!" Cookie added. "Not everyone can wear black as well as you!" Cookie gave her an appreciative look.

Mic smiled. "Thanks, Cookie. It takes me longer and longer to look good these days. Gone are the days when I plastered on some lipstick and mascara and took off."

"You'd never know it," Cookie insisted. "Let's go check on the countess."

Mic nodded and entered the grand hallway with Angel at her side. "I don't know what happened, but I'm going to find out. Just be sure she eats to balance the wine and gets to bed safely. No need for a broken hip."

Cookie shuddered at the thought. "The countess with a broken hip could be the death of me."

Mic laughed and nodded as she looked around at the grand entry foyer as she removed her black leather gloves. Even though she'd been there a million times, she was always impressed with the beauty and architecture of the mansion. It was like having a bit of Rome in Richmond. The grand foyer boasted a curved staircase, priceless objects d'art on antique tables and Renaissance murals adorned the walls. The furniture was vintage Italian from Dottie's ancestral home outside of Rome and many impressive pieces of Italian marble served as pedestals and tabletops. Opposite the living room, the dining room offered mirrored Fresno ceilings with a motif similar to the Sistine Chapel. Mic swore she could see all the miracles of the Catholic Church along the walls. The dining table seated an easy sixteen for dinner, and a beautiful terra cotta floor completed the authentic look of an Italian dining room fit for royalty who did, of course, live there.

Cookie accompanied Mic and Angel as they walked through the grand hall to the back of the mansion and made a right as they entered the library. The library had a beamed ceiling and arched library shelves and floor-to-ceiling

160

windows that overlooked Dottie's beautiful, snow covered courtyard. Dottie sat next to the fireplace, a crystal goblet of sherry in her hand and a cut glass decanter on the table next to her. She had on a navy blue silk dressing gown and rested in a Queen Anne leather recliner. She raised her glass in greeting when Mic entered.

Chapter 36

Dottie placed her wine glass on the coffee table and stood when Michaela and Cookie entered the room.

"Good. Finally, where have you been, Michaela?" she asked as she greeted Angel with a tug on his ears. "I've been waiting for you for over two hours!" Dottie's voice was anxious and peeved at the same time.

Mic noted Angel's ears. He was bothered by the anxiety and sound of Dottie's voice. He was on full alert. Mic was annoyed, and her voice was sharp. "Settle down, Dottie. Angel is upset, and what do you mean where have I been? I've been at home getting dressed, and I'm on my way to Biddy's. You know it's Thursday night, and I always make an appearance."

Dottie nodded and reseated herself in her recliner as Angel relaxed and sat on the floor next to Mic.

"Besides, I'm meeting Slade there to go over the findings in Allison's case," she said as she patted Angel on the head and watched him relax.

Cookie interrupted her. "Michaela, I have a plate of sandwiches and hors d'oeuvres that I'll bring you in just a few seconds. Is there anything else you need?"

"Thank you, Cookie," Michaela said. "I would love a bite to eat and a glass of mineral water."

Cookie nodded and glanced over at Dottie, "Countess, would you like some Perrier or a cup of tea?"

Dottie glared at Cookie and shook her head, giving her an icy look. "No. I am having my before-dinner drink."

"Or drinks," Michaela said, as she moved her chair closer to Dottie and put her high-heeled boots up on the end of

Dottie's recliner. "What's up, Dottie? I was worried about you when you were in the car. You sounded short of breath."

Dottie rolled her eyes. "I'm fine, Michaela. I told you that. I was excited about what I've learned. Now would you please be quiet and let me tell you."

Mic stared into Dottie's blue eyes and admired the energy and vitality. "Okay, I'm all ears, Dottie. But before we begin, I want you to know it worries me when you go off on your own and do crazy, dangerous stuff. Whether you want to admit it or not, you're over eighty years old, and you're not quite as fast as you used to be."

Dottie glowered at her but said nothing as she arched her eyebrows into a scowl.

"End of lecture," Mic said. "I promise."

Dottie held her tongue and that was hard for her. She was used to speaking her mind. She hated it when Michaela said things about her age, as if she didn't know she was old. She knew exactly how old she was, but she refused to give up things that were important to her. In fact, she was thirty-five on the inside. It was the outside of her that had visibly changed.

"Okay, just hold your tongue until I'm finished," Dottie grumbled.

Michaela smiled weakly and said, "Okay."

Dottie settle back comfortably in her recliner. "Well, after I left Margaret's house this afternoon, I decided to pay Dr. Dude's office a visit. I saw your car there and the police cruiser, so I parked across the street. And, oh, by the way, some stupid Richmond police officer gave me an improper driving ticket for no reason."

Michaela smiled. "Were you parked illegally?"

Dottie glared at her but said nothing. Michaela had her answer.

Dottie began again, "Okay, so after you and the detective left, I parked next door to Dr. Dude's office, walked through the snow-covered bushes and snuck into the back door."

Michaela was mortified. "You did what?"

"Just what I said," Dottie glared at her defiantly. "I hid my car, walked through the bushes and went into Dr. Dude's office by the back entrance. No one saw me, I can assure you."

Michaela's brain exploded as she shook her head. She fought to keep control of her temper. "Okay. Then what happened?"

"I snuck into the storage room, you know, the room between Dr. Dude's office and the staff kitchen. It's where they store all the dental supplies, like toothbrushes, mouthwash, and the stuff they make those impressions from."

Mic nodded impatiently. "Yeah, I know. Then what?"

Dottie continued to stress the point. "I'm talking about the room where they keep the metal plates they stick into your mouth when you can hardly swallow or breathe."

"Yeah, I got it. Go on." Mic was irritated and afraid of what was coming next.

Dottie's ice blue eyes widened, and she whispered, "Dr. Dude came into his office and got a call on his cell phone."

Mic noticed that Dottie's hand was shaking as she reached for her glass of sherry.

"A phone call? From whom?"

Dottie's voice was low and she said quietly, "I don't really know, but I'm sure the man was Russian. He said something to Dude about 'taking care' of Allison. He also said to have her ready tonight or else."

Michaela felt her heart race, and her stomach sank. Oh my, this is sounding more and more like international crime. My friend from the state police is right. "Or else, what?" Mic held back her excitement to keep Dorothy on track. She didn't want her to forget what she had to tell.

"I did hear most everything, but I was so excited I may have forgotten some of it… but I did hear the man…oh, by the way, did I mention that I think he was Russian?"

"Yes, yes you did. What else did you hear?" Mic hoped her voice didn't sound as impatient as she felt.

"I'm sure he threatened Dr. Dude. As a matter of fact, he called him 'Nickolov'. I believe that's a Russian word for Nicholas."

"Yes, go on," Michaela urged, eager to hear what was next.

"He told Dude that if he didn't 'take care of Allison' tonight he would hurt Dr. Dude's children and his new wife."

Mic was quiet for a moment as she processed this information.

Dottie took a break and settled against the cushions in her chair, exhausted from telling her tale. Just then, Michaela heard a knock on the door, and Cookie entered with a crystal goblet, her mineral water, and their hors d'oeuvres.

"Thanks, Cookie," Michaela said as the faithful housekeeper set out the food and prepared to leave. "It looks just great. Thank you so much."

Cookie turned around, smiled, and waved at Michaela. "You're welcome, Detective. Any time."

Angel stood and walked toward Cookie and looked at her expectantly as the housekeeper removed a plate of especially prepared "healthy" treats for him, made of oatmeal, peanut butter, roast beef, and carrots.

"Here you go, boy, made especially for you," she exclaimed as she placed the platter of treats on the oriental carpet.

Angel wagged his tail furiously and gave her his best doggie smile — broad, wide, and comical — then he proceeded to devour the treats. He was in Heaven every time he came to Dottie's house. Mic and Cookie grinned at each other, and Dottie smiled thinly.

"Cookie, don't forget. I retired. I'm no longer a police detective. Just a civilian, like you."

Cookie smiled at her. "Oh yes, you are, Michaela. Sure 'nuf you are, but you'll always be a detective," Cookie promised in her wise way.

The door closed, and Michaela moved her chair even closer to Dottie. "Okay, what else can you tell me about Smirkowitz? And the Russian?"

Dottie thought back over her afternoon before continuing. "There're a few more things. Let me eat a little bit so I can get my brain cells working again. Things seem a bit foggy now."

Michaela could tell that Dottie was exhausted and tired of talking.

Michaela carefully checked out her friend. She seemed calmer. She reached for Dottie's thin wrist and counted her pulse. It was one hundred ten, not too bad for an eighty-two-year-old.

166

Dottie reached for a small sandwich. "I'm hungry. I haven't eaten since I had that sandwich over on Cary Street this afternoon."

Michaela nodded, and the two women continued to chew silently for a few minutes until Dottie was able to continue.

Chapter 37

Tilda drove quickly down the highway and felt her blood pressure and heart rate decrease as she finally reached the place of pure pleasure she always felt after she'd committed a malicious or violent act. Ever since she could remember, even as a young child, she'd loved to hurt things and been fascinated by torture. In fact, it was a behavior she'd learned to control most of her life. Several times her parents had shamed and punished her for cruelty toward others, especially people less fortunate than her.

Her mother told her she was mean, but all her life, she'd hurt others on purpose, through her mean-spirited behavior disguised by her actions, made-up stories, and lies. She'd spent her young life in church getting prayed over, delivered, and punished.

Strangely enough, Tilda wasn't mean to animals, and in fact, was an animal lover, but she hated birds and chickens. Wilbur had realized her predilection for cruelty and had worked tirelessly throughout their marriage to "rid" her of the curse he felt was directly from Satan. In fact, he'd had her "delivered" several times by their deacons and had even called in a special theologian to "cleanse" her soul several times through the years. Tilda's stomach soured as she remembered the torturous process of deliverance and the humiliation that followed. Her brain pushed back the revulsion she felt toward her husband, but the memories fueled her anger.

Tilda forced herself to calm down. She wanted to relish and relive the pure sense of pleasure and sensuality she felt from the kills. She smiled in satisfaction and caught a glimpse of herself in the truck's rearview mirror. She looked pretty, really pretty, in fact. Her normally dark brown hair shined, and her curls were more bouncy than usual as they tried to escape from her stocking cap. Her brown eyes were bright and shiny with excitement, and her cheeks were flushed with pleasure. Her soul was elated, and she'd never been happier. She reached for her cell phone and told Siri to call Dr. Dude. She couldn't wait to give him a report of what she'd done. Ah, the evening would be sweet. They'd meet back at the office, party, and make love all night long.

Dude's phone rang and rang, and for a moment, anxiety gnawed at her and a touch of fear entered her pleasure zone. Suppose Nicholas got mad at her for killing Sarah. There really wasn't much she could've done. The kid was simply collateral damage, and besides, she reasoned, Nicholas hadn't liked the kid anyway. Hadn't he always said she was ugly and a pain in the ass? Oh well, he'd just have to get over it. Tilda continued to drive down the road, careful to obey the speed limit as she listened to the mournful ring of her lover's cell. Where the hell is he? A wave of sensuality and then anger overcame her as the phone continued to ring. Then she thought about the look of terror in Constance's huge eyes when she had come for her with the knife. The feeling was so carnal and erotic, Tilda almost pulled off the road.

Oh my God. I loved killing her.

Tilda closed her eyes for a moment as she relived the thrill of the knife sinking into Constance's soft flesh as she watched the look of bewilderment in her victim's eyes. She watched the bewilderment in her nemesis turn to fear and pain as she grasped the knife and pulled it upward sharply, using her upper arm strength to be sure the knife severed Constance's aorta. Chills of pleasure ran over her body, and she closed her eyes to relive the scene.

She felt the truck hit the shoulder of the road, and her eyes flashed open just as she turned the wheel one second before she crashed into the guardrail. Tilda righted the truck

169

on the shoulder and reentered the highway without even looking for other cars.

Am I this excited because I killed Constance? Or is it because I've found another way to pleasure myself besides Nicholas?

Tilda continued to muse and missed the blue lights of a Virginia State Trooper in her rearview mirror as he quickly approached her vehicle. She jumped when the trooper blasted his siren. When she saw him, she smiled to herself and zipped her jacket with one hand as anxiety flushed her face. She hadn't checked herself for blood splatter, and her eyes swiftly searched the truck for the murder weapon. Where'd she thrown the knife when she'd jumped into the vehicle? She slowly pulled off the road into a closed, deserted gas station and frantically looked into the backseat through the rear-view mirror.

The trooper approached her truck as she slid open her window, her license and registration in her hand.

He tipped his hat and said, "Evening, ma'am."

Tilda nodded and flashed him her brightest smile, her porcelain veneers gleaming, the same perfect smile that mirrored the teeth of anyone in Richmond who'd had an opportunity and enough money to visit Dr. Smirkowitz's office.

She responded in a soft, silky voice. "Hello, Officer, is anything wrong? I was sort of in a hurry to get home before it got too dark. I don't want to run into any black ice," she added as she pulled up her jacket sleeve to see her watch.

"Driver's license and registration please, ma'am," the officer answered his gaze unwavering as he stared at her, until his eyes swept the backseat.

Tilda handed him her documents and sat back in her seat. She watched him in her side mirror as he returned to his vehicle. She turned, opened the center console and peeked into the compartment. Sure enough, that was where she'd put her Glock. She stroked the gun fondly, smiled to herself and shut the console quickly as the smell of gunpowder wafted out of the small space. She turned the key and cut on her engine, setting the heater fan as high as she could to dispel the scent. She lowered the truck window allowing the smell to escape and reached into her purse. She grabbed the Sugared Fig body spray she knew Nicholas loved.

I'll have Nicholas spray me with this tonight. He loves it. She sprayed herself and her clothes with sugared scent. The scent was strong and heady. She lay back against the leather seat, savoring the intoxicating aroma and dreamed of her evening to come with Nicholas. Then she relived the exciting and stimulating five minutes at Constance's house. The minutes ticked slowly by. What the hell was that cop doing? She peered out the rear-view window. He was in his cruiser.

Bored and antsy, she inspected her nails and shook her head in disapproval as she noted the ragged cuticles and broken nail on her index finger on her right hand. There was dried blood under her fingernails. She considered buffing her nails but decided against it since the cop might perceive her as a smart aleck, at least that's what Wilbur would say. She decided to stay quiet and respectful. Her voices told her that would be best. She placed the offending hand in her jacket pocket.

The minutes creeped by, and Tilda's anxiety crawled up her spine. The noises in her head were so loud and restless, they popped her ears, and she placed her hands over her ears to drown out their sound. It didn't help, so she put her mittens on and tried to pad her ears from the sound of the voices.

I've got to hang on, got to keep it together, she told herself over and over. She checked her rear-view mirror and pretended to fluff her hair. She saw the officer slowly returning to her car treading carefully on the slick, icy terrain under the darkened sky.

Tilda stepped out of the truck. The last thing she needed was the cop checking out or searching her vehicle. She couldn't be sure there wasn't blood on the floorboard where she'd tossed the kitchen knife. She hunched her shoulders and crossed her arms in front of her chest and stared at a frozen puddle on the graveled asphalt.

"Ma'am, please return to your car," the officer directed, his voice tense and authoritative.

Tilda's hand flew to her ears as the voices in her head screeched at her.

"Get in the car, ma'am, get in the car," the trooper's voice was loud and harsh in her head.

Tilda was paralyzed with indecision. The sound of her inner voices screamed at her. KILL HIM, KILL HIM, KILL HIM! The noise blocked any reality and judgment she still possessed.

"In the car, NOW," the officer demanded, moving closer and closer as he pulled his radio from his pocket and spoke into it rapidly. He looked up and stared at her, his face suspicious.

Tilda turned and stumbled towards the car but slipped on the ice. It was then she noticed the blood on the side of her boot. Sarah's blood. She grabbed for the door, catching the door handle just before she went down. She flung herself into the front seat, her torso over the console. She shielded the console with her body as she pulled out the Glock and tucked it under her arm.

The officer bent over and inspected the pink smear in the snow. He squatted to examine it closely.

Her game was up. She saw the cloud of suspicion cross the trooper's face. He stood up. She straightened her body and reached for her seat belt as the trooper shined the light directly into her face. The light communicated intense pain into her brain as she raised her arm to shield her eyes from the light. She turned away from him as the voices screeched, Kill, Kill, Kill!

"Stop it, stop it, STOP IT," she screamed as the weapon discharged, putting three slugs in the officer's chest. He fell to the ground, his blood outlining her heavy truck tires as it pooled, bright red in the frozen snow and ice.

Tilda backed her truck up and screeched out onto the highway.

Chapter 38

Michaela glanced at her watch and checked the time as she watched Dottie devour one and a half sandwiches. She knew better than to hurry her, because if she did Dottie, either from stubbornness, or perhaps belligerence, would take her time telling Michaela the events of the day. It wasn't an artifact of Dottie's age, it was an artifact of Dottie's stubborn personality.

"Wow, you ate a lot. Must've been pretty good stuff," Mic observed as Dottie placed her tray back on the table. Michaela reached for a piece of roast beef and offered it to Angel who was lying at her side.

Dottie nodded. "Yeah, Cookie makes the best food in the world. Even though she totally gets on my nerves. I do have to admit I don't think I could do without Henry and Cookie."

Mic jumped on that observation. "You're darned right, you need them more than you'll ever know," Michaela assured her. "And you need to tell them that. Cut the royal crap and tell them how much you appreciate them."

Dottie contemplated this as Mic continued. "Now, can we talk about the rest of your afternoon with Dr. Dude?"

Dottie leaned back against the cushions in her recliner, picked up a glass of water "Yes. Let's do that before I forget. Where was I?" she asked as she reached for her sherry and put the mineral water down.

Michaela shook her head. She was glad she wasn't taking care of Dottie that night. "You'd just told me about Dr. Dude and the Russian. You told me the Russian had threatened Dude's wife and children."

Dottie nodded as she chewed. "Right. He only threatened Dr. Dude's new wife though. Not the mother of his children. The man seemed to like the first wife." Dottie paused for a moment to swallow. "I think he said 'they' picked Smirkowitz's first wife."

"Interesting, I wonder what that means?" Michaela asked.

Dottie shrugged her shoulders. "I've no idea. Maybe they picked her as his Russian bride," she suggested and gave a short laugh. "Just like in the movies."

Mic thought for a moment, before responding. "Who knows, she could've been. For all we know, they're both Russian spies although that's a huge stretch."

Dorothy was quiet and covered her mouth with her hand to hide a yawn. "I did hear the words 'family business' mentioned today, but I can't remember whether Dude said it or the Russian."

Mic's eyes bored into her. "Well, try. Think back over things," she encouraged.

Dottie yawned. "Can't, too tired. You just check it out. I've got confidence in you, Michaela."

"So what else do you remember from today?" Mic prodded. "Was there anything else you need to tell me about?"

"Oh yes." Dottie suddenly sat up straighter. "The Russian said that Dr. Dude must make Allison ready for tonight. Tonight is…" Dottie paused for a moment. "Well, I think he said that tonight was the bidding? Does that make sense to you?"

Mic was quiet, hoping Dottie would remember more.

Dottie hesitated for a moment and gave Mic a frustrated look, "I don't really know for sure. I couldn't hear that well, and half of the time he spoke in Russian."

Michaela nodded, her mind racing a mile a minute. What in the world was going on? Of course, Dottie could be a little confused. It was getting late, and she'd had a very stressful day plus a couple glasses of sherry.

"Don't you have to be going soon? You said you had to get downtown to Biddy's?" Dottie stifled another yawn.

Mic stood to leave, and Angel stood with her. "Yeah, I do need to leave, Dottie. Will you promise to write down anything else you remember on a pad of paper, no matter how important or unimportant you think it is?"

Dottie nodded, gray with fatigue. Mic was concerned about her. "Are you okay, Dottie? Do we need to call the doctor?"

Dottie yawned, "No, I am fine. Just tired and the sherry makes me sleepy."

"I'll have Cookie bring you a pad of paper and perhaps you can sit here and rethink the conversation."

Dottie nodded. Her silver head bobbed up and down. "Yes, I'll be glad to do that, Michaela. I must say I'm tired right now, and I think I'm going to go take a nap. Or maybe just go to bed for the night."

Mic nodded her approval. "I think that's a great idea! You've had a big day." Mic glanced at her watch. "I really must go. I'm already late." She leaned over and gave Dottie a hug. "Don't you ever do anything again like you did today. That was dangerous and very foolish." Angel yipped in agreement and licked Dorothy's hand.

In her usual stubborn manner, Dottie refused to agree. Instead, she sat defiantly, stiff as a board and didn't hug her back but managed to scratch the magic spot behind Angel's ears. Michaela saw anger flicker over Dorothy's face, but her voice was contrite when she finally spoke. "Okay, Michaela. I won't. It was a bit upsetting."

Mic hugged her again, gave her a peck on the cheek and said a final good night. She loved the way Dottie always smelled of Chanel No. 5.

Dottie sniffed as she watched Mic and Angel leave the library and then smiled to herself. No one would ever control her, no one. She'd see to that.

Chapter 39

Mic pulled out of Dottie's circular drive and turned right as she headed down Monument Avenue towards downtown Richmond.

"Hey, boy," she said as she reached out to scratch Angel's ear as he sat at attention on the seat next to her. "Do you think Dottie's mad at us?"

Angel gave his mistress a mournful look and turned his head slightly toward her. Michaela knew he understood everything she said to him.

"Yeah," she smiled. "I think you're right. I think she's pretty pissed, but we both know she'll get over it, right?"

Angel licked her hand to show agreement.

"Okay," she smiled at him as he wagged his tail. "Enough of that. I'm gonna have the cook give you a great bone when we get down to Biddy's. What do you say, old boy?"

Angel thumped his tail enthusiastically against the leather seat in the truck and gave Mic his happy look, which Michaela swore was a dog smile. "You just love the word 'bone' don't you, buddy?"

Michaela's police radio squawked loudly on her dash interrupting the Jimmy Buffet network on Sirius radio. She heard reports of a Virginia State Trooper being gunned down on Route 33, just west of Richmond. Her heart plummeted, and she gripped the wheel tightly. Angel's tail slowed, and he looked at her for direction.

"That's not good, Angel. That's the fear of all state troopers. You never know who's gonna be in that car." She listened carefully. The trooper had taken three rounds in the chest.

Overkill, Mic thought to herself as she maneuvered the car around the piles of snow and ice.

Chapter 40

Slade McKane ran his fingers through his thick dark hair as he studied the computer screens on his desk. He'd spent several hours looking at everything there was about the eminent Dr. Nicholas Smirkowitz. He'd perused every local, state, and federal database, and while there was considerable suspicion and innuendo about Richmond's eminent dentist, in truth, there was no proof. His gut gnawed and pained him. He reached for his anti-acid pills and popped two, just in case one wasn't enough. He smiled as he remembered Mic telling him he was addicted to Prilosec. Slade stood, stretched, and checked his watch. Soon he needed to leave to meet Michaela at Biddy's. He stretched again as he looked out his window at the darkened sky. He was angry and frustrated. He knew Dr. Dude was guilty, but he wasn't sure exactly what he was guilty of, but he knew he'd find out.

His cell rang and displayed the number for Charlie Thor, one of the best detectives in his precinct. Charlie had left earlier to investigate a home invasion.

"Charlie, what's up man? You got nothing better to do than bother me when I'm up to my eyeballs in copperheads and coon asses?" Slade stood and walked over to his window and examining the darkened sky.

Charlie gave a short laugh. "Hey, McKane, you're the coon ass."

Slade smiled broadly into the phone and said, "Indeed I am. What's up?"

"Aren't you workin' on something to do with that TV dentist, Dr. Smirkowitz, the fancy tooth dude with the office in the Fan District? "

Slade's heart rate increased, "Yeah, what's up? I got the man's life on two computer screens in front of me. Right now, I've got everything, but I've got nothing... except a lot of suspicions."

Charlie was silent for a moment. "Yeah, man, but what I got are three dead bodies. One is Smirkowitz's ex-wife, Constance, a kid, who we think is his daughter, but there is no positive ID."

"Somebody offed Dude's kid?" McKane was shocked as he felt his stomach ball up in anger. "Who the hell would kill a kid?"

Charlie replied in a terse voice, "I'd say somebody with a real vendetta against the guy. The kid was beaten, kicked, and shot in the face. Appears she had some sort of a head injury prior to the gunshots." He was quiet for a moment as he allowed his news to sink in. "It looks like the perp body-slammed the girl on the marble dining room floor."

Slade interrupted, "Damn, that's bad. Who's the third body?"

Thor paused. "We're not sure. It's a guy. Maybe Constance Smirkowitz's boyfriend. His driver's license says he's John Traynor, and his business card says he's a securities investment broker with one of the downtown firms."

"What the hell? What's his part? Collateral damage?" Slade sifted images through his mind. Three bodies. A triple homicide. Richmond hadn't had a triple murder in ages. "What the hell happened?"

"Beats me, Slade. It's vicious and violent. You need to get out here and see this. Place is a bloody mess."

Slade tapped his mechanical pencil on his legal pad. "On my way, man. Any sign of Dr. Dude?"

"Nada. Whoever did this was angry or just plain crazy. The perp beat the kid, threw her on the marble floor in the dining room and then shot her, a kid in her school uniform." He paused for a moment. "She could've taken more than one in the head as well. Can't tell. Too much blood. Haven't moved the bodies yet."

"Is the medical examiner there?"

"Nah, not yet. On her way. Crime boys are here. Lots of uniforms. Medical Examiner's ETA is about seven minutes."

Slade struggled into his jacket, held his cell under his chin and reached for his office doorknob. "How'd the wife die?"

Slade heard Charlie expel a breath. "Man, it's a mess. You need to get out here. Looks like she was strangled and stabbed in the chest. Then the perp threw her on the dining room table and dumped wine on her."

Slade shook his head. "On my way, man. Stay cool. Be sure the crime scene remains intact until I get there. Give me twenty or twenty-five minutes in this ice and traffic."

"Got it," Charlie said and clicked off.

Chapter 41

Things were popping down at Biddy's Irish pub in Shockoe Bottom. Michaela parked her Land Cruiser in her reserved spot behind the bar and entered through the back door. She reviewed the messages on her desk and hung up her coat. She inspected her face in the mirror, rearranged her hair, and walked into the taproom with Angel at her side. Mic loved this bar—the smells, the polish, the scent of Murphy's oil soap, and the décor. She loved the way Biddy's had turned out. It had taken her three years, all the money she had saved for twenty years, and several architects and contractors to build the exact bar she remembered from her childhood home in Ireland. Biddy's bar in Dublin had been her dad's bar, and it had been one of the most hoppin' watering holes in Dublin. Seumas McPherson was a legend in the pub world, and Mic had spent her childhood in a booth doing her homework and eating vanilla ice cream after school each day. She had loved being the daughter of a pub owner. It had been great.

Michaela waved at Sean, her Irish bartender, complete with brogue, and walked over to the long mahogany bar that extended over thirty feet on one side of the restaurant. The mirrored wall of shelves, home to every kind of Irish whiskey, reflected beautifully in the low light. A Celtic string quartet played Irish music across from the bar on the small stage. The restaurant was beautiful, with the highly polished tables gleaming in the light. Sean waved back at her and deftly poured her a pint of Guinness.

Mic watched him carefully. Sean had the qualities of the ideal Irish bartender. He was expert at the true, five-step Guinness pour process. He deftly tilted the glass, pulled the tap forward for a carbonated beer blend and filled the glass just below the harp symbol. Then he waited for the beer to settle, tapped back and topped her beer off with pure beer just below or at the rim of the glass. He waited for the rising stream of bubbles to settle to the top and handed it to Michaela with a flourish and bow, the bubbles just a millimeter or so above the rim.

Mic nodded and accepted the beer. "How're things?" she asked.

"Busy, been busy since lunch. The Shepherd's pie was a huge hit. We've a little left if you are hungry." He glanced down the bar and saw a man push his glass forward and mouth the word, "pint." He smiled at Michaela and said, "Duty calls."

Mic flashed him a brilliant smile and glanced over to the corner of the bar to what staff affectionately referred to as the "friends' corner". She saw a group of her old police buddies drinking and talking. Lieutenant Steve Stoddard raised his glass in greeting. Mic raised her glass in return and walked through the crowd to the corner table.

Stoddard gave her a long, appreciative look. "Honest to God, Mic, you look ten times better since you retired from the RPD. Much better than you ever looked on the job! What've you done to yourself?"

"Yeah," another guy agreed, and two others raised their pints in agreement. "To Michaela and Biddy's ...mostly Biddy's, the best pub in town."

Mic laughed and looked for a seat.

"Sit down, Michaela," Ted Matthews said as he smiled at her. "Tell us what it's like to own a gold mine restaurant."

Michaela grinned at Ted, an old friend from the third precinct. "It's got a gold mine mortgage and it's as big a pain in the ass as being a Richmond City cop. Only difference is the coffee's better, and the beer is plentiful." She raised her glass to salute the men in blue who frequented her bar.

"There's two reasons to quit the RPD right there," Steve opined.

Michaela grinned again and asked, "Anybody seen Slade McKane? I'm hoping to catch up with him tonight."

Ted raised his eyebrow and winked. "Uh huh, you and Slade gonna give it another try?"

Mic shook her head, even though she felt heat crawl up her neck. "Nope, we're working on a case together. I'm private on the Allison Massie case. I'm hopin' he has some info for me."

Steve shook his head. "That's bad business. Family's having a hard time. No contact with anybody. You see Smirkowitz?"

Michaela nodded. "Yeah, and he's definitely involved. I hope we'll get him this time. My gut went into triple time just lookin' at him."

Ted raised his pint again, "Yeah, that slimy bastard's been gettin' away with stuff for years. Get him, Mic. He needs to go."

Mic nodded. "That's my plan, Ted. No one wants him anymore than me."

"Not true." a voice behind her said, "I want him more than you do, Mic. I've been after the creep for years."

An excited shudder ran through Mic at Slade's voice and she made room for him to sit.

Chapter 42

Dimitri Kazimir paced the scarred, wooden floor of the old warehouse, his anger escalating with every step. Where the hell was Oleg? When had he left, and most importantly, where'd he gone? Dimitri had called all the phone numbers several times but couldn't find him and was getting angry. He sat at the desk and watched the shadows darken the tall windows. His gut burned. He knew something was wrong, very wrong. His head throbbed from too much vodka and too little food. He hadn't eaten in hours. He pulled open all the desk drawers and found an old pack of peanut butter crackers that he devoured in one bite.

The vodka bottle was directly in front of him. He craved a drink to calm his nerves. He could feel anger pulsating through his body. He reached for the bottle and took a long drink. The fluid washed down his throat burning all the way, until it came to rest on top of his angry, burning gut.

I've gotta get out of here.

He slammed the vodka bottle against the desk. He grabbed his coat and hat and left the warehouse to look for some place to eat.

The weather was biting cold and felt like his years in Siberia. He walked down the block as the wind pierced his body. He hunched his shoulders forward from the cold and passed tall buildings on either side. He didn't see the man walking toward him, who was also hunched from the cold. Suddenly, he heard a voice.

"Dimitri, Dimitri, wait up," the voice hollered, but could barely be heard in the wind.

Dimitri turned his head and saw Oleg walking toward him as quickly as he could, dodging patches of ice and snow.

"Dimitri, how long have you been up? We need to go grab some dinner. Aren't you hungry?"

"Where the hell have you been? Are things straight for tonight?" Dimitri growled into the freezing wind. "I've been waiting for you, and I've tried to call you. What the hell is going on?"

Oleg touched Dimitri's elbow. "Let's duck in here and have a drink and get some dinner. We've a long night ahead of us, and I haven't eaten for hours."

Dimitri nodded his head as his anger dissipated. He nodded in agreement. "Yes, yes. Let's get some food. I'm famished as well."

Oleg opened the door to the small restaurant, and the two men entered, taking comfort in the warmth and the smell of fine cigars. A man pointed for them to take any table they wanted. The two Russians slid into a booth on the side of the restaurant, far enough away from the kitchen so their conversation wouldn't be overheard, but close enough to the front window where they could check the traffic going up and down the side street.

"The steaks here are good," Oleg recommended. "I eat here often. The waiters are discreet and there's nobody in here at night. As a matter of fact," he said as he checked his watch, "they close early at night. It's mostly a lunch spot, and they pick up a few folks at happy hour."

Dimitri nodded, relieved to be out of the biting cold and screeching wind. "Good, I'm starved. Gimme a steak, baked potato and salad, just like Americans eat in restaurants every night," he said with a half-smile.

Oleg returned the smile, pleased Dimitri's mood seemed to be improving. He motioned for the waiter, ordered two double vodkas on the rocks and their dinner. He reached into his pocket and pulled out a package of Rolaids.
187

"Sometimes I get heartburn when I drink during the day. These help me. Would you like one?"

Dimitri smiled blandly. "Don't mind if I do. My stomach is burning. Where'd you go and where is Smirkowitz?"

Oleg sighed deeply. He gestured helplessly with his hands. "I don't know. I've been looking for him ever since I left you this afternoon. I've been to his home and office and learned he has a lady friend named Tilda who's his mistress. She works at the dental practice so I called her husband and ..."

"Smirkowitz has a mistress?" Dimitri's voice was loud and angry, and his lip curled in disgust.

Oleg nodded. "It seems that way." He rolled his eyes.

Dimitri's face was red from anger, and Oleg felt fear crawl up his backside. He saw the snarl on Dimitri's face and stared into his narrowed eyes as they stared back at him. The waiter appeared with their vodkas and salads and a large basket of freshly baked bread and butter.

Dimitri grabbed the bread, ripped two large pieces from the loaf and stuffed it in his mouth greedily. He took a swig of his vodka and reached for another hunk of bread, which he buttered and crammed into his mouth as well. Oleg watched him with amazement. He had never seen anyone cram so much food in his mouth at one time.

"Okay, what's this about Smirkowitz having a mistress? How did you find out? A better question would be," he snorted, "why didn't you know a long time ago?"

Oleg shrugged his shoulders. "I didn't consider it. The man just married a much younger woman a few years ago, and I assumed that he was in a monogamous relationship."

"You assumed?" Dimitri snarled as he crashed his fist on the table so hard that the ice cubes in the vodka rattled. "In our business, we never 'assume' anything."

188

"I'm sorry, Dimitri, if I have disappointed you. What matters now is that we know about the woman. I stopped by her house on my way to come here to meet you, and there were no vehicles in the driveway. I also looked for her at Nicholas's office, and she wasn't there either. I don't know where she is, but after dinner, I suggest that we go back to his office again because I understand they often have their trysts after hours there."

Dimitri nodded and said, "That's a good idea. What about tonight's cargo? What do you know about the women we'll be transporting?"

Oleg's gut burned like it was on fire. He shook his head. "Nothing. I don't know for sure. I haven't been able to reach Nicholas all day, so I don't know where he's holding the women. I told our contact to get us women from another source."

Dimitri looked hopeful. "What'd he say?" He reached for his vodka.

Oleg lowered his head, and murmured his answer. "He said he'd try, but he wasn't hopeful. The weather will keep him from driving any long distances to pick up the women." He noted the scowl that crossed Dimitri's face. "But he did say that he'd round up some cargo for tomorrow night."

Dimitri nodded. "And so it will be, but then we will still go tonight just in case Nicholas shows up. The trawler is coming anyway, is it not?"

"Yes. The boat will be there. It'll be a good time for you to meet those on that end of our East Coast operation." Oleg smiled. "This is a very good idea, Dimitri. Perhaps we can plan for future transports."

"Good," Dimitri said as he rubbed his hands together in anticipation. His eyes lit up as he saw the waiter approaching them with two cheap gigantic porterhouse

189

steaks with baked potatoes and sour cream. His broad mouth watered in anticipation. Oleg thought he saw drool gather at one corner of Dimitri's mouth.

The young waiter set the plates down. Dimitri signaled for two more vodkas, and Oleg asked for cup of coffee.

Dimitri cut into his steak took a big bite and smiled with pleasure. "Aw, this tastes good. I'm starved." He slathered butter and sour cream on his large baked potato. He gave Oleg an appreciative look and murmured, "Good food, my droog. If the rest of my day is as good as this meal, perhaps you will redeem yourself for losing Nicholas Smirkowitz." His eyes were as hard as coal.

Oleg remained quiet.

Dimitri said nothing else but continued to eat his dinner. Oleg watched him, and then said, "I have other news though. Do you want to hear it? "

Dimitri smacked his lips and rolled his eyes. "Of course, I do. I hope it has to do with finding the women no one seems to know about." His voice was laden with sarcasm.

Oleg shook his head. "No, it does not concern that directly," he said quietly as he stared at Dimitri.

Dimitri, his mouth full of food, gestured with his hand for him to continue.

Oleg took a deep breath. "I've learned an hour or so ago that someone broke into Nicholas's former home and murdered his ex-wife and his daughter."

Dimitri stared at him. "What?"

Oleg nodded as he picked up his napkin and wiped his mouth. "Yeah. I heard it on the radio, and then I turned on the police scanner in my car."

Dimitri stared at him, his gaze fixed and his eyes bugged out of his head. "You're saying that someone murdered Constance, is that correct?"

"Yeah, that's correct." Oleg said. "The same person killed her daughter and a man who was in the house. Police presume he was her boyfriend. It happened about five o'clock. About three or so hours ago."

Dimitri was shocked. He put his fork down and stopped eating to process the bombshell Oleg had just dropped. "What do you think this means? Why would someone kill Constance and her daughter? It makes no sense at all. Constance, to my knowledge, had no idea about Nicholas's relationship with Bratva now or ever," he stated as if trying to convince himself.

Oleg shook his head. "No idea who did this. It would seem to me that you and I would be Nicholas's Smirkowitz's worst enemies. Who could be worse than us?"

Dimitri sat still as he considered what he knew. He shook his head. "There is more to this than we know. Perhaps his mistress, this Tilda, or whoever she is, killed them? What do you think?"

Oleg shook his head as eyes narrowed. He shrugged his shoulders and clenched and unclenched his fist. "I suppose that's possible. But I don't understand why she would do that, particularly since they are divorced, and he has a new wife. Jealously is a green-eyed monster."

Dimitri picked up his fork and resumed eating. "Eat up, tovarich. You and I are going to search for Tilda because I think that when we find her, we'll find Nicholas."

Oleg nodded and shoved food into his mouth. No time for manners now. He reached for his coffee and took a deep drink. It would be a long night.

Chapter 43

The approaching bright lights blinded Danielle as she looked out of her rear view mirror. Fear consumed her, and her heart bounded in her chest. She was certain she was being followed. She drove her Jetta quickly down Broad Street, made a left turn over to Marshall Street, and pulled in behind a historic church on Leigh Street. She cut her lights off and pulled in the furthest corner of the parking lot. Sure enough, the car turned as well. It was a late-model black sedan, but she couldn't make out the license plate. The car continued down the street, driving slowly, looking for her as she huddled down in her seat at the far end of the church parking lot.

Danielle's chest hurt from the pounding of her heart as she fumbled through her purse for the business card of the lady she'd met earlier that day ...the one she'd met when she'd been crying in her car outside Dude's office, after Tilda had chewed her out for nothing at all and said her work was unsatisfactory.

She couldn't find it, and dug deeper into her purse. Her anxiety skyrocketed. Where'd she put it? She couldn't call in to her boss. They'd never be able to help her. She was too far away. Her home in Maryland was over three hours away. She should've never agreed to this assignment. Danielle's heart thudded in her chest. She could hardly breathe she was so scared. She saw the black sedan's headlights headed toward her.

She ducked down in her seat to hide and saw Michaela's card on the console. She grabbed it and punched the numbers into her cell. Voicemail picked up on the third ring. "Hello, this is Michaela McPherson. Leave a message and I'll get right back."

"It's Danielle. We met today. Help me. Someone is after …"

Danielle screamed as someone broke her car window with a pistol, unlocked her door, grabbed her by her hair and dragged her out of the car. Pain and darkness. That's the last thing the young woman remembered.

Chapter 44

The waiter bought a pint and a basket of chips for Slade, and he raised the mug to his lips for the first sip. He looked at the cops sitting around him. "Listen up, guys. We've gotta triple homicide in the west end."

Stoddard stopped his glass midway. His eyes bulged. "Triple? That's big. Who?"

Slade caught Michaela's eyes and held them. "Constance Smirkowitz, her twelve-year-old daughter, and a guy named John Traynor, who we think was Constance's boyfriend." He reached for his Guinness again.

"Oh my God," Michaela whispered, "Someone killed a kid? What kind of maniac did this? Who kills a kid?"

"Was this the home invasion that came in a couple of hours ago?" Stoddard asked.

Slade nodded. "Yeah. Far as I know. In the West End. High-end neighborhood. Looks like Smirkowitz's son, the sixteen-year-old, heard all of the noise downstairs and activated the alarm." He shook his head. "The family was eating dinner when they were attacked."

"Why wasn't the son eating dinner? Where was he?"

Slade fiddled with his silverware "Apparently, someone tried to kidnap the son from school today."

He glanced at Stoddard and saw the look on his face. "Don't worry. We're tracking that down now."

Stoddard nodded.

"Anyway," Slade continued as he picked up a chip, "the son wasn't feeling well, and that's why he was upstairs in his room."

Mic mulled this information over in her mind. "What has Dr. Dude done to piss off someone so much they'd try to kidnap his son at school, and then murder his wife and daughter?"

"We've gotta couple of theories on that and are still working it up," Slade said. "Whatever it is, it's bad business."

"Yeah, for sure. Photos?" Mic asked.

"Yeah, a bunch." Slade handed her his phone. "Dr. Altman caught the case and she's still there along with the crime team boys."

"Good. Mary's the best medical examiner we have," Stoddard said. "What's she sayin?"

Slade chewed his chip before he answered. "Thinks the perp entered through the back door and the boyfriend... or whatever he was, John Traynor, left the dining room and came into the kitchen to see what was going on. That's apparently when the perp shot him in the chest. We think the killer used a silencer on his gun. Then the ME thinks the perp entered the dining room with a gun and a knife and came toward Constance. There's a missing knife from the block in the kitchen."

Mic shook her head. "That sounds disorganized to me. I'd have thought the perp would have had a better plan. There're all kinds of ways a scenario like that could go wrong."

"Yeah, agreed," Steve added. "If I were gonna brazenly walk into someone's house with the intent of killing them, I'd have thought about it a little more. Have a more orchestrated plan." He scratched his head. "It makes me wonder if the perp even knew who was in the house."

Slade offered a tight smile, drank deeply from his pint and said jokingly, "I'm impressed. You guys are sharp tonight."

Mic gave him a dirty look, and he smiled at her.

"That's exactly what Mary said, and I agree," Slade continued. "The killings were not random, and they weren't well planned. The entire scene in the dining room is chaotic. It's violent, haphazard, and bloody. Whoever killed Constance Smirkowitz and her daughter either hated them or had a vendetta of some type … or, it was a crime of passion."

"How so?" Michaela asked, pushing her dark curls behind her ears as she leaned in closer to Slade. "What else did the scene tell you and Dr. Altman?"

Slade shook his head and shrugged his shoulders. "Violence, passion, disorder, hate, not random. That's about it. Isn't that enough?" His voice was acerbic.

Mic gave a short laugh and raised her glass. "Yeah, Slade, lighten up. We'll give you all a couple more hours to solve it," she teased as she touched him on the arm lightly. "There's that black Irish temper again."

Slade nodded. "I've got Charlie Thor running down Dr. Dude's new wife to try and figure out whether she had a part in this or not. We're also looking at Dude's financials to see if he had any recent money problems. It looks as though the newly deceased Mrs. Smirkowitz had not changed her style of living one iota."

Anger surged through Mic as her eyes flashed, "Why should she? For all we know, she put Dr. Dude through dental school. She also birthed him two children. She deserves everything she has, and more as far as I'm concerned …or at least deserved. Why is it all you guys think that once divorced that a woman should live with less?"

Lt. Stoddard touched her shoulder. "Pipe down, Mic. Nobody said that, and nobody implied it, so give it a rest."

Mic took a deep breath and gave Stoddard an apologetic look. "Sorry, Lieutenant. You know that's a hot button for me. I've worked far too long at the women's shelters with their fear, pain, and poverty. Most women are crippled financially when their husband takes off." She looked around at her former colleagues, her friends, and said, her voice small and contrite, "Hey, guys, forgive me?"

"Sure, Mic," Slade said, after looking around the table. "We know you work hard for women. We'll forgive you for another round of Guinness, won't we, guys?"

Mic sighed deeply and signaled the waiter for fresh round. Then she looked at her friends. "You guys make me sick. I don't know how I lasted there for twenty years."

An old buddy guffawed and said, "The only reason we ever put up with you at the station, Mic, was because we knew that one day you'd own a bar, and you'd give us free drinks."

Laughter erupted, and Lt. Stoddard raised his glass in a toast. "To Michaela, to the best damned homicide detective RPD ever knew."

"Hear, hear," her friends said as they raised their glasses in a toast.

Mic did her best not to blush, but she could feel it creeping up her neck.

"And," Slade said, "to Biddy McPherson's, the best watering hole the RPD has ever frequented." He grinned as he raised his glass in tribute.

Michaela knew her face was bright red as she looked around the table at the smartest and bravest men she'd ever known. She stood and raised her glass in respect. "To the best Guinness drinkers in the Richmond Police Department. May you live long, solve crimes, and visit Biddy's forever."

"Hear, hear, I'll drink to that," several guys said in unison and clanked their glasses together.

When the cheering died down, Stoddard turned to Slade. "Is there anything else you need to tell us on these triple murders? Was forensics turning up anything?"

Slade shook his head. "Nope. Too early. No murder weapons located at the scene, so the perp must've taken the weapons with him, or at least we couldn't find them, but we did get some good footprints entering and leaving the house. The uniforms are canvassing the neighborhood now to see if anyone saw anything. Charlie Thor will call me with any changes."

"Dr. Altman say anything else? Did she speak to the order of the killings?" Michaela asked as she shredded her napkin. "Who died first?"

Slade nodded. "Yeah, she thinks the killer shot the boyfriend, went for Constance, but the daughter jumped him, and the killer slammed her onto the floor. It looks like she hit the floor hard because the back of her head was pretty banged up. Lots of blood. The kid took three rounds up close, so the doc thinks, and so do I. The killer shot her on the floor. Also looked as though the kid had a broken rib, so we guess the perp kicked her in the ribs. We don't know if the kid was conscious or not when she was shot."

Stoddard groaned and shook his head as a look of disgust shot across his face, "Shot the girl three times when she was on the floor? That's pretty cold." He slammed his mug on the polished table, and the dark brew spilled over the rim of his mug and spread toward the center, "This isn't an intruder. These murders are up front and personal."

Slade nodded, his eyes smoking rage. "Yeah. No question." He paused for a moment, then continued, "The girl has a bloodied footprint on her chest, so the way I see it, the perp tracked through Traynor's blood in the kitchen and held the kid down with a foot on her chest when he shot her."

Stoddard nodded. "Man, that's cold. To do that to a kid." He grunted as the other men nodded.

"Anything else?" Mic asked as she looked into Slade's eyes, conscious of the angry sounds and low conversation from the rest of the police officers at the table as they cursed and discussed the case.

"Perp has a small foot. Man's size ten- perp wore work boots. Not sure yet."

Michaela thought about this. "Small feet? That's pretty weird. Most people wear snow boots in this kind of weather." She paused for second. "I wonder if we're possibly looking for a woman?"

The men quieted down as each considered the possibility that a woman could have murdered two adults and a twelve-year-old child.

Stoddard looked pensive and spoke slowly. "A woman in work boots? Sure, it's possible. I wouldn't have thought that, but it's always possible."

"Lieutenant, everything about this scene is different," Mic persisted as she ran her ringers through her curls as she often did when she was thinking. "Time of day, disorganized, chaotic, child murder. It's a crazy, cruel scene."

"If a woman was angry, she could've very easily taken charge of the scene, especially if she killed the man in the kitchen," Slade added.

"Yeah, she used the element of surprise on two unsuspecting adults and a kid," Mic said "We've gotta keep that option open." Mic knocked her pint over with her elbow.

Mic was silent as the waiter cleaned up the table with a brilliant white towel. Mic watched the towel turn color as it sopped up the brown Guinness spills. She turned to Slade and Steve.

"I'm sure it was a woman," she said. "All of the rage at the scene and killing the girl …maybe she killed the daughter because it wasn't her daughter." She turned to Slade and said, "It's just a hunch but I wonder if Dude has any long-term woman friends …women that go back fifteen or twenty years. This feels like a 'woman scorned' case to me. Pure jealous rage."

Lt. Stoddard and Slade McKane stared at each other as Mic watched their expressions light up.

"She's on to something," Stoddard said. "No question. The brilliant intuition of Michaela McPherson strikes again."

Slade nodded. "Damned right. Never left her, even after she retired. I'll call the ME and Charlie Thor. I'll tell her what Mic thinks and get her reaction. Dr. Altman rarely misses stuff, and I think Mic's right on."

"Yeah," Stoddard agreed and bottomed-up his pint.

Chapter 45

It was cold as the wind whipped around the tall buildings in downtown Richmond where Redman waited for Oleg on a street corner.

Redman jumped in at the corner as Oleg slowed the car.

The tension between the two was palpable.

"Where've you been, Branislava? Where's Dimitri? I've been freezin' out here for over twenty minutes," Redman snarled, between the chatter of his teeth.

"I came as soon as I could. I've gotta move carefully around Dimitri. I took him out to dinner, and he's back at the warehouse takin' a nap. We'll pick him up later and take him to the dock. He's suspicious about the exchange tonight." Oleg looked at Redman out of the corner of his eye as he turned onto the interstate ramp. "How's that comin'?"

"It's not, it's not coming along at all, Oleg," the younger man scowled. "We ain't got nobody to transport."

Oleg pulled the car off to the side of the road and stared at him without speaking.

Redman flinched in the passenger seat. "Okay, Oleg, what the hell do you want me to do? Manufacture women for tonight? Conjure up some female flesh? Maybe some mystical women without bruised faces and ligature marks?" His voice was tinged with sarcasm.

"We've gotta pull it off tonight. I can't find Smirkowitz, and you know Dimitri Kazimir will kill us or have us killed if we come up short."

Redman shrugged his shoulders. "Screw Dimitri. He's not the only oar in the water," he spat with anger in his voice. "Just postpone tonight's rendezvous. I'll round up some women for tomorrow night, even if I have to drive to hell and back to get them."

Oleg couldn't believe what his comrade had said. "Are you out of your mind? Do you know who Dimitri Kazimir is? He wants women tonight and more women tomorrow night."

A flicker of anger flashed across Redman's face. "Yeah, I know who he is, but things happen. And, we're not gonna find Smirkowitz until we go to his house and check out his wife, so drive," he ordered.

Oleg pulled off the shoulder of the interstate and exited left. "Dimitri Kazimir is the boss of human trafficking for Bratva." Oleg paused for a moment for his statement to sink in. He continued, his voice threatening, "You never anger or insult a Bratva boss. Especially if you value your life." He ended with his voice several octaves higher than normal.

The man ignored him. "Cut the gangsta crap. I don't care, and I'm not scared of some Russian mob boss."

"You damned well should be. You're new in this organization, and you've got a lot to learn. Isn't this your first 'real' assignment?"

"Where're we goin'?" Redman demanded. "Where does Smirkowitz live and is his new wife there? Or, has somebody has offed her too?" he added sarcastically.

Oleg said nothing.

"Well, did your goons kill the first wife and kid?" Redman asked harshly. "I heard it was a bloody mess over there."

Oleg shook his head. "I know nothing about Constance's death, and I doubt Dimitri does either. He'd have told me earlier today if it had been the plan. I've no idea who killed them."

Redman looked at him and laughed sarcastically. "Of course you don't. I just bet. Isn't it a bit ironic that you've gotta major Bratva contact on your hands who isn't performing, and his ex-wife and kid are killed?" He shot Oleg a suspicious look.

Oleg shrugged his shoulders. "I got you, but you're a contact who 'isn't performing well' to quote you," he said as he glared at Redman wondering if he could develop this arrogant man into a competent soldier for Bratva. He guessed he'd have some sort of clue if Redman could pull off his current double agent assignment.

Redman stared at Oleg, who noticed the younger man's Adams apple working in his throat.

"I don't think Bratva is involved in the murders," Oleg said. "Dimitri was fond of Constance Smirkowitz. They were friends in Russia before she was ex-patriated. He selected her to be Nicholas's wife several years before they actually married."

Redman rolled his eyes, "So ...where's Smirkowitz? Where'd he go?"

Oleg shook his head. "I've no idea."

"He's close to worthless, but you all covet him like he is some kind of hero."

Oleg let out an exasperated sigh. "Parents were big in the Communist party and protected the assets of Bratva during the Soviet era. They offered their son to Bratva shortly after his birth. Nicholas, like you, was bred for this work. Nicholas's parents were well respected, and we honor them by honoring their son."

"That was eons ago. No one cares about that crap anymore. It's a new ballgame," Redman said smugly. "Nicholas is expendable, no question," he added with a sneer.

Oleg was silent as he turned his car into the lavish, high-end subdivision where Nicholas Smirkowitz currently lived with his second wife and baby. The paved driveway was empty, and two gas front porch lights were burning brightly. He rang the bell and could hear Corinthian chimes echo through the vast downstairs. He pulled his coat tightly around him as he waited on the snow-covered front porch.

Chapter 46

A beautiful young woman with long blond hair and violet eyes pulled open the heavy door and stared at the two men. She wore a lavender sweat suit that matched her eyes. Oleg was taken aback by the beauty of the young woman. She held a baby, who was less than a year old, in her arms.

"Yes, can I help you?" the young woman asked.

"We're looking for Nicholas. Is he home this evening?" Oleg's voice was low and gruff.

The woman shook her head, her blond hair moving from side to side. She studied them. "No. He's not. I'm looking for him myself," she admitted as her eyes filled with tears.

"You're Dawn, correct?" Oleg asked.

The woman nodded her head

"When did you last see him?" Oleg questioned as he looked into her strange eyes that now appeared more of a blue shade than violet. "It's very important that we find him, Mrs. Smirkowitz," he added gesturing to Redman.

The woman hesitated for a moment. "It was late this afternoon, maybe 'round three o'clock or so, I think. He said he would be back before dark,"

Redman broke into the conversation. "That was a long time ago. It's way past dark. Where'd he go?" he demanded in a harsh voice.

"I ... I don't know," Dawn stammered. "He said he had a few errands to run, and then he was picking up some wine for this evening."

Redman moved closer to her. "Cut the crap," he said rudely. "We need to find him. Tell us everything you know and spit it out now." Redman's tone was abrasive and loud. The baby started to cry.

Fear flooded her eyes and tears flowed down her cheeks. She shrank back in the doorway and bounced the wailing infant in her arms. "Is this about Constance's death? The police just left a little while ago." Her voice quavered.

Oleg put his hand out to prevent Redman from moving closer to the woman. "No. It's not about that. We've business with Nicholas and had planned to meet this evening. He didn't come, so we thought that perhaps something had happened." Oleg tried to make his voice as reassuring as possible.

Dawn looked at him but said nothing.

"I've been calling Nicholas for hours. No answer. Do you know where he is?" Oleg asked Dawn gently.

She shook her head, her violet eyes filled with tears.

"Is there anywhere you can think of he may have gone?" Oleg continued.

"No, not really, but we own a couple of tracks of property, sort of a farm, between here and Gordonsville. He bought them a few years ago. He goes there sometimes and rides his tractor, plays with his ATV, that kind of thing."

"Would he go there with snow and ice on the ground?"

She shook her head. "No, I don't think so. There'd be nothing for him to do," she admitted. "The barn doesn't have heat, so I doubt he'd go there."

"Where is the farm or farms?" Redman asked.

Dawn shot him a frightened look. "I'm not sure. Off of Route 33 somewhere. Before Gordonsville."

"Can you be more specific?" Redman growled, an angry look on his face. "That's a lot of miles to cover."

Dawn looked apologetic. "I …well, not really. It's near the Barboursville winery. We went there last year, and the other track of property is close by. I saw the barn. He wants to build a horse farm there in a few years." She forced a smile through her tears.

"Is there anything else you can possibly tell us that may help?" Oleg asked kindly. "We wouldn't bother you unless it were really important."

"No. I've told you the same thing I told the police. They're looking for him, too," she said. "They want to question him about Constance and Sarah," she said as her eyes filled with tears again.

Oleg handed her his card. "Please call us when you hear from him, Dawn. It is very important."

Dawn accepted the card and nodded.

"Thank you, and good evening," Oleg said as he and Redman turned and left the porch. They heard the door shut, and the dead bolt click into place.

"Well, that was useless," Redman growled as he lit a cigarette and threw the match in a pile of snow.

Oleg scrunched the match with his boot. "Pretty much was. As you said, that's a lot of area to cover. I guess we need to go on the Internet and search the county deed book."

"You may, not me. I'm busy," Redman shot back. "Get me back to our meeting place."

Chapter 47

Michaela and Slade moved away from the booth filled with police officers to a smaller table where they could talk privately and discuss the deaths of Constance and Sarah Smirkowitz. Mic hadn't missed the "knowing" looks several of her old buddies had given her. She watched Angel struggle into a comfortable position on his cushion next to the wooden table. She needed to take him in to the vet to see if there was another medicine for him. His hip was giving him such pain.

She looked down at her plate and studied her Shepherd's pie. It was pretty tasty so she took another bite. She tried to put her thoughts about Dottie in order. She filled him in on what she could remember.

Slade devoured his dinner and pushed his empty plate aside. "Okay, Mic. What else did Dottie say she overheard in Smirkowitz's office? I've got two guys trying to track down info on the Russian guy, but it might be a couple of days before something pops."

Mic nodded and sipped her water. "I think I've told you everything. What do you think about the state police investigation that didn't go anywhere? Do you think this is an international crime incident?"

Slade continued. "Yeah. I do. I called in the feds because, from what you told me via Dottie and your friend from the state police, it sounds like some sort of a human trafficking or sex trade scheme is goin' on. Especially, if they're talking about bidding."

Mic shuddered when she thought about the possibility of young women being sold into slavery. "Are you all working on anything else that involves human trafficking? Is there evidence of that happening here in Richmond?"

Slade slouched in his chair. "We get reports of it from time to time, but we chase it down and there's nothing. Frankly, I'm of the opinion that happens a lot, especially with illegals that enter the U.S."

Mic listened as her stomach soured. "Yeah, I'm sure it happens more than we want to know," she answered as she reached for the water glass.

Slade nodded, his dark eyes flashing, "Human traffickers prey on the poorest people in the world, recruit young men and woman and promise them the world ... jobs as fashion models, movie stars, a college education, just name it." Slade noted the look of revulsion on Mic's face. "I can see you get my drift."

Mic nodded, a pain in her gut. She'd lost her appetite. "What else? What else is happening here?"

Slade was quiet for a moment as he collected his thoughts. "There's some speculation that young women are smuggled into Richmond because it's a port city. Generally, they're smuggled to Egypt, the Mediterranean, or the Middle East, or just about anywhere else in the world, especially if they're American women with blond or light-colored hair. Do we have proof? Nope, not really," Slade reported. "I do think it's happening a lot." He mopped up the spreading beer with his napkin and signaled for a waiter.

Mic watched the Guinness spread over the table. She shook her head and said, "That disgusts me and boils my blood," she retorted angrily.

Slade nodded. "Yeah me, too. I hate the exploitation of anyone for someone else's gain, animal or human. It just pisses me off."

Mic was quiet for a moment as she reached down and patted Angel who was busily chewing on a steak bone. "I guess we've got to assume that this is what happened to Allison. There's a real possibility that she's been abducted to be trafficked to another country as part of an international human trafficking ring? Maybe an international trafficking ring that Nicholas Smirkowitz runs?" She gave Slade an uncertain look.

Slade pondered her question. "Yeah, that's possible although I hope not, but we've gotta consider it." He was quiet for a moment and continued, "That's why I called in the FBI. An agent from the Richmond office is gonna meet us here in about forty-five minutes. Is there a quiet place we can go and talk?"

"Sure. We can use my office," Mic advised as she played with the Shepherd's pie on her plate. It'd been a good ten minutes ago when she'd had her first bite, but now she'd lost all appetite. She looked at her cell phone and noted she had a voicemail. She picked it up and listened as her face paled.

"What is it?" Slade demanded. Mic handed him the phone. "It's a message from the young woman, Danielle, the young girl I met today outside of Smirkowitz's office. She left it a few minutes ago. She thought someone was after her, and then I heard her scream."

Slade grabbed the phone and listened to the message. "We'll find her," he advised as he called for backup. He gestured toward Lt. Stoddard's table. "Tell Stoddard what's happened, and our suspicions about human trafficking. See if he'll meet the FBI guy in a half hour or so."

Mic nodded, and she and Angel headed over to Stoddard's table with the message. Stoddard agreed to wait for the FBI although Mic knew he hated to work with them.

Slade joined them. "This FBI agent sounds like a royal pain in the ass. I guess I'll have to owe you one." He grinned sheepishly at his boss.

Stoddard scowled, his handsome face scrunched up in a mock frown. "Yeah, for sure. You will owe me. You know I hate the feds," he said then grinned broadly, "but for you, Slade, I'll do it just this one time." He winked at Michaela.

Slade returned the grin and grabbed Michaela's arm as they quickly left Biddy's through the back door, Angel at Michaela's side.

"Be careful, Mic. It's icy out here. You don't need to fall," Slade cautioned.

Michaela nodded. "Yeah, I know. I should've worn rubber-soled boots. Will you open the backseat door for Angel so he can jump in?"

"Sure, come on, ole boy," Slade clicked his fingers, and Angel jumped in and lay on his blanket in the back of the cruiser. Mic and Slade were quiet on the ride uptown toward the church on Leigh Street in Slade's cruiser.

Chapter 48

Dottie tossed and turned in her bed, unable to sleep. Her mind raced as she replayed the events of the day in her head. What had she forgotten to tell Michaela? It was important, and it nagged at her incessantly. She sat on the side of her bed and tried to remember everything she'd overheard in Dr. Dude's office. It just wouldn't come. She looked at her alarm clock. It was after midnight.

Damn, I shouldn't have had that third glass of Sherry. It's keeping me up. She decided to go into the kitchen and make herself some hot chocolate.

Dottie stood but had to hold onto her bedpost for moment. Sometimes she got dizzy when she first stood, and she didn't want to take a chance on falling. A new right hip reminded her she wanted no part of the inside of a hospital room. When she felt steady, she looked beside her night table and sure enough, Cookie had placed her walker where she could easily reach it.

I hate this damned thing and I don't want anyone to know I have it, but I do know that when I get up at night I'm a little rocky.

Dottie grabbed the walker angrily and held on to it as she slipped on her slippers and robe and padded across her bedroom into the hall. She pushed the elevator button, and the door opened immediately. The elevator made a quick sweep to the first floor, and she exited in her kitchen. A voice startled her and she almost jumped out of her skin.

"What are you doing out of bed, Countess?" a surprised and concerned voice demanded. Cookie stood across the kitchen, her face a mixture of anger and concern.

Dorothy turned and smiled when she saw Cookie in her robe standing near the opposite entrance to the kitchen.

Dottie tossed her head and her silver hair, free from its bun, danced around her head. "I couldn't sleep. There's something I forgot to tell Michaela, and I thought if I had some hot chocolate, it might jar my memory. I know it's important and I think it might be the final piece to the puzzle." Dottie was so frustrated she was close to tears.

Cookie walked across the kitchen and took Dottie's arm. "Countess, sit at the table, and I'll make your chocolate for you. The next time you need help this late at night please ring for me," she added in a reproachful voice.

Dottie sighed but remained silent as Cookie ranted a bit longer, "Henry and I are happy to help you anytime you need us. You do know that," she said in an accusing tone, as her right eyebrow arched. Dottie knew that when the eyebrow arched, she was in deep trouble with her housekeeper. She sat quietly as Cookie continued to chastise her, but her mind wandered to more important things.

"Countess, are you listening to me?" Cookie demanded.

Dottie waved her hand and dismissed her. "Seriously, Cookie. This is important. I overheard a conversation today in Dr. Smirkowitz's office, and it had something to do with Margaret's granddaughter."

Cookie went over to the refrigerator and removed a gallon of milk. Then she retrieved the cocoa powder from the walk-in pantry. "Of course, you did," she interrupted Dottie. "It's Allison Massie, you told Michaela about it when she was here a few hours ago."

Dottie shook her head. "No, no, no. I did not." Dottie protested sharply, her voice caustic. "Stop telling me what I said because you weren't even in the room," she added, her voice belligerent.

Cookie shot her a stunned look and opened her mouth to speak, but before she could get the words out, Dottie spoke again.

"Oh, yes, I apologize. I didn't mean to sound so rude." Dottie gave Cookie a pained look. "I'm just anxious because I'm sure I've forgotten something important."

Cookie gave her a brief smile and gestured for her to continue. "Go on. Tell me what you remember," she encouraged. Cookie prayed for patience and hoped she didn't smack the arrogant old lady, something she'd never done but dreamed of often.

Dottie thought for a moment. "I did tell her about Allison, but there's another young woman who's in danger, and I cannot remember her name to save my life," Dottie continued as she pounded her delicate, blue-veined fist on the table. "It makes me so mad," she wailed.

Cookie laid a reassuring hand on Dottie's shoulder. "You'd best settle down so you'll be able to think more clearly. I'm going to have some chocolate, too, and I'll sit here with you, and we'll try to remember together."

Dottie nodded stiffly.

"Sometimes two heads are better than one," Cookie added, but Dottie remained silent.

As Cookie busied herself at the stove, Dottie slowly sipped her hot chocolate. It was warm and comforting and the milk felt like velvet in her mouth. She felt her blood pressure and pulse slow down. She turned to Cookie, and said, in a rare moment of appreciation, "Cookie, I hope you know how much I appreciate you and Henry. You are the only family I have now... and Michaela, of course, and I don't know what I would do without you."

"Thank you, Countess Borghase. That means a lot to us. We love you and that's all the more reason why you should call us at night when you need help." Dottie thought Cookie sounded like she might cry.

"For heaven's sake, can't you just let it rest," Dottie blurted out.

As soon as the words escaped her mouth, Cookie wished she could stuff them back in. Dottie rarely said anything that touched her heart, but Cookie had replied like she were speaking to a child. Cookie turned away from the stove and faced Dottie who rolled her blue eyes. Cookie ignored Dottie's angry look and carried the hot chocolate over to the large oak kitchen table and sat down.

"Would you like a refill? I made a full pot," Cookie offered.

Dottie stared steadily at the table but pushed her cup toward Cookie. "Yes, it's really good, and it hit the spot."

Cookie smiled and refilled Dottie's cup. The two women drank their chocolate in silence as Dottie thought about her eavesdropping escapade at Dr. Dude's office. Suddenly, a light bulb went off, and she smacked the table and said happily. "I remember the girl's name. I know her name. It's Danielle, and the Russian said he was going to get her tonight before she talked to anyone. Oh gosh, Cookie, please give me the phone so I can call Michaela."

"Yes, ma'am, I'll get it right now." Cookie scurried across the kitchen, as fast as her buxom-full frame could carry her, returning with Dottie's house phone. She pushed the redial button for Michaela's cell.

Michaela answered on the first ring. "Dottie, what's wrong?" Mic's voice sounded strained and tired.

"Michaela, Michaela, nothing is wrong. I remember something else from today. The Russian man was also after a young girl named Danielle."

There was long silence. Michaela was unable to speak.

"Mic, do you hear me. There's a young woman, who probably works in Dr. Dude's office, and she's in trouble. I know it. I just remembered." Dottie's voice was excited, and she seemed a bit short of breath.

Michaela said softly, "Thanks, Dottie. I knew they were after her."

"He said he was going to find Danielle tonight and take care of her," Dottie added as she paused. "Does that mean anything to you?"

"Yes, I know. I've found Danielle," Mic said sadly.

"What's wrong, Mic? You sound funny," Dottie said.

"I'm okay. Go to bed and get some rest. I've got to go, Dottie. I'm pretty busy now, but I'll talk to you tomorrow." Michaela stared at the bloodied body of Danielle Alvarez. She could hardly hold back the tears.

Chapter 49

I should have known. That bastard. Her heart twisted in pain as she examined the mangled, battered body. Michaela bent to pet Angel, who was standing at her side, was unruffled by the sirens, blue lights, and the smell of blood. He looked expectantly at Michaela for orders, but his mistress was quiet.

"Are you ready to go, Mic?" Slade asked as he stood by her side.

Mic shook her head. "In a minute. I want to talk to the paramedic."

Slade walked over to the stretcher, tapped the young paramedic on the shoulder, and signaled for him to come over. The young man had blood all over his hands. He'd just placed a breathing tube in Danielle's throat.

He looked at Michaela and said, "Ma'am, can I help you?"

Mic flashed her police identification shield, the one issued to retirees and asked. "How bad is she? How badly is Danielle hurt? Do you think she'll make it?" The questions tumbled out of her mouth before the man had a chance to respond.

He shook his head as he stared at the still form on the frozen ground. "I don't know. She's been badly beaten, and it looks like blunt force trauma to her head. She's unconscious, most likely in a coma. She has a broken arm and leg."

Michaela stood still and waited for more.

The paramedic scratched his head and continued, "I don't know about her internal injuries, but I suspect she's got some bleeding going on somewhere. Her blood pressure is dropping, and her heart rate is picking up." He shook his head and said sadly, "I'd say its touch and go."

Michaela was silent and the paramedic continued, "We've stabilized her and we've got to move her over to MCV."

"So what do you think?" Michaela persisted.

The young man shrugged his shoulders. "I don't know. It's like I said… touch and go. It could be either way. They do perform miracles at MCV as you know, and they have the best head team in the country."

Michaela nodded and the young man returned to Danielle's stretcher and continued to stabilize her.

Mic gritted her teeth, turning to Slade. "Let's go. I can't stand it here any longer. We have to stay on this, Slade, because finding who attacked Danielle is the key to finding Allison."

Slade nodded, grabbed her arm and the two of them watched Angel as he sniffed Danielle's still body and gave Mic a mournful look. Mic was visibly upset as the three of them made their way through the snow and ice toward Slade's cruiser.

Chapter 50

Mic and Slade sat outside the busy waiting room at the Medical College of Virginia Hospital's Level I emergency department. The blue and red flashing lights of police and emergency vehicles were reflected in the windows. Mic stared into her coffee cup and watched the cream and sugar crystals slowly dissolve and thicken the hot substance. Slade stood and went over to the emergency room desk clerk and asked how Danielle was doing. A few minutes later, a young physician approached them.

"Are you here for Danielle Alvarez?"

Michaela stood and offered her hand. "Yes, we are. This is Detective Slade McKane of the RPD, and I'm Michaela McPherson.

"Are you relatives?" the young man asked as he peered at them over his glasses.

"No, we're not," Slade said quickly. "I only met Danielle today. We are investigating a case we believe she is involved in."

The young man nodded.

"How is she, Doctor?" Mic asked in a breathless voice. "It looked bad at the scene."

The ER doc nodded. "Yes. She's stable and we're running tests.

"Will you keep us in the loop?" Slade asked doctor as he handed him his card. "I'm the investigating detective. Will you call us when she wakes up?"

"I will indeed," he answered as he accepted Slade's card. His cell phone rang. He checked the number and looked apologetic, "Gotta get back."

"Thank you, Doctor," she said.

The physician touched her shoulder. "We'll take care of her, I promise. She won't get better care anywhere else on the planet."

"Now, that I do know. Thank you again."

Slade placed his arm around Mic's shoulders and said softly, "Let's sit down for a few minutes and figure out where we go next."

Michaela nodded and sat again in the hard, turquoise plastic chair. She needed comfort so she leaned down and scratched Angel's ear. He responded and licked her hand. She leaned forward and nose to nose, the two looked at each other. Angel licked the tears from Michaela's face and kissed her on the nose. Slade noted the connection between Michaela and her dog. It was beautiful. No one could question the loyalty between the two. The moment was so pure and serene, tears jumped into the sentimental Irishman's eyes that he quickly brushed away.

Mic continued to stroke her dog as she remembered the night Angel had saved her life. They'd been chasing a pimp years ago when she was working vice. The chase had turned dirty when an accomplice had trained his weapon on her. Angel had leapt over a police car to get to the assailant and when the man fired, Angel took the bullet mid-air in the hip. The bullet threw the powerful dog against a brick wall and knocked him unconscious. Mic's partner had taken down the pimp and rushed to Mic's side who knelt, unhurt and crumpled next to Angel's body.

It had been touch and go for Angel but after intensive treatment, Angel was retired with honors from the RPD, and came to live with Michaela full time. The two were inseparable. There wasn't a finer police dog on the earth than Angel. No RPD officer could ever have a finer partner than a highly trained working dog like him. She reached into her pocket and gave him a treat as tears fell down her face.

Slade touched her shoulder gently, "Mic, we don't need to stay here any longer. Wanna head back to Biddy's?"

Mic shook her head. "No, Slade. I'm pretty tired, and I think Angel and I would just like to go home. Can you give us a lift?"

Slade hugged her gently. "Yeah, and I'll have a unit drive your car back to your house."

Mic nodded in appreciation. "Thanks. You never know when I'll need to go out, and I surely don't want to drive my other car in this weather.

Chapter 51

Richmond homicide Lt. Steve Stoddard ran his big hands through his coarse salt and pepper hair as he stared across Mic's desk at the smooth-skinned, fresh-faced young FBI agent, a plate of fish and chips between them. The young man touched a raw nerve Stoddard couldn't identify. He wondered if the fair-headed, baby-faced agent shaved. Irritation or maybe impatience shot through him as he studied the young man. The Fed was impressed with himself and had an air of superiority. But for some reason, he wasn't quite genuine. Stoddard sized him up as a cocky, pain in the ass at first glance. The RPD lieutenant stifled a yawn as the young man droned on and on about the FBI and his law degree from Stanford.

Just the facts, man, just the facts. I don't need a lecture on the history of the FBI.

Stoddard checked his phone, hoping for a text from McKane.

"Lt. Stoddard, did you hear me?" The young agent's voice was persistent, and it bothered Stoddard beyond imagination, but instead he smiled at the cocky agent.

"Of course, I did, Agent. You were telling me that the FBI had the bead on Smirkowitz. Is that correct?" Stoddard hoped the annoyance in his voice wasn't too apparent. He had nothing against the young agent, but for some reason the fresh-faced kid irked him beyond reason as he drummed his fingers impatiently on Michaela's desk. The man seemed fake.

"Yes, but I wondered if Smirkowitz is known to you here in Richmond?" the agent asked.

Stoddard decided not to answer. "Are you new to the Richmond office?" he said, suddenly curious about the response.

"Yes, I'm new to the Richmond office, but I was assigned to the human trafficking task force in Baltimore last fall," the man said.

Stoddard could swear his chest puffed out as he continued.

"I was sent down to Richmond a week ago to give you all a hand," the agent finished.

Stoddard nodded as he checked the clock on the wall and watched the second-hand crawl past each number. "A hand? What kind of a hand are you gonna give us?" He hoped the smirk didn't show on his face.

The agent stared at him, not trying to disguise his smirk. "I'm gonna help you catch the bad guys, of course. What do you think I'm gonna do?" he said, his voice arrogant as he reached for a piece of fish.

Stoddard's eyes narrowed. "A hand? Generally, when someone offers me a hand, I hear about it from my higher-ups command, and not when I'm at my local watering hole."

Baby-face seemed ruffled for a moment. "Your man, Slade something or another, called the Bureau ...something about human trafficking and a Dr. Smirkowitz. I was the agent on duty. That's why I'm here." Stoddard could swear the youngster sneered.

Stoddard paused for a moment, studying the cocky young agent. "Human trafficking? I'm an officer in the first precinct and that's my command area. No trafficking problem I know of." He stared at agent who picked at his fish and chips but said nothing. Perhaps the man was arrogant because he looked like he was twelve years old. "We've heard a few rumors, but nothing's panned out,"

Stoddard continued. "You think we have a trafficking problem?" Stoddard gave him a tight-lipped smile and leaned back in Mic's chair as he steeled himself for another display of arrogance or brilliance, or whatever from the young man.

That kid thinks I'm a moron. Screw him.

The agent smiled benignly, a smug look on his baby face, as he glanced at the older officer, but he remained silent. He offered a brief nod.

Stoddard felt his heart rate pick up. He was pissed, and he wanted to crush the little twerp's skull. "Tell me about our trafficking problem. Go on and educate me," he said rudely and gestured with his hands.

Baby-face puffed up again, took a deep breath and began, "The trafficking problem is huge, enormous, actually. Human trafficking is modern-day slavery and involves everyone — especially children and young women. They are forced into prostitution, labor, and domestic servitude."

Stoddard nodded. He was bored and angry but tried not to show it. He stifled a yawn as he checked out his salt and pepper hair in Mic's wall mirror. He scanned his phone for messages and texts, hoping for a reason to leave. "Yeah, I figured. So, what about the task force in Baltimore?"

The agent nodded and continued. "The FBI is the lead agency that investigates human trafficking, and it's a top civil rights violation. The task force in Baltimore has found that traffickers target poor and unsuspecting families, and that many victims don't speak English. Most are smuggled into the East or West Coast, told they have to pay $10,000 to $20,000 for the cost of being smuggled into the country. If they buck the system or refuse to pay the debt, they're told their families in their old country will be murdered."

Stoddard nodded. "Yeah, that's stuff anybody can read on the Internet. What can you tell me about the task force... and our trafficking problem in Richmond?" he asked as he leaned in towards the young agent.

The agent's young face darkened with contempt. "A lot. Our human trafficking cases have increased over three hundred percent in less than three years. We made almost five hundred arrests last year, three hundred and thirty-six indictments were issued, and we got two hundred and fifty-eight convictions. We've partnered with local law enforcement and the community and developed an extensive outreach program to raise awareness."

Stoddard picked up his Guinness and mused over the information. "Interesting, but I'm not a social worker. That's not tellin' me about the task force. What's happenin' in Baltimore?"

Baby-face offered him a shrewd smile. "This is where it gets exciting." Stoddard noticed a flicker of anger cross the agent's face and his eyes wandered. "We rounded up some perps we think were smuggling young women into D.C. and Northern Virginia via Baltimore Harbor. We think the operators of this large trafficking ring may open a new shop in Richmond."

Stoddard's face flushed with anger. "When were you guys gonna tell us at the RPD? Thought we all had the same goal of catching the bad guys," he added sarcastically, anger in his voice.

The young agent said nothing but reached for the fish and chips platter and chewed thoughtfully. He walked over toward the door and opened it as he turned his attention to the musicians who had hauled in a couple of base fiddles, a few violins, and a synthesizer and watched them set up. "When we were damned good and ready," he said and turned to face Stoddard.

Stoddard turned red as anger rushed to his brain. He wanted to flatten the kid's smart-ass skull, but he held his temper, as he mused over the possibility of Richmond becoming a port for human traffic smugglers. There was no way he was showing this idiot his true feelings. He enjoyed a good game of cat and mouse, so he baited him.

"I'm surprised about Richmond being a desirable port for trafficking. The port is barely operational these days. We have barges that travel the James River with consumer goods, frozen seafood, and other supplies each day. The port is easily accessible by truck, car, and rail. Other than that, it's been pretty much closed for months."

The agent gave the older cop a sly smile. "Exactly my point. Good port, easy in, easy out. Minimal security. A perfect place to smuggle. Buy yourself a railroad car or truck, and you're good to go." He smiled smugly to himself.

Stoddard gritted his teeth and realized the enormity of the federal agent's words. It was true. There was barely a Richmond police presence at the quiet port of Richmond.

Damn, we need to look into this soon.

"Let me think about this and talk to the higher-ups. You know resources are tight," Stoddard said as he eased back into his chair.

The agent was about to respond as his cell rang. He looked over at Stoddard. "Gotta take this, be back in a minute."

Stoddard looked at him strangely. Did he detect an accent in his voice? An accent that he'd covered up earlier in their conversation? He waited a couple of minutes and followed the man, peering at him through the windows at the front of the bar, his presence blocked by folks bellied up to Biddy's bar.

Stoddard watched as the agent stood outside in the freezing cold. The man was clearly pissed. He paced the cobblestones outside the bar and gestured wildly with his arms. The cocky young man was agitated, talking loudly into his phone. Stoddard walked by the table full of his RPD friends, who laughed and taunted him about hanging out with the feds. As he stood at the bar and watched, the baby-faced agent reentered with an angry scowl on his face that instantly changed to a smile when he saw Lt. Stoddard.

"Hey, man, sorry about that," the agent apologized. "You know how it goes sometimes."

"Everything okay, man?" Stoddard asked.

"Yeah, everything's okay," the agent assured him as he put his cell in his pocket and held on to it tightly. Stoddard could see the outline of his fingers clenching the phone through his trousers. "You know how girlfriends can be, right?" he asked giving him a feigned painful look.

"Nope, don't think I do," Stoddard replied. "I've had the same wife for twenty-five years, and all we do is sleep together and pay bills." He paused for a second. "And you?"

"Well ...," the agent paused for a moment, "I have this girlfriend, and she's wants me back in Baltimore, and I can't get there tonight, and she's mad, that's all," he said. "Let's go back and finish our talk," he said as he gestured towards Mic's office in the back.

Stoddard had a funny feeling. The funny feeling he got whenever people were lying to him. "Tell me about your girlfriend. Is it a serious relationship because if — "

"Nah, not at all," the agent interrupted him. "It's hardly worth discussing." He signaled the barkeep for two more drafts as they passed.

Stoddard took the same seat he had occupied earlier as they reentered Mic's office. "So, where were we?"

"Talkin' about the port tonight," Baby-face reminded him, his tone irritated. "Remember what I told you earlier, about Baltimore and the trafficking?" He stared at the lieutenant as though he was a moron.

Stoddard heard the accent again. It seemed to occur when the man was angry. "Oh, yeah, that's right," Stoddard said and smiled brightly as he lifted his beer. "Tell you what. We'll do a little surveillance ourselves and call for backup, if we need it. I'll keep you in the loop," he said dismissively as he stood to rejoin his friends. "I'll tell Det. McKane your concerns. You don't need to contact him. Now, I've gotta get out there with my buddies while it's still happy hour," he said as he shuffled through the door.

"What the hell, man. Have you forgotten what I told you? This is important." The agent's face was red with anger.

"No, I remember," Stoddard said as he turned and faced him at the door. "Close and lock Michaela's office door when you leave," he instructed. "It's party-time for me and my friends," he added.

The agent stood and walked a few steps to him and faced him eye-to-eye. "Listen up, Stoddard. Just answer my question. Are you all looking at Nicholas Smirkowitz for anything? The Bureau wants to know."

Stoddard shrugged his shoulders. "Don't know. You'll have to ask Det. McKane, but I think he's tied up now. He's in vice. That's not my area ...so, why don't you just go back to Baltimore and see your girlfriend."

Baby-face glared at him but remained quiet. He knew a brush-off when experienced one.

Stoddard smiled to himself.

That kid's a real prick. But he's right. Richmond's a perfect location. Close to D.C., Virginia Beach and Norfolk, and there's a lot of "gentlemen's" clubs there with all of the military in Tidewater. But I'll be damned if I'll let him know.

The agent opened his mouth to object again, shrugged his shoulders and hunched forward toward the plate of fish and chips just as the phone in his pocket rang shrilly.

Stoddard smiled. "See, there she is now."

Baby-face glowered, cursed under his breath and reached for the phone. "What now?"

Stoddard's phone signaled a text from Slade McKane.

MEET US DOWNTOWN. TROUBLE.

"Gotta go. Lock the door," Stoddard said as he left Mic's office and headed to the table of off-duty police officers. He motioned to two of them.

"Drink up, we're rollin'," he said when they joined him.

He texted McKane back and said, "ON OUR WAY. FBI GUY IS TROUBLE." Of course, when had an FBI agent been anything other than trouble? Stoddard smiled as the three cops met a blast of cold air as they left through the front door of Biddy's Pub.

Chapter 52

The music was deafening in the strip club. The tattooed man signaled for a waitress. He was in a sour mood and beginning to hate his favorite strip joint. They needed some new women. All these women were old, nasty skags.

A waitress with big hair and big boobs sauntered over and knelt down, her breasts in his face, "What can I getcha, honey? That's a great tattoo on your hand. Snake, right? It's nice work," she said as she admired his ink.

The man nodded, "Git me a beer, a tall one, now."

The waitress smiled at him. "You been in before?"

He nodded. "Yeah, lotsa times."

"Well," she purred in his ear, "You're new to me, and I love the colors in your tattoo, and you look really hot in those scrubs. You work over at the hospital?" she asked in her most sexy purr.

"Yeah," he roared. "Leave me alone, I'm gonna use the phone."

The waitress scurried off, angry with her head held high. What a bastard. Maybe I'll spit in his beer.

"Man, you there?" the tattooed man spat into the phone, his face in a snarl as he watched the retreating back of the waitress, who he'd most likely pissed off.

"Yeah, where're you?" Oleg asked with an impatient edge.

"Don't worry 'bout it," he barked. "Did you call that crazy woman from his office ...the ugly one he sleeps with?"

"Who?" Oleg was clueless. "The mistress? I can't find her."

Tattoo man was impatient as he watched all shapes and sizes of women bump and grind at the bar. He had work to do, and it was cold and he was sick of screwing around with stupid people. "The one that's the office manager, the psycho bitch."

Oleg was quiet for a second. "The office manager. Can't find her."

"Where the hell is Smirkowitz?" Tattoo asked.

"Smirkowitz is missing. I just learned about the office mistress, but I don't know much about her," Oleg admitted. "I'd never heard of this until today.

"She lives somewhere in the area on a farm. She is part of some religious group, but I also heard she is crazy," Tattoo added. "Why don't you know about her?"

Oleg was speechless. "I had no idea. How do I reach her?"

The tattooed man was irritated. His voice dripped with mockery. "What the hell, Branislava? Aren't you Smirkowitz's handler? Haven't you been his handler forever?" Tattoo's voice taunted him.

Oleg didn't reply, but he was angry. He didn't consider this man his equal, "Yeah, asshole, I'm his handler and have been for four years. No one ever told me about a mistress. Why didn't you tell me? You're the grunt and you're supposed to report in." Oleg was fuming, ready for a fight. He'd never liked the cocky low-life guy he was working with now. He wasn't Bratva, just hired muscle.

Tattoo examined his snake-tattooed hand and replied. "Nah, not now, but you're incompetent. How can I know about the woman and you not know?" the man asked, his voice tinged with sarcasm.

Oleg was furious. "Just get the women, and get them to the rendezvous place tonight. Or you'll pay with your life when I tell Dimitri you're responsible," he promised.

232

Judith Lucci

"And just how in the hell do—"

"Figure it out," Oleg hissed as he hung up the phone.

Chapter 53

Mic stared into the nasty, foul smelling grounds at the bottom of her Styrofoam coffee cup and sighed deeply. Slade had gotten a text to report to the station immediately and they hadn't made it home yet. The precinct was as dismal as ever. The place hadn't changed at all. If anything it was more archaic and dreary than she remembered. Angel whined softly as she reached down to comfort him. It was late - almost midnight - and way past Angel's bed time. She cooed softly to him, "Is your hip hurting you, boy?" She rummaged through her purse and searched for the pain reliever he took twice a day for pain. She knew Angel was tired, plus he'd been out in the cold for hours. She rubbed his ears and offered him a jerky snack with his medicine, which he accepted gratefully.

Michaela continued to talk with him and rub his head as his tail thumped steadily on the floor. "Okay, boy. We're gonna head out. Neither of us are as young as we used to be." She picked up her briefcase.

Angel struggled to his feet and favored his right hip. Mic leaned down and massaged his hindquarters carefully as Angel stood stoically and offered her a wet tongue and a grateful whimper. She stood and grabbed his lead just as Slade entered the squad room, half of a sandwich in one hand. His face was angry, and his dark eyes glittered. Mic knew that look. He had information.

"What's up? What do you know?" she demanded as she stood with Angel at her side.

"Just talked to MCV. Danielle is still in a coma and on a ventilator in the surgical intensive care unit. They may do surgery tonight because they think she's most likely bleeding somewhere. They're watching her blood work."

234

Michaela's shoulders sagged. "Yeah, I figured they'd do something. She was barely breathing at the scene and the paramedic said one side of her chest wasn't moving air well." Mic shuddered as she remembered the beaten body of the young, beautiful woman who'd been so alive and healthy yesterday afternoon.

Slade nodded as his eyes smoldered with anger. "They said she's pretty beat up, but they'd do what they could. Her head injury is pretty bad, though."

Mic shook her head as tears filled her eyes. "I'm heading out. Angel and I are whipped. Can you get a blue and white to take us home? I'll get my truck from Biddy's tomorrow."

Slade reached down and gave Angel the remaining half of his egg salad sandwich. "Here, boy, need a snack," he said. Angel gobbled the sandwich before Mic could protest. She gave Slade a dirty look as he grinned his sexy smile at her and flashed his perfect white teeth. Michaela felt her heart flutter.

Stop it. You've been down this road. The last thing you need now is a volatile relationship.

Slade nodded. "I just talked to Stoddard. He met with that FBI guy who's supposedly an expert on human trafficking." He grinned broadly. "Stoddard didn't like him. Said he was a smart ass, and he doesn't think the kid shaves yet."

Michaela grinned and shook her head. "Yeah, I can bet where that conversation went. What else?"

"Guy says they have their eye on Smirkowitz — think he's involved in a trafficking ring. Also thinks the port of Richmond may be the new distribution and transfer point."

Mic's face registered surprise. "The port of Richmond? Since when? That place has been dead for years except for a few barges hauling vegetables and beer."

Slade nodded. "Yeah, really. I agree. Only the feds have turned up the heat in Baltimore so the smugglers are looking for new entry and exit ports. I guess Richmond looks good."

"Terrific," Mic said sarcastically. "So, what's the plan?"

"Don't know for sure yet, but Stoddard said something didn't quite add up with the FBI guy. He's tall, blond, and has a baby-face. The lieutenant said he was agitated after a couple of phone calls. Stoddard said the guy gives him a bad feeling."

Mic mused over this tidbit of information. "Well, Stoddard's got a good gut, so I wouldn't discount anything he thinks. He's been around the block a bunch of times."

"Yeah, I agree, but we gotta pick and choose. We both know Stoddard hates fresh-faced, cocky FBI agents tryin' to tell him what to do, or maybe just FBI agents in general," he said as he smiled broadly. "So, we gotta factor that in."

Michaela laughed. "Now, that's the truth. Is he gonna check out the FBI agent's story and set up surveillance at the port?"

"Yeah. Stoddard sent an undercover van down an hour or so ago to sneak and peek. We're going down shortly."

"Tonight?" Michaela's heartbeat accelerated.

Slade smiled as his eyes questioned her. "Yeah, didn't you tell me Dottie told you Smirkowitz said something about getting someone tonight?"

Mic frowned as she remembered back. "Yeah, she did, but I'm not sure how accurate she is. She said something about Danielle earlier when she phoned me... right after we found her." Mic paused, "She was tired this evening."

Judith Lucci

"Tired or in the sherry bottle?" Slade gave her his famous lop-sided grin.

"Stop it, Slade," Mic protested as she glared at him. "Dottie is, after all, eighty-two-years old. Tired is the state of life at her age, and if the sherry bottle helps with that, it's okay in my opinion."

Slade gestured "back off" with his arms as he shuffled his feet impatiently.

"I just hope I live to be eighty-two and am able to drink sherry, although it will take me at least twenty-five years to acquire the taste."

"Pipe down, Mic. You know I love Dottie," he admonished sternly, his dark eyes piercing her hazel ones.

Mic felt a tingle work up her spine. He was so sexy. "I gotta get outta here. We're both tired."

Slade smiled. "I'll run you home. I'll have someone drop off your truck in a little while."

"Deal," Mic said.

"Angel's tired, too... even though he's been sleeping a while," Slade noted as he scratched Angel's neck and ears. Angel gave him a happy look and continued to chew his rawhide.

Mic stood and gathered her coat and briefcase. "Has anything come in on Allison?"

Slade shook his head, "Afraid not, and we are almost out of time. We've been watching Dude's office and there's no sign of him or anyone suspicious around his office."

Mic nodded. "We need to do something soon. Her doctor told me a little earlier that if she's being held some place cold and if she's able to exercise, her insulin may hold out another fifteen or twenty hours. Apparently, exercise

237

decreases the need for insulin. That's hoping she took her after lunch dose before her appointment with Smirkowitz."

"That's good, assuming she's not frozen to death somewhere," Slade muttered. "We've just gotta find her and that's it."

Mic nodded. "If she is unconscious, I hope they don't hurt her because she can't talk to them."

Slade gritted his teeth. "If she's being trafficked, we'll be lucky if they don't kill her or beat her to death trying to wake her up. They want the women to look beautiful, seductive, and sexy so they can bring the best price… you know, like a bidding war."

Mic sat back at the old battered desk and remembered the bloodied body of Danielle. Nausea crept into her throat. She stood. "I'm ready. I need fresh air. Let's get out of here."

Slade stood. "All right. It's getting late."

"I'm sick of this place and besides, I'm not getting paid," she quipped as she reached for her boots.

"Okay, let's go."

Mic pulled on her boots as Angel woke up, scouted out the water bowl and drank heartily.

They moved toward the door, Angel in tow when Slade's cell rang. Mic shook her head as she reached down and patted Angel's ears as he sat at attention.

"Yeah," Slade barked into the phone as Mic kneeled next to her dog and locked eyes with him. He licked her nose with his tongue.

"What! Who? Who's she working for?" Slade's voice was angry, his face attentive as he gripped the phone and turned his back on Mic. Angel stiffened and sat quietly.

238

Michaela rose to her feet and walked around the chair so she could face Slade. She saw Slade's white-knuckled grasp on the cell.

She touched his shoulder, giving him a questioning look.

He ended the call and stared at her. "You're not gonna believe this ..."

"Why? What's happened?" Michaela asked softly, her voice barely a whisper, almost afraid to hear his answer.

"Danielle's an undercover cop. The Baltimore PD placed her here. They've got the bead on Dude and put her in his office as a dental tech," he said, his eyes smoking with rage.

The implications of this smacked Mic in the face. "Oh my God, Slade. She was targeted."

"Yeah," he grunted. "And she was nowhere close to ready for the assignment. She's little more than a rookie, and she'd never worked undercover before."

Angel's fur bristled as he felt the anger roll off his mistress.

"What the hell?" Michaela was furious, her face red and her Irish temper as hot as it'd ever been. "Who the hell did this to her? She's been sacrificed," she finished as she threw a paperweight against the wall in anger.

Slade's voice was brittle with rage. "She was assigned to the local FBI task force investigating human trafficking."

"You mean that straight-laced fibbie you put off on Stoddard, the creepy guy, the guy the lieutenant doesn't trust? She must've been working with him."

Slade shrugged his shoulders. "Yeah, I guess so. I'm sure that agent must know about her. Danielle's from Baltimore, she works out of the Baltimore PD."

Slade was silent for a moment and continued, "She was just what they were looking for …age, geographic location, ethnicity except she had no experience," he finished, cursing under his breath. "By the way, what was this baby-faced feds real name?"

Michaela was so enraged she had tears in her eyes. "Except she had no experience. She must have realized she was out of her league earlier today when I found her crying outside Dude's office." Mic picked up the broken glass and put it in the trashcan. "Let's get the hell out of here and do something."

Slade put his arm around her shoulders to comfort her, and the three walked down the dark hall to the door.

As the cold air hit them in the face, Mic said, "Take me down to MCV. I want to sit with Danielle in case she wakes up and has any info. Besides, I don't want her to be alone when she wakes up."

Slade shook his head "Mic, you need to go home. You and Angel are both tired, and besides, the hospital said she was in a coma and unconscious."

Michaela stared at him and repeated, "I want to see her, just for a moment. Who knows, maybe she'll wake up," she added hopefully.

Slade punched a number in his phone. He shook his head. "She's having tests done. They've postponed the surgery since she isn't any worse. I put a cop outside of Danielle's room …just in case the killers learn she's still alive."

"Okay," Mic said as she looked at Angel. "Let's go home then. Angel and I need to rest a while, right, Buddy?"

Angel wagged his tail, and the trio left the precinct by the back entrance.

Chapter 54

"Who's this?" Oleg barked into his cell as he sat in his parked car outside of Nicholas Smirkowitz's dental office.

"And who is this?" an equally irritated voice responded. "You called me, and I don't know who you are."

"I'm looking for Tilda," Oleg admitted as he attempted to lower his voice. "She's the emergency contact for Dr. Nicholas Smirkowitz. Her name's on the door of his office, and this is an emergency."

Wilbur was bone tired. He'd returned from the budget meeting at his church an hour ago where he'd listened to a bunch of "God's people" argue with each other and point fingers to blame for the financial woes of the church. He was powerless and all he'd wanted to do was come home, have a cup of tea to relax, and go to bed.

"Hello, hello, are you there?" Oleg persisted.

"Yeah, I'm here," Wilbur said quietly. "What kinda emergency. What's wrong?"

"I must speak to Tilda, and only to Tilda. Please put her on the line," Oleg insisted, his voice anxious.

"What kinda emergency?" Wilbur asked again.

"Ah, a dental emergency. A tooth emergency." Oleg stuttered and lied. "My tooth hurts me, and I need the doctor," he insisted.

A sense of relief came over Wilbur. "Call the office number and they will direct you to an on-call dentist who will see you," Wilbur assured him as he prepared to hang up.

"No, no. I must talk to Tilda. Dr. Smirkowitz is missing." Oleg's voice was insistent and his accent more pronounced. "I heard she knows his personal cell number. I must reach him," Oleg pleaded with Wilbur.

"I dunno and Tilda's not here. Just call the office in the morning. I am sure he'll be in then."

"You must help me, you have to help me. I've no one else to ask. Please let me speak with your wife," Oleg begged him. "If I can't find the doctor, many people will die."

"People die? I thought you had a toothache. You're lying to me," Wilbur added, his voice reproachful.

Oleg was silent.

"Who are you?" Wilbur demanded. "What do you really want?"

Oleg responded in a slow, steady voice. "I need to find Dr. Smirkowitz or many bad things will begin to happen," he promised in an ominous voice.

"I'm hangin' up and callin' the police," Wilbur answered angrily. "That is, unless you wanna tell me more about this."

Oleg sighed loudly. He could make sure Wilbur never woke another morning with no problem. He took the chance. "Dr. Smirkowitz is involved with very bad people. I'm worried about him and think he could be in great danger."

"So what? I don't care about Nicholas Smirkowitz. Why're you telling me this?" Wilbur questioned in an irritable tone.

Oleg took a chance. "Your wife helps Dr. Smirkowitz sometimes in the evenings. Perhaps she stays late to assist with patients or to work on the bookkeeping. Perhaps she's involved in the bad business. That's why I'm looking for your wife."

Wilbur sighed, and Oleg could tell he was getting somewhere with the moron. "Tilda's not home, I dunno where she is." His voice was quiet and discouraged.

"When did you see her last?"

"Late this afternoon. 'Bout half after four or so. She left to go to Walmart."

"Walmart? You think she went to Walmart?" Oleg's tone turned incredulous and sarcastic.

When Wilbur spoke again, Oleg heard the defensiveness. "That's what she said," he repeated slowly. "She was goin' to Walmart to pick a few things up and be back shortly."

"That's been hours ago. Any idea where she is now?"

"No," Wilbur said, and then Oleg heard the click of the call ending.

Chapter 55

Oleg was pissed. How dare that country bumpkin hang up on him? Obviously, the man had no idea who he was dealing with or where his wife was. As he backed out of the parking space at Smirkowitz's office, he remembered Redman had placed a GPS chip in Nicholas Smirkowitz's car. He dialed Redman's number.

"What do you want?" Redman growled into the phone.

Oleg pushed back his rage and spoke quickly as his stomach pulled itself into a tight ball, "We're almost out of time. Did you get any women for tonight?"

The man laughed sarcastically and said harshly, "Sure, Branislava. I just picked 'em up. A whole busload from Virginia Beach. Good lookin' too."

Oleg didn't reply. The silence was ominous.

"Hell, no," Redman said when Oleg didn't say anything. "I have no way to get any women, unless I call my buddy with a bar a few miles away. But it's getting late. Did you find Smirkowitz's girlfriend?" he asked with a tinge of hope in his voice.

"No. Husband said she went to Walmart hours ago. Has no idea where she is, but I think he's pretty sure she's with Smirkowitz."

"Yeah, bitch probably is, but she's a bonafide nutcase. She's gonna turn around and kill him one night."

Oleg ignored him. "Any ideas on where Nicholas could be holding up? Any idea at all?"

"Nah, my guess is he's with the woman, but I gotta go. I have to tie up one loose end… if you know what I mean."

"Loose end? We don't need any other loose ends. What's up?"

Redman paused, "Well, the woman we took, the one from Nicholas's office? The undercover cop from Baltimore..."

Oleg felt his belly knot, "Yeah, you and your partner with the tattoo. Danielle, right? We talked about transporting her. Where is she?"

Redman signed deeply, his voice rough, "She got a little too smart too quick, so we took care of her earlier tonight."

"Smart how?" Oleg felt a deep foreboding.

"She was smarter than we gave her credit for. She caught on to what was happening at Smirkowitz's office quickly. She made friends with the other techs, and they told her about the women disappearing and warned her to be careful. They told her about the blonde we snatched yesterday."

"She knew about Allison?"

"Yeah, she was pretty good at puttin' two and two together."

Oleg shook his head. "Where is she?"

Redman was quiet for a moment and said, "She had an accident this evening."

"Accident? What kind of accident?"

"Mugged, beaten in her car, left for dead."

Oleg groaned. "Damn, we were gonna transport her. She was beautiful. Why didn't you just take her to the barn?"

"She was trouble," Redman spat defensively. "We had to know who she'd blabbed to. That's why we took her... for information. We beat her, thought she was dead."

"What'd you learn?" Oleg was pissed. Redman and his buddy were a couple of goons. Redman was looking less promising as a Bratva soldier.

"Nothing. Our friend got too happy with the brick before we found out anything."

Oleg shook his head. "You've got to control him, Redman. He's bad news. Is she dead?"

Redman hesitated for a moment. "We think so. We haven't heard it called a murder yet by the media or Richmond police. Nothing on the scanners. We're gonna look around the local hospitals. Figure out what's up."

"Keep me posted," Oleg directed as he hung up.

Chapter 56

Mic lay on her side in her four-poster bed, looking out of the window at the rooftops of her neighbors. As hard as she tried, she just couldn't get to sleep. Fortunately, Angel was snoring softly next to her bed. She reached down and scratched his ears and, after counting sheep, she drifted off into sleep.

The sharp ring of her home phone woke her from a dead slumber. She looked at the alarm clock next to her bed. She'd only been asleep for about forty-five minutes.

"Hello," she said softly. "Who's this?"

"Mic, its Slade. Just wanted to tell you the emergency department called me, and said Danielle's awake. They said we could talk with her first thing in the morning. Are you up for that?"

Mic breathed a sigh of relief. "I'm absolutely up for that, Slade. Thank goodness. I didn't know if she'd recover." She remembered the mangled body of the beautiful young woman.

"Yeah, I know," Slade agreed. "She looked pretty bad. But the doctors say she should be more alert in the morning. There's no indication she has brain damage at this point, so that's good for us."

"Yeah, we've got a lot to be thankful for. Are you keeping her condition secret?"

"Hell, yeah. We've got an officer on duty outside her room. I don't think there's any question based on what the doctors have said, and from what I saw, whoever did this wanted her dead. If they had any idea that she was still alive, I imagine they'd be back to finish the job."

Mic pressed her lips together as she considered this and thought about someone attacking the helpless, almost lifeless form of Danielle Alvarez.

"That's very possible," she said as anger coursed through her veins. "You think one officer's enough? I don't mind going down there sitting in the room with her the rest of the night. I'm not sleeping anyway."

Slade considered this for a moment. "Thanks, Mic, but I don't think that's necessary. We'll be okay. If anything changes, I'll let you know."

Michaela felt a vague feeling of disappointment. Perhaps she did miss the excitement of being a Richmond homicide detective. "Okay, I'll be here if you need me. Anything new on Allison?

"Nah. We've got some patrols out looking through buildings on Smirkowitz's properties west of town. Nothing specific yet."

"I'd hoped that would pan out. I'm sure Allison and Danielle are connected and the key is Smirkowitz," Mic said, her voice disappointed. "What's up with the stakeout?" she asked.

Slade took a breath and said, "We're headed down that way now. We've got Intel that suggests some sort of transport of women tonight. We've got a couple of guys on foot, and one guy in the old guard booth right at the dock. We've also arranged for eyes and ears on site, specifically, Big Dawg and his mighty sneak and peek van will be with us."

"Wow, that great. They're the best. Backup?" Mic asked. "You've no idea what you're walking into. You've arranged for backup to be on site, right?" she questioned.

"Of course we did," he snapped. "You think I'm a rookie or something?"

"No, no, not at all. I just want to be sure you're safe," she said in a soft voice. "We both know that drug runners and human traffickers are the worse criminals out there. Just want you to be safe."

"I promise, I'll be safe and I'll check in with you when all's said and done," he assured her, his voice softer and almost apologetic.

"Thanks, Slade. Be careful, I'll see you for coffee in the morning. You're buying."

Mic turned off her lamp and settled in for what was left of the night, the details of Allison's abduction and Danielle's attack playing over and over in her mind.

Chapter 57

Tilda woke up in her truck and looked around. *Where was Nicholas?* She looked down at her clothes and saw blood on them. Then she remembered she'd killed Constance and her daughter. She smiled smugly. She looked out of the truck window and noticed she was in a small thicket of trees off a secondary road. It was pitch black outside. *How in the world did I get here?*

She pulled up her sleeve and looked at her watch. The face on her watch was bloodied, and she couldn't tell the time. She wiped the blood off on her jeans and looked again. It was late - after ten o'clock. She cut the interior lights on in the truck and searched for her phone. She found it on the floor, and immediately dialed Nicholas's number, but the number rang and rang with no answer. She cursed the phone, threw it back on the floor and beat her fist against the steering wheel. Where in the hell is he?

He should be ready to go celebrate with me. I've done what he asked me to do. She sat there for a few minutes and realized how cold she was. It was amazing that she hadn't frozen to death. *How long have I been asleep?* She picked up the phone off the console and called Nicholas again. It went straight to voicemail. Rage spread through her body. Either he's not taking my calls or he is out of juice. She sat in the car willing herself to be calm and not overreact.

She leaned her head back and relived her afternoon. It had been glorious. A perfect day. She savored the quiet in the truck and noticed her head didn't hurt. Her brain was quiet. There were no voices telling her what to do, and for this, she was imminently grateful. She closed her eyes to think and savor the darkness and her hiding place.

Her phone rang and the sound jerked her out of solitude. The digital readout displayed her home number. It was

Wilbur. Tilda answered the phone on the second ring, her voice low and sexy. "Hello, honey, she murmured. "Betcha wondering where I am," she added with a half laugh.

"Of course, I'm wondering where you are," Wilbur growled. "You told me you were going to Walmart to pick up a few items. That was hours ago. Where've you been?" he asked with fear in his voice.

Tilda pictured him, his eyes squinted, his face furrowed in anger, and the unruly shock of hair falling across his forehead. He was irate and disgusted with her. If she were sitting across from him or face-to-face, she doubted he'd even look at her. She decided to wait a few moments and let him stew in his own juices.

"Tilda, are you there?" This time Wilbur's voice was louder and more insistent. "Where are you? Tell me right now," he demanded in an angry voice.

Tilda sniffed loudly and manufactured crocodile tears that actually slid down her face. She said with a half sob, "Honey, why are you so mad at me? All I did was go to Walmart, and I ran into an old friend ... you remember her — Sally Jean Shoemaker from church? From a long time ago? She was in charge of the Wednesday night dinners," she prodded softly.

Wilbur remained silent.

"Wilbur, honey. Please talk to me," Tilda pouted. "You know it upsets me when you don't answer me," she whispered with hurt in her voice, "Please answer me, honey. I haven't done anything wrong." She sobbed into the phone. Silence. She knew she was getting to him. She smiled to herself. *I'm such a good actress.* The crocodile tears flowed.

"You left hours ago. Why didn't you call me?" Wilbur's voice was softer. Tilda thought he sounded contrite.

Tilda smiled. She'd known she'd be able manipulate him. "Why, honey, you were at church. I didn't want to call you and interrupt you during your vestry meetin'. All I did," she began sobbing again. "All I did was go out for pizza with Sally Jean. It's been so long since I've seen her, and we had five years of catchin' up to do. I'm so sorry, honey. I didn't mean to make you mad, I really didn't," she said in a mournful voice as she choked back a sob.

"Why didn't you call me?" he asked, his voice cold. "The weather's awful, and the roads are treacherous. You should've called," he insisted.

Tilda signed. "Honey, I was gettin' ready to call. I just left the pizza restaurant a few minutes ago. We talked and talked and talked and lost track of time," she said in her best contrite voice.

Wilbur again remained quiet. She knew he was contemplating her explanation.

Tilda continued. "We were just sittin' there drinking coffee and joshing just like it was yesterday. Please don't be mad at me. You have no reason to be mad at me," she said a hint of anger in her voice.

"Have you seen Dr. Smirkowitz?" Wilbur asked her.

Tilda's heart jumped. "Of course not. I haven't seen the doctor since early this afternoon. Why'd you ask?"

"Because some foreign man with an accent called here looking for Nicholas Smirkowitz. He said he had a dental emergency, but I'm not so sure. It sounded fishy to me." Wilbur's voice exploded. "I think he was up to no good. And he is looking for you too, Tilda."

Tilda took a deep breath. What the hell was going on? Wilbur was really pissed. "Honey, why would a man, particularly a foreign man, be looking for me? I don't know any foreign men, except a few that are patients at the office."

Judith Lucci

Wilbur exploded. "I've no idea, but I can tell you this, the man was up to no good, and he's been looking for you as well Dr. Smirkowitz." His voice was rigid. He was as angry as Tilda had ever known him to be.

Tilda was quiet and thoughtful for a few moments. "Well, I've no idea who this is, but I should be home in a little while. But first, I'm going to go by the office and check to see if everything is all right. You know Dr. Smirkowitz keeps a lot of medicine and anesthetics and painkillers in his office. We couldn't handle it if someone broke in and stole something."

"No, hell no. I want you to come home right now, Tilda. I mean it." Wilbur said in a frustrated voice. "I demand you come home."

"What? Honey, honey, I can't hear you? You're cracking up on me," Tilda said with a sly smile. "What, what did you say? You're all garbled, and I can't hear you. I think I might be out of cell service 'cuz I only have one bar. But I'll be home after I check the office. Love you, Wilbur. Bye."

Tilda clicked off her cell and smiled to herself. I'm so smart. She headed to the office to take a shower and change her clothes. She smiled to herself when she thought of how wonderful it would be if Nicholas was there waiting for her.

Chapter 58

Michaela snuggled under her down comforter and clicked on her Kindle to do a bit of reading. She had made herself some warm milk because she couldn't get to sleep. Her mind was too alert from recent events to focus on the new historical fiction novel she'd just downloaded from Amazon. And there was a sick feeling in the pit of her stomach that something just wasn't right.

After a few minutes of tossing and turning, Michaela threw back the covers, jumped out of bed and pulled on her sweats and tennis shoes. She patted Angel on the head.

"I'm going out for a while, buddy, to see our friend Danielle at the hospital, but I'm gonna leave you here to rest up."

Angel thumped his tail weakly against the wooden floor in her bedroom and laid his head back down on his huge orthopedic bed.

"You remember Danielle, don't you, Angel? She is the pretty lady we met earlier today."

Angel looked up at his mistress, searched her eyes and licked her hand. Mic knew he was concerned about her leaving him at home.

Mic smiled and leaned down as Angel offered her a nose kiss. "I'll be okay and yeah, I knew you'd remember her. You never forget anyone, do you, boy?" Michaela squatted down and gave her beloved dog a big kiss on his head. "Get some rest, I'll be back shortly."

Angel rose from his bed and followed her to the front door. He didn't want her to go alone.

Mic pulled her warm vest, hat and gloves from the hall closet and put them on. She squatted and ruffled Angel's ears, reassuring him she'd be back soon. She dressed as warmly as she possibly could but was still unprepared for the blast of frigid air that almost knocked her down when she opened her front door. The temperature was in the single digits. For once, the weatherman had been right. She walked carefully down her wooden steps and jumped over piles of snow and ice. Thank goodness, Slade had delivered her truck quickly from downtown. She felt an urgency to get to MCV, and that sense of urgency bothered her. Her gut was her sensor, her barometer, and she trusted it implicitly. She had a strong feeling something was wrong at the hospital.

Mic drove quickly and pulled her vehicle up to the emergency entrance, spoke quickly to the security guard, who checked out her creds and badge and took her keys. He promised to park the truck for her. A blast of wind snatched her scarf, and she quickly chased it to the sidewalk and grabbed it. She noticed a man in scrubs talking on his cell. He wore a dark hooded sweat shirt and had a strange tattoo on his hand. She shook her head and wondered why he didn't move into the warmth of the hospital. She quickly walked back to the double doors and entered via the emergency room as she savored the blast of warm air that enveloped her. The emergency room clerk was busy shuffling papers but promised Mic she'd get the doc who had treated Danielle as soon as she could.

Mic took a seat in the corner of the emergency room and looked around the large, busy waiting room filled with patients and families. The place was jammed. An elderly lady walked in through the front door, her right foot leaving large puddles of blood with each step she took. Mic ran to get a wheelchair and called for help when she noticed the puddles of blood that stretched for about fifty feet, outside on the concrete and in the snow. Two nurses rushed toward the elderly woman with a stretcher. One nurse caught her just before she crumpled to her knees, probably from dizziness and loss of blood. Mic shook her head as she watched the team of nurses work. *I could never do this kind of work. I don't have it in me.*

The nurses rushed her quickly to the back, one nurse calling for five units of O negative blood, while the other monitored the woman's vital signs. Gradually, the noise died down as the double doors separating the acute care area from the waiting room closed. Michaela watched absently as a cleaning lady appeared with a bucket of water and mop and started cleaning up the trail of blood the woman had left.

Michaela returned to her seat as a thirty-something-year-old white male entered the emergency department. It was the same guy she'd seen outside the entrance just before they'd parked her car. He had on a pair of dirty scrubs and an old down jacket with a hood that hid his face. Her gut tightened as he spoke to one of the cleaning people and headed toward the patient care entrance. The guy bothered her, and there was that weird tattoo on his hand. Mic had seen it outside when he'd been on his cell phone. It looked like a tattoo of a snake. Hadn't someone called him Snake Man or had they called him Tattoo? She heard someone call her name, and she turned to face the emergency department doctor.

"Hi, I met you earlier. You were with the police. I don't remember your name, I'm sorry," the young physician said and smiled at her.

Mic extended her hand and said quietly as her eyes followed Snake Man towards a bank of elevators. "I couldn't sleep, and I was wondering how Danielle was doing, so I decided to come back downtown and check on her." She gave him a bright smile. "Do you think it's possible for me to see her?"

The young physician scratched his head. "I'm sure you can. But we transferred her upstairs to the trauma intensive care unit a while ago." He smiled at her, "I'll call up there and persuade the nurses to let you see her."

Mic nodded. "That'd be great."

The physician gave her a concerned look. "You look upset. Is there something we should know?" He watched as fear flickered and uncertainty registered on Mic's face.

Mic shrugged her shoulders. "I don't know how to say it, but I'm a bit concerned about her," she admitted. "I'm concerned for her safety." Her eyes locked with those of the emergency doctor.

The physician nodded. "Then, by all means you should go see her. She was doing quite well, and she was stable when we discharged her upstairs," he assured her.

"I just have this feeling in my gut. I appreciate your letting me see her for a few minutes."

The doctor nodded and pulled out his cell.

"I guess my years as a homicide detective taught me to pay attention to my gut," she said apologetically.

"You don't need to apologize to me about instinct and gut," the young man said. "I depend on my gut all the time, regardless of what I see in a patient or on diagnostic tests. That's what I've learned from being an emergency room physician."

Mic smiled at him. "I guess we have that in common," she said as she waited while he talked to the intensive care unit.

"Hold that thought," the doctor said as he talked on the phone.

"I think it's simply about the kind of work we do," he said, when he ended the call. "Go past the sofas and take the bank of elevators on the left to the third floor and follow the signs. They're expecting you. I hope your friend is doing well," he said as he pointed to the direction of the elevators.

Mic flashed him a grateful smile. She found the elevators, pushed the button, and watched as the elevator slowly descended from the top floor. Her anxiety increased as the elevator got closer to the ground level. *I just know something's wrong.* Mic's stomach was churning, and the hairs on her arms were standing up, all clues pointing to danger. It was the sixth sense she'd inherited and honed over the years. The elevator door opened and Mic quickly covered the distance between the elevators and the trauma ICU. She rang the bell at the door. A voice answered, and Mic identified herself as "with the police" and gained entry. She sprinted toward the double doors of the intensive care unit and waited while they slowly opened. A young, dark-headed nurse met her at the door.

"You're here to see Danielle Alvarez?" the nurse asked.

Mic nodded and looked at the young woman. She was young, attractive and appeared competent in green scrubs that matched her green eyes. "Yes, yes I am. How's she doin'?"

The nurse smiled as her eyes searched Michaela's face. "She's doing better. I think she'll wake up again soon and be even more alert."

Mic's heart leapt with hope.

"We're noticing a lot of rapid eye movement, and that's usually a really good sign," the nurse told Mic. "By the way, my name is Patricia." She offered Mic her hand.

Mic sighed in relief and clasped the nurse's hand. "Wow, that's great news. This place really is the Miracle College," she said with a broad smile. "Do you think I could see her?"

"Absolutely, let me take you to her room. Would you like to stop for cup of coffee?"

"No, I'd better not. It'll keep me awake, and I really am hoping to go to bed sometime tonight."

"We have decaf," Patricia said, "though we rarely drink it up here. I can bring you a cup of decaffeinated into Danielle's room if you'd like." A generous smile lit her face.

"That'd be great!" Mic exclaimed. "Lots of cream and sugar. If I can't have the caffeine, I'll just have a sugar high."

The nurse laughed. "Sounds good to me. Second door on the left, pull up a chair, and I'll be there in a moment with your coffee, and I'll explain what's going on with all the tubes in her room."

Mic walked to the door and paused for a moment outside, gathering the strength she needed to see Danielle and imagining what she would look like. Even though she was a hardened homicide detective, hospitals gave her the willies because she didn't understand them and they were out of her comfort zone. The tubes that snaked around the bodies and all the machines with their mysterious beeps, bangs and gurgles, and the hanging bottles and plastic bags totally unnerved her. She didn't understand them and felt out of control.

Mic took a deep breath. She figured that Danielle probably had a head bandage and black eyes. *Where was the police officer guarding Danielle?* She entered the room and saw someone standing by Danielle's bed. *The officer must be on break since someone's in the room*, she assured herself.

Mic moved closer and stood next to the caregiver. It was a man with a syringe in his hand. He was searching for a port, a rubber stopper in Danielle's IV tubing, so he could inject the medicine.

"How is she doing?" Mic asked. "Does she look like she's going to wake up to you?'

The man turned sharply and looked at her.

"I'm sorry," Mic said when she saw the startled look in his eyes. "I guess you didn't hear me. These tennis shoes are quiet," she quipped as a huge pain of recognition doubled her over. The man uncapped the syringe and started to inject the medicine into the IV. Something was wrong. She saw the tattoo on his hand. It was Snake Man.

Mic screamed, grabbed the man's hand and attempted to grab the syringe. Her elbow turned over Danielle's water pitcher and knocked a stainless-steel basin to the floor. The man gripped the syringe tightly and pushed the plunger and squirted the medication into Danielle's vein so it would quickly spread throughout her body.

"You bastard," Mic screamed. "You're not going to get her."

Mic shot her knee up into the man's groin, and he bent over in pain and fell to the floor. She kicked him in the back and shoved him under the bed with her foot as she reached for the first shut-off clamp on Danielle's IV to prevent the spread of the poison the man had injected. She then instinctually moved to the code emergency button and rang it as she screamed for help. *Thank God for my CPR training.*

The man slithered out from under the opposite side of the bed, and clutching his groin, ran quickly from the room.

Several moments later, nurses, doctors and respiratory therapists poured into Danielle's room. Danielle's cardiac monitor was going crazy, and Mic watched as her blood pressure quickly fell.

A nurse screamed at her and shook her. "What happened?" as another nurse reached for Danielle's IV to put something in it.

"No, no," Mic said loudly. "A man just injected a drug in her IV. Look, the syringe is on the floor," Mic pointed to the syringe halfway under the bed. "I clamped it off as best I could."

The first nurse ripped out the tainted IV line just as another nurse started a new IV line.

Suddenly, the loud speaker went off again. "CODE BLUE, CODE BLUE. Surgical ICU, Bed 4," and more and more people entered the room.

Mic ran from the room, to alert hospital security, but a man in a business suit stopped her.

"Come with me, now," he ordered.

Mic ducked into an empty patient room with the man who asked harshly, "What the hell happened in there? Who are you?" His face was red and ugly, his voice demanded answers.

Mic pulled her identification from her pocket and shoved it at him, her shield shining in the florescent light. "I'm a retired homicide detective, RPD. I'm working on her case. Where's the officer who was guarding Ms. Alvarez? He wasn't outside her room when I got here."

"I don't know," he said looking around for a staff member who wasn't involved in the Code.

"Who are you?" Mic snarled.

"I'm the night superintendent for the hospital, and I'm in charge of the entire facility." He spotted Danielle's nurse racing through the hall. She'd been on a coffee break and returned when the Code was announced."

"Where's the police officer who was guarding Ms. Alvarez?" he barked.

Patricia was white as a ghost. "He went on a bathroom break when he saw us walking toward the room. He'd told me he was going," she said gesturing toward Michaela.

Fear almost paralyzed Mic, but she asked quickly, "Where's the bathroom?

"Follow me," Patricia commanded. Patricia and Mic ran to the staff restroom around the corner. They jerked open the door and immediately saw the young cop crumpled in the corner of the large, handicapped bathroom, his body bent behind the door.

Patricia checked his carotid pulse. "I can't get a pulse. Pull the Code alarm next to you."

Mic felt sick as she looked at the young man. She pulled the alarm and helped Patricia straighten the young man on the floor. Within seconds, a second Code team appeared and Mic and Patricia left the restroom and returned to the nursing station.

Mic sat down for a moment and said, "I've got to call this in. We're looking for a medium tall man with dark hair and a tattoo of a snake on his right hand. He has on blue scrubs." She checked her watch. Less than three minutes had passed.

Patricia nodded and called the hospital switchboard and security and relayed Mic's information. Then she went to check on Danielle.

Mic explained what had happened to a security guard and ran towards the stairwell, taking the steps, two at a time in pursuit of the tattooed man.

By the time she reached the emergency room door, she knew they'd lost him. Hospital security was standing there, as were several members of the Richmond Police Department. Mic recognized one of the officers.

"Brenner, a guy upstairs, white guy in a pair of scrubs, just tried to kill a young woman and a police officer from

Baltimore. I think he'd beaten her up earlier this evening. He's about five feet eleven, with dark hair. That's about all I can tell you right now. Oh, wait. He has a tattoo on his hand. Have them put out an APB." She faltered for a moment and added, "I think he killed one of our officers as well, the uniform who was protecting Danielle. I just found him in the bathroom with no pulse. They're working on him."

Brenner nodded and said, "We're on it, Mic. We'll get him."

Mic nodded and fished her phone out of her jacket pocket and dialed Slade. He answered on the first ring. "Mic, I thought you were asleep by now, what's up?"

Mic was breathless. "I'm at MCV. Someone tried to murder Danielle. A man, I've given a description to Brenner."

"How's Danielle, did she make it?" His voice was a low bark. Mic knew he was furious and could picture him standing at his desk, fists balled in defiance, and his black eyes glittering with hate.

"I don't know. I'm going back up there to see. I'll call you. But it gets worse."

"How can it be worse?" Slade asked, confused.

"I think he killed the police guard, the policeman who was guarding her," Mic said, her voice tight with fury. She paused for a minute to take a breath. "Oh, Slade, he was such a young officer," she murmured. "I've gotta go." She hung up the phone and walked toward the elevators.

Slade McKane cursed like a sailor.

Chapter 59

Tilda sighed with contentment as the warm water pounded her body, washing away the sweat, blood, gore, dirt, and uncertainty. It had been a long day, but all in all, a great day with very few worries. As she lathered soap all over her, she thought of Nicholas and the many times they had showered together in his executive bathroom attached to his office. She reached for her own specialty shampoo that smelled of violets. Nicholas loved the smell of the richly lathered shampoo and always said her hair smelled divine. She applied the thick concentrate to her hair and massaged the soap into her scalp. It felt so good.

She sat on the tile bench in the shower and picked up her razor and shaving cream. She shaved her legs, paying careful attention. The last thing she wanted was a scar from shaving on her long, tanned legs. She loved the feel of the razor against her flesh. A razor was great little tool. There was a lot of power in one little blade. The power to maim, disfigure, and kill, all with one or two swift movements. Tilda had cut herself a few times, probably from the emotional pain she suffered from not seeing Nicholas enough. Once he had seen where she'd cut herself and had been disgusted. He told her to never do it again. Tilda had hung her head in shame and promised him she wouldn't. Ever since then, she had been good about it. She hadn't cut herself, but she had cut other things.

Her favorite thing to do as a kid had been to break chicken necks... she hated chickens. When she turned sixteen and started to shave her legs, the razor had opened up a whole new spectrum of opportunity. Her favorite tools of all time were box cutters, and she always carried a box cutter with her. And, she used them a lot. She used the box cutters on things she should cut and on things she shouldn't. She loved razor wire, too. It made a perfect slice. She

264

continued to dream and lather herself. She'd be beautiful for Nicholas in just a few more minutes.

She stepped out of the custom-designed shower, stepping on the luxurious bathmat and toweled her hair dry. She reached inside the secret panel drawer built under Nicholas's closet, and removed a black Victoria's Secret bra and thong and put them on. She strutted in front of the mirror and admired her body. *I look great.* She touched her skin, and it was soft and moist. She reached for her signature body lotion and slathered her arms and legs and other "special" parts. As she massaged the lotion into her skin, she remembered one of the special times she and Nicholas had spent. They had ordered Sushi and dined by candlelight on his desk, showered together, and then spent several hours enjoying the benefits of his nitrous oxide tank. They'd made love, laughed and giggled for hours, and then done it again. She smiled when she remembered how much fun that had been. Tilda applied fresh makeup and slid into a pair of tight jeans, boots, and a silk blouse. She picked up her cell phone and went into Nicholas's office.

She decided she needed a glass of wine. She walked over to Nicholas's midsize refrigerator and removed a bottle of pinot grigio. She deftly removed the cork, selected a glass from the cabinet, and poured herself a glass of the white wine. She seated herself on a beautiful upholstered antique Jacobean revival chair in radiant viridian green and sipped her wine as she repeatedly dialed her lover's cell phone, her anxiety mounting each time the voicemail picked up. Tilda poured herself a second glass and drank it quickly. She was startled when her phone rang.

She picked it up quickly and spoke in her most sensual voice. "Hello, who is this?"

She was shocked when Wilbur responded.

"Where are you, Tilda?" he questioned, his voice quiet and subdued.

"I'm busy," she said. "I've just now gotten to the office, and I'm going through the messages. I need to see if that man has called. I'll be home sometime soon," she promised.

"I had a call from the police, and they want to talk to you."

"The po-leese?" Tilda laughed aloud. "What could they possibly want with little old me?" She paused and waited for Wilbur to respond, but he was silent. "That's ridiculous," she added when he didn't respond.

Still nothing.

"Wilbur, are you there? Answer me." Tilda raised her voice. It was then the voices started again. *You're in trouble, you're in trouble, you're in trouble,* they chanted in rhythm, over and over again. The sounds started in a low pitch, but by the time the word trouble came around, the voices were screeching in her head. Tilda covered her ears to block out the sound.

"Get home, Tilda, now, they're coming back to see you." When Wilbur finally spoke, his voice was ominous.

Tilda was silent as she tried to block out the voices.

"For God's sake, Tilda, what've you done?" Wilbur cried with fear in his voice. "Have you hurt someone?"

"I haven't done a damned thing," Tilda screamed as she slammed her phone to the floor. She reached for the wine bottle and poured another glass. Anything to make the voices stop. She sat there for about a half an hour and her cell phone rang again. She checked the digital display to see if it was Wilbur. It wasn't. It wasn't a number she recognized. She took a chance and clicked the green button.

"Hello," she said in a subdued voice… a voice that didn't sound like her own.

266

"Come and get me, sweetheart. I'm hurt," Nicholas cried, his voice weak and exhausted.

Tilda's heart jumped for joy. "Nicholas, Nicholas, is that you? You sound so funny." Fear edged up her spine.

"Yes, I know. I'm badly hurt. Please come soon. I've lost a lot of blood," he said in a shaky voice.

Tilda's heart raced in the anticipation of rescuing her man. "All right, I will. But where are you, sweetheart?"

"At the barn, the one near the winery, near the river where we had the picnic. Bring my gun, don't forget, and some bandages."

"I will, my love, I will," Tilda said wildly, furious because someone had dared hurt the love of her life. "Who did this to you?"

"Later, just come. Hurry and don't forget my gun."

"I'll be there soon. Hang in there. I'm on my way," Tilda promised as she searched her purse for the key to Nicholas's desk. The keys were in the zippered compartment of her purse. She quickly opened his bottom drawer and pulled out his Glock and several magazines of ammo. Then she ran into the utility room, grabbed a laundry basket full of towels and picked up antiseptic from the medicine room. And a handful of narcotics.

She reached for a canvas bag with Dr. Smirkowitz's picture and the office logo printed on the side and dumped the antiseptic and gauze bandages in the bag. Then she noticed the large silhouette of a man in the outside light near the office front door. She heard a knock and stood in the front office debating what to do just as the voices started to scream again in her head. GET IT. GET IT. GET IT. ANSWER THE DOOR. ANSWER THE DOOR. ANSWER THE DOOR.

The knocking was deafening as Tilda dashed down the hall and left quickly through the side door, with the gun, canvas bag, and laundry basket in her arms. The voices were screaming in her head. They were so loud she could hardly think. She pushed her way through the bushes and moved quickly and quietly to her truck. She opened the door, got in and started the engine, just as she saw the large man directly in front of her with his hand in front in her vehicle as he signaled her to stop.

Tilda pressed the unlock button and lowered the side window. "What do you want? I'm in a hurry," she growled at him. She noticed the man was hatless and bald.

"You're Tilda, aren't you?" the man said. "I'm Oleg, I'm Nicholas' friend. I must find him. He's in grave danger," the man pleaded. "Do you know where he is?"

Tilda could barely concentrate on what the man said, but she noticed the Russian accent. She pressed her hands against her head to try to quiet the voices. "What did you say?"

The man moved closer and looked into Tilda's eyes. Her eyes were huge, her pupils dilated, and she appeared confused, crazed. Perhaps she is a psycho just like they said. He tried again, "I am Oleg and Nicholas is my friend and I must find him. He's in danger."

Tilda stared at the man as his face became distorted and unrecognizable. He was the enemy. The voices changed their tune, KILL OLEG, KILL OLEG, KILL OLEG. Tilda gave Oleg an uncertain look as her heartbeat rose rapidly. He was the enemy. She knew it.

The man walked closer to the truck, his hands held up in surrender.

"Please, let me help you," he said gently. "We both love Nicholas. He's like a son to me. Let us go search for him together."

Tilda was uncertain. The voices persisted. KILL, KILL, KILL. DO IT, DO IT, DO IT. She couldn't stand it anymore. She reached for the Glock on the seat beside her and put two slugs dead center into Oleg's chest. He fell immediately, blood pooling on the white snow. Tilda stared at what she'd done and backed up the truck and ran over his body on the way out of the parking lot.

The voices were quiet. She picked up speed and headed toward the 295 Bypass as her body gradually relaxed.

Chapter 60

Allison Massie was chilled to the bone and her throat was raw from inhaling the freezing air. She'd been walking on foot for what seemed like forever, and her legs felt heavy and bulky. She had walked aimlessly in the cold, and for a while, she'd gotten lost in the woods. Fortunately, she finally found her way out and crossed over the highway. As she walked down the road, she spied a barn with lights on. She walked through the door and was enveloped with warmth. She was surprised and pleasantly pleased at the change in temperature. She looked around and noticed that she was in some sort of a chicken-hatching facility. Cages of chickens four feet deep and three levels high looked down at her from both sides of the barn. It was weird to have hundreds and hundreds of pairs of beady eyes staring at you as they sat on their eggs. Allison held her arms close to her body and walked the length of the barn and back, and she could feel the chickens watching her. It was an eerie feeling but certainly preferable to where she had been.

Allison stumbled over to several bales of hay and sat on the floor. She noticed two tarps stored on a shelf, shook the dust off of them, and covered herself with them as she snuggled against the bales. As she warmed, she thought about the past few days. Her need for insulin made her brain hazy, and she had difficulty sorting memories. She realized she didn't even know the date or how long she'd been missing. She wondered if Dr. Dude was dead. She didn't know what had compelled her to hit him in the head with the shovel, but she was terrified he'd be able to get up and follow her. Why had he kidnapped her? Why hadn't he hired her for the dental hygienist job in his office? What had her interview even been about? Allison shook her head and tried to focus, as she examined her jumbled mind for clarity. She lay against the hay, closed her eyes and then opened them quickly. Did she hear voices? She listened closely, afraid to breathe.

Yes, it was two men, farmers, dressed in overalls and warm jackets for the weather. They were talking and moving down the rows of cages and collecting eggs and cleaning out cages. Her heart beat sharply, and her lungs burned. She needed to cough, but held it back. As she watched the two men work their way toward her, she frantically looked around for a place to hide. It was difficult to see in the low light of the barn, but she spied a wheelbarrow turned on its side and inched her way toward it. Perhaps her slender body would fit into the body of the wheelbarrow. She curled up into a fetal position, and in the process, knocked loose part of her diabetes medical-alert bracelet.

"What are these tarps doing down here on the floor?" one of the farmers asked the other.

"Doan know. Beats me. Think the wind could've blown 'em off the shelf?"

"I wouldn't think so. It'd have to blow two of them down, and that's jest not likely," he surmised as he looked around the barn.

Allison's heart was hammering in her chest. She knew the farmer could hear it. Should I identify myself and ask for help? No. I only want the police to help me. She willed herself to settle down and tried her best to quiet her breathing, but her breath kept coming in short, sharp breaths. I need some insulin, I need insulin. Her mind panicked when she thought of her need for insulin. She knew she couldn't keep active without her medicine.

My blood sugar is low and I'm freezing cold. I know Dr. Smirkowitz gave me some insulin, but I don't think it was long acting. That's why I can't breathe or focus better. My head and

271

brain feel like cotton. Allison's anxiety level climbed and she found it more and more difficult to breathe in her cramped position.

"Well, I'm gonna walk around and take a look," the first farmer announced.

"You help yourself, but who do you think would be out hiding in a barn on a freezing, snowy night like this?"

"Doan rightly know but suspect it's someone who wants to get in out of the cold, a squatter, something like that," the first farmer answered as he moved the ladder closer to the next bank of cages.

"Well, you keep on lookin' if you want, but I'm gittin' the rest of these eggs, checking the generator and goin' home. I got plans to sit by my woodstove and have a snort, maybe a couple of little snorts, of Jim Beam," his friend announced.

"Yeah. I like that idea," the first one said as he scratched his head. "I might join you. Whoever's here, if anybody is, can spend the night and try to stay warm. If the person is still here, we'll git 'em tomorrow."

His friend gave a short laugh and nodded his head in agreement. "You're getting' smarter every day, Bert. You get the eggs, I'll check the generator. We sure don't want the chickens too cold to lay tonight," he muttered. "That'd be a real problem."

"Ain't that the damned truth," Bert said as he moved the ladder to the final row of cages, opened each door, and carefully collected the eggs and changed the straw.

Allison took a deep breath and watched until the men finished their work, bolted the door, and left the barn happy at the prospects of warmth and whiskey. Then she slithered out of the wheelbarrow and returned to the bales of hay. She removed the tarps again from the shelves, wrapped them around her as tightly as she could so maximize body heat.

I'll find help in the morning. I've got to rest. If I sleep, my body will not need as much insulin.

Then she fell asleep.

Chapter 61

Tilda stayed below the speed limit as she drove towards Nicholas's farm west of Richmond. The last thing she needed was police attention because she'd had more than her share in the past couple of days. The snowplows had been down Route 33, and the roads were clear except for patches of black ice. She slipped and skidded several times. Thirty minutes later, she pulled Wilbur's truck up to the door of Nicholas's barn situated off a side road near the old estate of General Barbour. Tilda grabbed her gun, slid out of her truck and quietly entered the barn. It was pitch black and quiet as death.

She returned to the truck and found Wilbur's flashlight in the backseat. She returned to the barn, closing the door behind her. She called softly, "Nicholas, Nicholas, are you here?"

There was no answer.

Tilda shone the flashlight near an old table and saw areas of congealed blood. She aimed the light on the nearby floor and saw reddened straw. Upon closer inspection, was shocked at the amount of blood on the floor. Her pulse quickened, and her fury escalated. Where was Nicholas? Where was the love of her life? Her heart pounded deep in her chest as panic crushed her soul. She called his name, but there was no answer. She continued her search of the barn. She passed an old tractor and a hay baler and other equipment she didn't recognize. As she walked the length of the barn, it was clear there'd been several major struggles. She saw a pallet and a rope where one of the women had been handcuffed to an old hay baler. The pallet was soaked in blood. She called Nicholas's name again and thought she heard a low moan. She ran quickly to the other side of the barn and found him, crumpled in a heap, barely breathing,

274

his jeans and flannel shirt soaked in blood. His face was badly bruised, his beautifully shaped lips were cut on one side, and a long gash extended across his forehead and down his cheek. Tears and anger over who could have done this paralyzed Tilda for a few seconds as she stared at her lover. The pain in her chest overwhelmed her, but she pushed it away.

"Nicholas, Nicholas, oh, who did this to you?" she crooned quietly as she held his bloodied face in her arms. She noticed the gashes weren't too deep and that a good plastics guy could fix him right up.

Dr. Dude opened his swollen eyes. "It's my leg, check my leg. I can't feel it."

Tilda ran her hands down his jeans and saw the long gash in his groin. She knew a little about first aid. She thought his injury had hit an artery. She untied the makeshift tourniquet and blood immediately saturated the cloth. She quickly tightened the tourniquet.

"You've a bad gash. I think it hit your leg artery. You've lost a lot of blood." She stroked his bloodied forehead.

"Water, do you have water?" Nicholas croaked. "Thirsty."

"Yes, I do. I'll get it," she reassured him.

Nicholas coughed and murmured with great effort, "Thank you, Tilda, you're always there for me."

Tilda cradled him in her arms. For the first time, she was in charge in their relationship. He needed her. "Baby, who hit you in the head? Who attacked you?" she asked softly as she bent down to listen.

"Allison, the girl from the office, remember her? You and Oleg snatched her a few days ago." Nicholas was in such pain, he could hardly speak.

"Allison did this to you," Tilda repeated with surprise as hatred entered her heart. The voices began again, KILL HER, KILL HER. The chant sent a shock wave of pain through Tilda's head. She grabbed her head to stop the sound and hissed, "If she did, she'll pay for it."

Nicholas stared up at her. "Please, not now, just some water," he begged.

Tilda kissed him on his bloody forehead. "Okay, I know. I need to get you to a hospital, but let me clean you up first. Water and bandages and painkillers." She stood up.

"Please, please don't leave me," Nicholas begged.

Tilda smiled down at him and said, "My love, I will never leave you. I love you now and forever. I'm gonna go to the truck and get water. I'll be back in an instant."

And she was. The next time Nicholas opened his eyes, Tilda was bathing his face with water. She offered him a straw to sip. He sipped the water slowly, swallowed. His body racked with a deep cough. Tilda helped him sit up, and he spit out another tooth.

She smiled at him and said, "Don't worry my love. We can always make you more teeth."

"Yes, we can." He lay down, gave her a sad look and whispered, "You're so good to me, Tilda. You smell so good, too," he added as he gazed at her through swollen eyes.

Tilda's heart warmed with pleasure. She offered him two Vicodin. "You can swallow these. They're no bigger than the teeth. They're pain pills."

Nicholas nodded and swallowed each pill, one at a time. "I need them. My face hurts like hell."

"I'm sure," Tilda said as she moved down to inspect his leg and groin area. It was then she noticed his right shoulder. It sagged way below the level of his left shoulder.

Was it a broken clavicle or a broken shoulder? "Nicholas, my love. What about your shoulder? Does it hurt? It looks injured." She touched it, and he winced in pain.

"Yes, yes, I think it's broken or dislocated. I can't use my right hand and can barely move my arm," he said with a grimace. "I'm all beat up, aren't I?" He managed a weak smile.

"Yeah, you are. Are you sure no one else was here? Allison did all of this?" Tilda asked. She remembered Allison as being a little over five feet tall. She couldn't have weighed much more than a hundred pounds.

Nicholas nodded. "Yeah, she did it, believe it or not. I don't remember how it all happened, but she slapped me, hit me in the head with a shovel and kicked my shoulder. I guess she knew karate or something," he said slowly as he tried to remember.

Tilda moved back down to examine his leg. "How'd this happen?" The tourniquet was saturated with blood. She removed it briefly and let the blood permeate his leg. She remembered that from her first aid course.

"I'm not going to lose my leg, am I?" Nicholas asked fearfully.

Tilda smiled brightly, "No, of course not, my love," she assured him. "Your leg is bad, but I am sure they can fix it."

He nodded, "Are you positive? I don't want to lose my leg," he whined. "I wouldn't look good with only one leg."

Tilda moved up and kissed him. "Your leg will be fine. And you will always be perfect to me." She smiled down on him. She adored him even though it'd become clear he couldn't fight his way out of a wet paper bag.

He smiled at her with his torn lips and broken teeth. "What would I do without you, Tilda? You've always been there for me."

Tilda nodded. "That I have. Now, how did Allison hurt your leg?" Tilda had to admit a grudging respect for the young woman.

Nicholas tried to think back. "I don't know for sure," he said, "but I think I fell on a pitchfork and it pierced my leg."

Tilda nodded as she remembered the pitchfork at the other end of the barn near the congealed blood. She reached for the bottle of water and held it to his lips. Nicholas moaned in pain as she moved his shoulder and tried to sit him up.

"No, no, stop it. I can't sit up. It hurts too badly," he said hoarsely. "Just give me the straw."

Tilda shot him a dirty look and handed him the straw and water. She watched as he struggled to drink. He does need me. He can't even get a sip of water without me. She took the bottle, bent the straw and held it to his lips, and he drank until the bottle was empty.

He looked up at her with a question on his mind. "What are we going to do now?"

"Where's Allison? Where's the girl?" Tilda asked abruptly, ignoring his question.

"I don't know. She left."

"How long ago?"

Dude attempted to shrug his shoulders and moaned in pain. He shook his head. "I don't know. I passed out. I've no idea what time it was, and I don't even know what day or time it is now. How long have I been out?" Nicholas's eyes filled with tears.

Tilda shook her head. She was disgusted. Nicholas was proving to be useless. She stared at him. "I'm taking you to the hospital, and then I'm coming back to find and kill Allison."

Nicholas's pupils dilated, "Don't kill her. Just find her," he ordered with the first sign of strength Tilda had witnessed since arriving. "They'll be pissed if she's dead. She's worth a lot of money. They might even kill us. She's their merchandise."

Tilda gave him a searching look. "By 'they' do you mean a tall man with a bald head?"

"Yes. Oleg. He'll kill us or have it done," he said with assurance.

Tilda smiled smugly. "Don't worry about Oleg. He's dead. I killed him tonight, outside your office."

Nicholas's pupils dilated. "What, you killed Oleg? Oleg's my friend, my protector. He's my godfather." Tears fell from his eyes.

Tilda stared at him with dead fish eyes. "Was your godfather and friend. He's deader than a doorknob." Tilda felt only pride. "No need to worry about him." She smiled down at him.

Nicholas shook his head, his eyes terrified. "But...there are so many more. They'll come for us. Dimitri will skin us alive. They are all Bratva. Russian mob. I work for the Russian mob. You know that. You've helped me. He will kill us. You've no idea..." his voice trailed off into a whisper.

Tilda shook his shoulder roughly, and he screamed in pain. "Shut up, Nicholas. I'll kill them, just like I killed Constance and her boyfriend. Just like you told me to."

Nicholas looked up at her bewildered, "You killed Constance? I never told you to do that. And what boyfriend?"

Tilda glared at him. "Some man in her kitchen, and you did tell me to kill her. This afternoon. I did what you told me to do, Nicholas," she assured him as she felt resentment consume her.

"NO, I NEVER told you to kill Constance. I told you to take care of things. Take care of the rumors, to scare her. Threaten her. NEVER kill her. Why did you ever think that?" Once again, Nicholas's eyes filled with tears.

"You ungrateful bastard," she hissed as she stared at him.

Nicholas shook his head. "No, no. I never would have said that. She's the mother of my children. You're crazy."

Tilda smacked him in the face and said in a vicious tone, "I killed your ugly little daughter, too."

Nicholas's eye widened before turning to his side and vomiting.

Tilda shook her head. "You're disgusting."

She stood, grabbed Nicholas by the feet and dragged him through the barn, and then hoisted him onto her truck bed.

Chapter 62

Redman cursed softly as he drove his white paneled van off the I-64 ramp into downtown Richmond. Where was Oleg? Why wasn't he answering his cell? He checked his watch. It was getting late, and he'd have to find Oleg and get in touch with Dimitri.

He was feeling pretty satisfied with himself as he looked in the rear-view mirror at the two gagged and bound women sitting on the floor in the van. He'd managed to pick up the girls from an old friend who owned a country and western bar east of Richmond. He'd called and the guy had invited him to a party, and these were the hottest chicks in the bar. The women were both "lookers," but the brunette was feisty, and she'd put up quite a fight even though his buddy had spiked both of their drinks with roofies, and then drugged them into unconsciousness. As he looked at the brunette in the rear-view mirror, her legs seemed to extend the full length of the van. She had the longest legs he'd ever seen. His wrist still smarted from where the woman had bitten him. In return, she'd gotten a black eye that was turning as dark as her hair by the minute. Now he could see her glaring at him through her swollen, half-closed eyes. He wondered if she'd woken up. The look of hatred she gave him excited him, and he felt a feeling of ecstasy float over him. She'd bring a fair penny tonight, and the two women would keep Dimitri's ire at bay. Where in the hell was Oleg? Perhaps he'd gotten a lead on Smirkowitz and was tracking him down. He speed-dialed Nicholas's phone but got no answer.

His cell rang. He picked it up and barked, "Yeah, Oleg. Where're you?"

"That's what I'd like to know. Where's Oleg?" The voice was cold and harsh.

Redman's heart raced and for a moment he was dizzy. He said quietly, "Dimitri, its Redman. I can't find Oleg, but I saw him a few hours ago. He's still trying to find Smirkowitz. Have you heard from him?"

The silence on the other end was interminable. "If I had, would I be calling you?" Dimitri roared, his voice tinged with sarcasm.

"No, I guess not. I do have some women for tonight's run. I'm gonna stop over to Smirkowitz's office. Oleg was headed that way looking for Nicholas's girlfriend. Thought she might know where Nicholas was."

There was no response on the other end. Only a long, painful silence. "Sir, did you hear me?" Redman repeated.

"Of course I heard you," Dimitri barked, his face red with anger. "Find Oleg, or even better, find Smirkowitz and meet me at that convenience store on Commerce Road before we go to the rendezvous." The voice was cold and steely.

"Yes, sir, I'll be there," Redman assured him with a sinking feeling in his belly as fear etched up his spine. Where the hell was Oleg? Redman needed him to interface with Dimitri. The man was cruel and ruthless and he was frightened of him.

"Find them. Bring them with you. No excuses. We don't do business like this in Russia." Dimitri clicked off, but Redman heard the threat in his voice.

Redman was burning from fear. He opened his window, sucked in cold air and coughed vehemently. He knew Dimitri had threatened his life.

He took a few deep breaths, picked up his cell, and redialed Oleg's number. He got voicemail. He threw his phone on the floorboard of the truck and headed towards Smirkowitz's office. Who knew, perhaps he'd catch Oleg and Smirkowitz in the vodka bottle. He smiled to himself as his phone rang. He checked the display this time. The Richmond Police Department was calling him. His heart beat quickly. What could those bastards want with him? Whatever it was, it was gonna complicate his evening.

He clicked on the green button. "Yeah."

"Yo, it's Stoddard."

Redman didn't respond.

Stoddard continued. "Yo, man. We talked at Biddy's. Stoddard from the Richmond Police Department."

Redman remained quiet.

"Come on, man. Do you remember me? We just had a pint at Biddy's a little while ago," Stoddard laughed. "I know I'm not that memorable, but it's only been a couple of hours."

Redman put on his cocky FBI voice and said, "Yeah, okay, what's up?"

"Just wanted to catch you up on the human trafficking end of things since you were good enough to bring it to my attention."

"Yeah, so what you got?" Redman asked his voice cross. He didn't have time for this local yokel now.

"We ain't got nothing. Nothing. We checked it though, and it doesn't look like there's anything goin' on. I sent a detail down to the port, and it was quiet as a mouse."

"Yeah, okay. Keep me in the loop," Redman said, smiling to himself as he clicked off. Thank goodness for one small success for the night. At least the police wouldn't be in the way later.

When he arrived at the office, he broke the sidelight panel in Smirkowitz's office and turned the door handle. He walked through all of the examining rooms and the front office looking for anything suspicious. There was nothing. He reentered Nicholas's private office to see if there was anything he'd missed. The smell of violets permeated the air. He entered the bathroom, and it was evident that a woman had showered there recently. He noticed the half bottle of pinot and figured it had been Tilda. He checked Nicholas's desk and messages but there was nothing. He decided to look outside just in case he had missed something.

He walked along the sidewalk side of the office and scanned the parking lot. He saw nothing so he went through the bushes on the right and found the crumpled body of Oleg Branislava. Redman rushed over to examine the body. Blood had hardened on his chest from the bullet wounds to his torso. Oleg's eyes were open in death. He had seen it coming. Redman continued to look at the body, cursing softly to himself when he noted that the bottom half of the corpse was anatomically displaced.

Redman shook his head and knelt in the snow. He reached for Oleg's warm, knitted hat in his pocket and put it on his bald head. Then he used his fingers to close Oleg's eyes. He decided that he was going to kill the person who had done this to his friend. And he was pretty sure it was the psycho bitch that Smirkowitz had been sleeping with for twenty years.

He walked back to his van in the freezing cold, pulling his jacket around him. His heart was heavy. He yanked his cell phone from his pocket and punched in numbers. Dimitri answered on the first ring.

"Where're you?" Dimitri asked, testy as always. "Did you find Oleg?"

Judith Lucci

Redman swallowed a lump in his throat. "Yeah. I'm over at Smirkowitz's office. Oleg's dead in the parking lot. He took two slugs to the chest, and then whoever shot him ran over him with their car."

There was a long silence on the other end. Redman could feel sweat pooling and running down his back and underarms, even though it was freezing outside. The silence stifled him.

"Dimitri, did you understand what I said?" Redman asked carefully.

"I understood perfectly. Come here now. We'll do business, and then we'll find Oleg's killers and take care of them." Dimitri's voice was frigid. "There will be hell to pay by the killer. Oleg was a good tovarich. I always demand retribution for a good friend."

"Yeah, he was," Redman agreed as he stared at Oleg's body.

"He gave his life for Bratva," Dimitri added with grit and hate dripping from his voice. Redman could imagine the rage that consumed Dimitri's body. He was glad he wasn't with him.

"Yeah, he did," he added less enthusiastically as his voice trailed off. Dimitri's voice chilled him more than the eighteen-degree weather and the freezing wind that whirled around his head.

"Are you there, tovarich? Come in now. We've work to do." Dimitri growled, "Do you hear me?"

"Yes, sir. I hear you. I think there is only one killer," Redman muttered.

"One killer?"

"I think one person killed Oleg," Redman said furiously. "I think I know who it is."

Dimitri shook his head. "One killer or ten. They'll die tonight, but first things first, business continues as usual. We save the killing for fun at the end," Dimitri snorted and laughed, "We are not kind to our enemies."

"Yeah," Redman agreed, and he wished he was anywhere but Richmond.

"I'll be waiting. Do not keep me waiting long," Dimitri threatened.

"I'll see you shortly at the same meeting place," Redman assured him. "I have goods to transport," he added and hoped that improved his boss's temperament.

"Just get here," Dimitri barked.

"What should I do with Oleg's body?" Redman asked in an uncertain voice.

"Leave him," Dimitri commanded. "The city will take care of him. He's no good to us now."

Redman shuddered at the indifference in Dimitri's voice. He gave Oleg's body one last look. He missed his friend already. With Oleg gone, there was no buffer between him and Dimitri. He knew the man only by reputation. He was unpredictable and cruel. The stories he had heard chilled him to the bone as he turned the key in the white van. He'd be lucky if he survived the night because Dimitri would kill him if no one else did.

Chapter 63

Slade McKane squatted behind a trashcan near the empty guardhouse at the Port of Richmond and watched the trawler make its way up the James River. The night was dark and a dense cloud cover added to   the poor visibility. Even though most of the snow and precipitation had moved out, the weather remained bitterly cold. The wind off the water was freezing, and he pulled his coat closer around him. He spoke softly into his headpiece to the men, "Here she comes… looks to be a couple of miles out."

Silence. He stared over at the surveillance van and spoke again into his headpiece, "Big Dawg?"

Monty "Big Dawg" McGraw was tracking the trawler on his monitor and answered. "Yeah.   It's a pretty big vessel. We see her. Got it covered, Detective. As soon as she gets a little closer, we'll have eyes and ears on deck."

"Roger that, Big Dawg." Slade smiled. Monty McGraw was the best eyes and ears a RPD crime team could ever wish for. Scottish by birth, Big Dawg commanded an amazing girth, a great sense of humor and was a brilliant technician and analyst. He had fifteen years of active police service and was a computer genius. Slade always felt good when he had the Big Dawg on his team.

"Who's ridin' shotgun with you in there, Dawg?" Slade asked.

"I got Smitty tonight, and we got us a fifth of Black Jack we're gettin' into as soon as this dance is over," Big Dawg informed him.

Slade grinned. Things couldn't be better. Big Dawg and Smitty were the best. Between the two of them, they didn't miss a trick. Big Dawg himself was the architect of

Richmond's impressive police security van, considered "heavy artillery" in the surveillance world. Dawg had designed the RPD van to provide for the upmost safety for surveillance operatives and police officers to get the job done and capture the bad guys. Dawg's van appeared like any other van from the outside, but it had a secret door hidden between the front and back seats. The "working" part of the van had its own heating and cooling system, and the technology in the van was capable of monitoring the four corners around the van to cover and protect officers from blind spots. The van boasted extremely sensitive listening equipment, night vision capabilities, thermal imaging, GPS and video surveillance. There were side and back state-of-the-art cameras capable of medium and long-range surveillance, and the video camera had wide-angle lenses with panning capabilities. The Richmond Police Department van was equipped with riflescope advanced night vision that lit the night like daytime. Photography, and video recording with superior performance and image clarity helped identify perps. The dashboard control center had a camcorder capable of taking night shots at 450X. A periscope located on top of the van was cleverly disguised and rotated 360 degrees to offer surveillance operatives greater vision.

"Hey, Slade," Big Dawg crackled, "let's take these perps down like we did couple of years back when that Turkish Trawler came through here with all the cocaine. We did good, 'member?"

Slade smiled. "Yeah, man. That was a great take down. We got over eight mil worth of coke. Our drug-sniffing dogs were amazing that night."

"Yup," Big Dawg said. "It was one fine night. We didn't find anything at first but when both dogs alerted, one in the captain's cabin and the other behind the kitchen galley, it was all over but the shoutin'."

Slade checked in with Lt. Stoddard about the vehicles he'd arranged for back up. Each vehicle was equipped with sensitive sound detection equipment as well as night scopes to easily enhance shadows on this dark, dreary night. Two officers manned each vehicle. Everyone was on high alert and ready for action. The canine van was parked in a grove of trees, and it would only take the two dogs a few seconds to attack if needed.

The minutes ticked by as Slade waited and his anxiety increased.

"Detective, we got a white Chevy panel van, Maryland plates, headed your way. I'm thinkin' it's the exchange vehicle." Big Dawg's voice hummed with excitement.

"Copy that," Slade said as he spotted the headlights reflected off the snow-covered trees as they approached the entrance into the port. He watched as the van passed the "Port of Richmond" sign and entered the gates. Slowly, the van moved closer and closer to the darkened port building. He watched as his officer dressed in overalls and a winter jacket moved into the shadow of the building, holding a snow shovel with thick heavy gloves.

"Thermal images suggest four bodies in the white van." The voice crackled through his headset.

"How about on the trawler? Can you tell whether it's armed and the number of bodies?"

Big Dawg shook his head. "Nah. Too far out. I'll let you know soon as I can tell," Big Dawg promised, his voice calm and steady.

Stoddard's voice crackled in his ear. "Slade, we got another van, dark color for a total of two vans. This one is over on the west end of the port, coming through the west gate."

Slade's heart pumped hard and adrenalin rushed blood through his brain. "Okay, can you see it, Dawg?"

"Yeah, I see it. No visual yet. Heat sensing suggests three images. Two in the front and one in the back. I'll keep sneakin' and peepin' and get back."

Slade repeated Big Dawg's update to his men. His heart was hammering in his chest. He in no way had expected a second van. This was getting interesting. They were ready to rock and roll.

Chapter 64

Dottie tossed and turned in her bed. She'd taken half of her sleeping pill, but for some reason it wasn't working. Of course, she didn't believe in that herbal stuff anyway. Melatonin was like taking nothing. She really wanted her Ambien back, but her doc wouldn't prescribe it. She flipped over in the bed and pulled the down comforter over her. It was useless. She couldn't fall asleep. She'd counted sheep, tried some meditation but nothing worked. Finally, she got out of the bed and sat in her large recliner by the window.

It was a little after one in the morning. Dottie shook her head and cursed softly. She'd be dead if sleep didn't come soon. She lay back in her recliner and looked at the street below.

There was very little traffic on Monument Avenue that time of night, and the lights from neighboring homes twinkled in the darkness and reflected in the snow. The street lights made the ice on the streets glisten. Snow was piled several feet high on both sides of the avenue, the aftermath of the snowplows that had cleared the roads earlier in the day. She listened intently but didn't hear anything. Dottie returned to her musings and replayed the tapes in her brain from the previous day, convinced she'd forgotten something important or that there was something she should or could do to help Allison.

She heard the elevator moving slowly to the third floor where Cookie and Henry lived. She listened to the slow drone of the motor as the iron monstrosity climbed. She supposed Cookie was finally going to bed for the night. Dottie's eyes closed again, heavy with the need for sleep and rest. Finally sleep came, and she slept deeply.

A while later, her eyes popped open. She heard something. She swallowed deeply and looked around her room. She could hear the soft ping of an alarm. There! She heard it again, and she looked quickly around her room for the source of the noise. She knew the sound, but she couldn't put it into perspective. It wasn't her cell or, iPad nor was it her alarm clock. She was puzzled as she continued to listen to the soft sound. It seemed to be coming from her highboy. She rose slowly from her recliner and moved as quickly as she could to her tall chest-of- drawers. She opened the top drawer. She saw it and blood rushed to her head and made her dizzy. She clung to the massive chest for support. She stared, mesmerized at the flashing glow of a tiny red light and the origin of a soft sound.

Her heart fluttered in excitement as her soul sprang to life. It was the medical-alert GPS tracker for Allison Massie. Margaret had given it to her last fall when she and Beau had traveled abroad and she had never given it back. Did this mean they could find Allison? Why had the alarm just come on? Dottie was so overcome with excitement, she was dizzy and took deep breaths as she moved back towards her four-poster bed, holding on to the posts as she moved. She eased herself into her recliner and elevated her feet. This meant she could locate Allison, or at least a specific area where Allison was being held. She steadied herself, grabbed her cell phone and called Michaela, who answered her home phone on the first ring. She heard Angel yip in the background.

"What's wrong? What's wrong, Dottie," Mic barked. "Are you okay?"

Dottie was so excited she couldn't speak.

"I'm gonna call 911 and I'll be there in a minute. Can you ring for Cookie?" Mic asked. There was silence.

"Dottie, Dottie, speak to me," she said in short gasps. Mic hadn't ever realized until recently how much she loved this woman.

"I'm, I'm okay. I think I know where Allison is. I have her GPS unit for her medical alert sensor. It'll tell us," Dottie said, a note of pride in her voice.

"Her med-alert has a GPS sensor? Huh?" Michaela's voice was dubious.

"Yeah, yeah, it does," Dottie said impatiently. "Margaret and Beau got her the very best system available. The medical alert system has GPS as part of its safety checks. The technology can track where you are at all times that is, if you press the help button on the GPS mobile alert device. I know, I have one."

Excitement shot through Michaela. "Who takes the calls? Is there an emergency number?"

Dottie turned the device over. "I have to get my glasses. The print's too small. Hang on."

Michaela sighed deeply. She put her landline on speakerphone, picked up her cell, and called Slade. He answered quietly, "What's up, Mic?"

"Where are you?" she asked breathlessly.

"Stakeout at the port." His voice was soft, his words terse. "We're getting ready to rock and roll."

Mic took a deep breath. "Listen, we think we know where Allison is. Dottie has her medical-alert device monitor. The device has GPS tracking, and it's beeping."

"Where? I'll get a unit out there immediately," Slade said softly, his heart pounding in anticipation. Finally, a break and maybe they weren't too late.

Mic could hear the veiled excitement in Slade's voice.

"Just a sec, Dottie's getting us the number on the back of the monitor. It rings somewhere into an emergency control center."

Slade could hear Dottie repeat the number to Mic. He committed it to memory.

"Got it, Mic. I'll follow up and get a couple of units out there. Will call you back," he promised. "Things are heatin' up here."

"Stay safe," Mic added but Slade had signed off.

Mic returned to her conversation with Dottie. "Okay, I'm gonna wait to hear back from Slade, and then I'm going out there to find her."

"You and I are going out there to find her," Dottie retorted crisply. "Don't think for one small minute that I'm not going to be a part of this."

Mic rolled her eyes. She could sense the intensity and determination in Dottie's voice and see the glare in her blue eyes. There was no way she was getting out of taking her, but it was worth a try.

She sighed deeply, "Dottie, for heaven's sake. It is after one in the morning, and you were exhausted at seven this evening. There is no earthly reason why you should be making this trip."

The silence was deafening.

"Besides, it's freezing cold, and the ice is treacherous," Mic added weakly. "If you slip and fall, you're a goner."

"Maybe in your mind I shouldn't be going, Michaela," Dottie said in her haughty Countess voice, "but I am... besides, I've had two naps," she snapped crossly.

Mic backed down. "Pick you up in fifteen minutes. Slade or Lt. Stoddard will back us up with a couple of units."

Judith Lucci

"I'll be at the front door," Dottie promised as she struggled into her long underwear, sweat suit and boots. Adrenalin pumping through her veins was a wonderful thing. She felt thirty-five again.

"If you're not out front, I'm gonna keep on driving, Dottie," Mic warned. "We're not dressin' for fashion tonight," she said in a fit of frustration. "I don't think this is necessary anyway. You should stay at home."

"I'll be downstairs," Dottie repeated as she clicked off.

For half a second, Mic considered calling Cookie and asking her to pull the plug on Dottie's midnight escapade. But she didn't have time and Dottie would kill her.

Chapter 65

Slade pulled on his night vision goggles and watched two men exit the white van and walk toward the darker van that had pulled into a parking place a short distance away. One man was tall and thin, and the other, short and stocky.

Big Dawg spoke into his ear. "Slade, hey man. We got facial rec on the short guy. He's Dimitri Kazimir, a high-up in the Russian mob, straight from Moscow. Homeland has him entering the country a few days ago. He's reputedly head of the human trafficking end of Bratva, the Russian Mafiya."

Slade smiled broadly as he looked at the short, powerful man through his night goggles, "Big cheese, eh. The Russian mob."

"Yeah, sending two close-up images to your phone."

"Got 'em," Slade reported as he checked out the mob boss. "Guy looks mean," he whispered to Big Dawg.

Big Dawg nodded, "Yeah, man, for sure. The guy next to him is a lower tier Bratva operative. We think he's a U.S.-born Mafiya. I'm sending pics to you."

Slade stared at Dimitri's image and flipped to the other. It was a blond guy with a baby-face. His heart flipped as well. "Dawg, send this one to Stoddard right away. I think this guy is a double agent of some sort." he gasped as realization flooded his senses. "Patch Stoddard through."

"On it," Big Dawg replied. "Stoddard, you know the guy with the blond hair?" he asked as his voice cracked through the headset. "By the way, I got Slade on the line."

Stoddard saw the image and cursed loudly. "Hell, yes, he's supposedly an FBI agent. Met him this evening. Talked to him a few minutes ago."

Judith Lucci

Slade interrupted. "Hey, Dawg, guy said he's FBI from Baltimore. Can you verify?" Slade asked as his stomach churned. Stoddard had said there was something wrong with the man, but he'd taken that to mean he'd been a cocky asshole. Not a guy playing the RPD.

"If he's truly FBI, we're into some serious shit. We'll check it out," Big Dawg assured him.

"Thanks, man. It looks like it's heating up down there," Slade observed.

"Yeah, We're about to dance. Check it out," Dawg said as he scanned the scene. He watched as two men emerged from the car. "Check out these thugs. You know them?" Big Dawg questioned, "Here are some close-ups."

Slade shook his head as he squinted into the goggles. "Negative. No recognition from this distance. Anything goin' on inside the trawler?" he asked as he watched the men on the dock greet each other warmly.

"Got twelve heat images. Could be anybody, crew, bad guys, contraband, slaves, who the hell knows?" Big Dawg guessed as he played with his camera equipment panning the view down to the shore.

"How long before trawler docks?" Slade asked as he watched the vessel rock back and forth in the freezing James River as it moved closer and closer to port.

"Less than five minutes. He's already cut the engines back."

"Thanks, man. Keep me posted," Slade said as he turned his attention to his headset to update his men.

Chapter 66

Dorothy stood in the enormous foyer in her Monument Avenue mansion. The crystal chandelier provided a dim light as she glanced at herself in the mirror. She was dressed in all black. She'd had time to pull on her fleece-lined long johns under her sweats and hoodie and had donned a black down sweater vest, black leather gloves, black snow boots with a heavy tread, and a black stocking cap that she'd pulled over her hoodie. She placed her Glock 26 into her vest jacket for easy access. Dottie loved the little Glock. It had the accuracy of her larger Glock in a smaller compact package and was much easier for her to handle since her hands had aged. Another good thing about the Glock 26 was its ability to pack plenty of firepower. It would shoot nine rounds of 9 mm ammo in rapid time. Dottie also appreciated the additional grip strength it provided for all three of her fingers, which helped her accuracy when shooting.

Michaela's headlights beamed down her driveway, and Dottie moved over to her elegant brass umbrella stand and picked up her pump twenty-gauge shotgun. She caught an image of herself dressed in black, holding her shotgun in the gilded gold mirror hanging over an Italian marble console. She placed her right hand in the side pocket of her down vest pocket and pulled out her Glock. She gave herself a big smile, picked up her ammo bag and opened her front door. I'm looking pretty hot tonight for an old broad, and, I feel thirty-years old.

She knew Mic would have a fit when she saw her. She looked at herself again. I'm badass with this shotgun. No one would think an eighty-two-year-old woman would pull out a pump twenty gauge.

Dottie was confidant with the weapon and had practiced with this shotgun just a few weeks ago at the range. She routinely went to the range with Henry at least every couple of weeks to target practice with her Glock and shotgun. What she loved about the gun was that it didn't have so much kick that it knocked her down. True, she was eighty-two, but she could shoot straight and run fast for her age. Her career as an Olympic swimmer had conditioned her to stay in shape her entire life, and it'd paid off.

She opened her front door and waited as Mic pulled under the carport and unlocked the electric locks for her.

Mic smiled broadly. "Wow. You look like you're a member of the RPD SWAT team," Michaela observed. "What's up with the shotgun?"

Dottie glared at her and pressed her lips into a thin line. "Leave it be, Michaela. I'm not droning on and on about the way you're dressed, so start the car and drive."

"But, Dottie —" Mic began.

Dottie glared at her, "I was at the range a couple of weeks ago, and I shot the Glock and my twenty gauge. Told you that yesterday. Henry took me. I have confidence in both these guns. There was nothing wrong with my aim then, and there won't be anything wrong with it tonight either. So, shut the hell up."

Michaela sighed. "Okay, you're fine. Just buckle your seat belt."

Dottie shot Michaela an icy look, probably colder than the temperature outside. "I don't need you to remind me about my seat belt either. I'm not senile."

Mic rolled her eyes and started the car.

Angel gave a soft whimper from his seat in the back. Dottie turned around and smiled at him. She reached in her purse and offered him a piece of jerky. His eyes shone as he devoured the jerky in one quick gulp.

"So, could you show me some respect, turn on the heat in the truck and drive so we can save Allison Massie. I'd hate to think she died while you quibbled about how I look and act," Dottie added in her snotty, countess voice.

Michaela groaned inwardly but smiled on the outside. "You're right. I'll call a truce, but are you sure you need that shotgun?"

Dottie gave Michaela, also dressed in black, the once over and sniffed, "A girl's got to have what a girl's got to have. And tonight I need both of my guns and regardless, I want them." Her face was set with determination and Mic knew better than to try to change her mind.

Michaela arched her eyebrows, held her tongue and smiled tightly. Oh, how she wished Dorothy had stayed home. She planned to have a chat with her about going out on nights like tonight when true danger could really hurt her. After all, she wasn't young anymore... a fact that Dorothy knew but refused to accept.

Dottie scowled at her. "Let's get moving."

Mic was silent as she entered the coordinates they'd received from the medical security facility that hosted Allison's medic alert device. Mic's dashboard gave the estimated time at thirty-three minutes based on road conditions, traffic, and weather.

"You talked with Slade McKane about this?" Dorothy asked.

Michaela nodded. "Yeah, he has two units headed out with us, and he and Stoddard are down at the port working another angle of Allison's case. He'll join us as soon as possible."

"What's the ETA of the units?"

Mic skirted a patch of black ice on the road and shook her head. "Don't know. They'll radio us. If we get there first, we're going in. As soon as we find Allison, we'll call 911. There's a good chance, she'll be unconscious from lack of insulin."

"Yeah, I know. I just hope we're not too late."

Mic glanced over at Dottie and noted the strong set of her jaw. She'd didn't look frail or old at the moment. She looked like someone Mic would rather not deal with.

Dottie glowered as her. "Whatever are you looking at now, Michaela? Can you just watch the road? There's ice everywhere."

Mic smiled. "I'm just lookin' at you. You're looking pretty tough… and sassy… tonight, I must say, as much as I hate to admit it."

Dottie snorted. "I'm badass tonight, Mic. Don't forget it, and don't get in my way," she added as she gave a short laugh.

Mic laughed as well, to relieve the tension in the car.

"You think Allison will be okay?" she asked.

Mic gave her a quick look and said, "Don't think like that, Dottie. For some reason, her medical alert device was activated, and that's only been about forty minutes ago. If Allison activated it herself, then it's good news. I think we'll get there in good time." Mic hoped she was right and that she'd reassured Dottie.

Dottie took a deep breath. When she spoke, her voice quivered. "I certainly hope so. Because if we don't find her, Margaret's never going to be the same, and I really don't want that to happen."

"I know what you mean. I think we're going to make it," she said as she turned on to Route 33 and accelerated her truck. The roads seemed to have improved.

Chapter 67

Tilda backed her pickup out of the driveway at Nicholas's farm spinning snow and ice twenty feet. She jerked the car forward as she turned around and headed for the main road. She was angry, and the voices in her head were screaming. Her hands shook so badly on the steering wheel the car jerked back and forth. She had almost reached the road when she slammed on brakes again and lowered her head onto the steering wheel and covered her ears with her arms. The voices had become her reality. KILL NICHOLAS, KILL NICHOLAS, KILL.

Tilda left the vehicle, got on her knees in the snow, and scooped handful after handful of the cold wetness, wiping each handful over her ears and head as she tried to freeze out the voices. Finally, they quieted, and the silence paralyzed her for an instant. Then she stood and went to the back of the pickup truck and opened the tailgate. Nicholas shook violently. She grabbed his feet, pulled him toward her, and tried to sit him up on the side of the tailgate. It was hopeless. Nicholas couldn't sit up; his injuries, particularly his shoulder, made it impossible for him to maintain his balance.

Tilda met his eyes and was stunned by the fear in them.

"Nicholas, Nicholas, what's wrong?"

Nicholas stared at her, his eyes enormous with fear. He was shaking so hard he could hardly speak. "What are you going to do with me?"

Tilda gave him a sweet smile. "I'm gonna put you in the backseat where it's warm. Then, we're gonna go find Allison Massie, and we're going to kill her."

"You're going to kill her?"

"Of course, I'm going to kill her, you idiot," Tilda snapped. "She knows way too much."

Nicholas shook his head, and his voice quavered as he spoke, "No, no, Tilda. Let's take her downtown to the port. Or we can call Dimitri. They want her. She'll bring them a lot of money," he begged.

Tilda shook her head. "There's no way. She knows us, and she'll finger us to the cops and the FBI. Let me help you into the backseat, and we'll find her. She couldn't be too far away. After all, she's on foot." Tilda reached to pull him from the truck.

Nicholas shook his head. "No, you don't understand. She'll never set foot on American soil again in her life."

Tilda ignored him and lifted Nicholas into the seat. The pain was excruciating, and Nicholas hollered with each movement.

"Just get in there, Nicholas. Don't be such a sissy," Tilda muttered angrily.

"No, no, please no seatbelt," Nicholas cried. "It will hurt too much."

"Okay." Tilda rolled her eyes and packed snow in his groin area to stop the flow of blood trailing down his leg onto the truck floor.

"Wilbur's gonna have a shit fit when he sees this truck." She blocked her mind against the metallic stench of the blood. "I've got to stop the bleeding, or you'll die," she told Nicholas.

Nicholas nodded as his teeth chattered and his shoulders shook, causing him even more agony.

Tilda started the truck and drove slowly toward the wood line, her headlights on low beam. The last thing she wanted to do was to bring attention to herself this late at night, especially with a brutally injured man in her truck, three bodies back in Richmond, and a dead state trooper. She shined her low beams into the snow and looked for tracks but didn't see any at all. She turned the heat on for just a moment to warm up her brain and spur her thinking. She didn't want Nicholas too warm or his leg would bleed more quickly.

She turned and asked, "Is Allison injured?" she asked.

Nicholas was so cold he could barely speak. His teeth chattered, and he shook with cold. "I... I don't really remember. I think she is. I kept her unconscious with insulin and drugs most of the time, but I don't remember if she is injured." he admitted, afraid to meet Tilda's eyes.

Tilda nodded and looked around. She spied a barn located across the road about a hundred yards down from her truck. "I bet I know where the little bitch is," she snarled, her face contorted with anger.

Nicholas was silent. It was the first time he'd ever thought of Tilda as ugly or unattractive. Her face was a caricature of evil.

Tilda leaned over and gave him a quick kiss. "I'm going over to that barn, the one with the lights on and take care of Allison. Then I'll take you back to the office, get you cleaned up and figure out if we need to go to the hospital.

Nicholas gave her an uncertain smile and closed his eyes. He looked at the barn out of his window. "That's a chicken hatchery. Two farmers own it together. It's full of laying hens. I'm positive she's not there."

Tilda smiled happily. "Oh, good. It'll be nice and warm. They gotta keep it warm for the chickens to lay eggs, and I'm sure all those chickens put off a little heat. And besides, I'll break a few chicken necks while I'm in there... after I take care of the little bitch of course," she chuckled.

305

Nicholas was silent.

"When we're done, I'll put the dead chickens in the back of the truck, and I'll make my chicken casserole you love so much." Her eyes danced with joy about the possibility of killing Allison and a few chickens.

Nicholas remained silent.

Chapter 68

Slade watched as a trawler edged closer to shore. He couldn't make out the ship's country of origin but figured that was info he could obtain later. These guys were gonna be toast, there was no way they were getting away, even if he died in the process. Big Dawg's voice rasped into his ear.

"Slade, you see what I see?" Dawg's voice pierced Slade's headpiece.

"Yeah. Think so. Looks like three guys got off of the trawler. Right?"

"Yeah, that's what we see, too. Still got nine heat images showing up on our monitors so should be nine other people inside the boat. Guessin' they're probably prisoners or victims."

Slade nodded as anger burned through him. "Yeah, probably so. Can you check with the Coast Guard to see if that trawler has an itinerary? Maybe we can figure out where they were taking the victims."

"Sure thing," Big Dawg agreed. "But right now, we're running these guys through facial rec. I got nuthin' on the men from the dark van, but one of the men that got off the trawler is a known human trafficker in Central America. I guess the other Central American is his sidekick. My guess is the first one is the boss and one of the major contacts for the Russian Mafiya in that area."

Slade nodded. "Yeah, probably. You see anything else? I'm about to give the order to move."

Big Dawg mumbled to his tech. "No, man, we've been panning all around and looking for other images, but we don't see nuthin'. I think what you see is what you get."

Stoddard's voice, harsh with anger, clamored into Slade's ear. "Detective, we just did a sneak and peek into the white van, and there are two women tied up and drugged in the backseat. One looks pretty beaten up. When're you movin' in?"

"Soon. Just waiting for surveillance to take one last video pan of the area. Don't want us to have any surprises on the backside."

"Gotcha, Slade. We move on your word."

"Get the men into position," Slade ordered. "Tell them to move quietly. As soon as I hear back from Big Dawg, it's party time."

"Roger that," Stoddard said. "I'll pass the word."

Static blasted Slade's ear as he tried to reach Dawg. "Is the perimeter safe? Can you pick up audio?"

Big Dawg nodded. "Nah, no audio. Yup. Surveillance is clean. They're talkin' in broken English so lip reading is hard." He paused for a moment and continued, "Sounds like they're talking about the cost of the cargo." Dawg stopped for a second, observed and added, "Oh, looks like Dimitri's getting pissed, he's kicking the ground and shaking his fist. Madder than hell."

"They're having a disagreement?" Slade asked.

"Yup. No question. We could have a problem over money," Big Dawg observed.

Slade smiled broadly. "Good." He gave a short laugh. "Let 'em duke it out so they're less likely to see us coming."

"Yup," Big Dawg said, "Lovin' it. Maybe they'll kill each other, and we won't have to even draw our guns," Dawg joked.

Slade watched for a moment as the two men continued to disagree. Dimitri took a giant step forward, pulled a shiny knife from his jacket pocket and, in an instant, slit the throat of one of the Central Americans. Slade could see the blood spurt from the man's neck through his night vision goggles. The man remained on his feet for several moments before he slid to the ground. Slade stared, mesmerized, at the scene below him until he heard a crackle in his ear. It was Dawg.

"Man, did you see that? I called it. I guess the shit we heard about Dimitri is true. I didn't 'spect that," Big Dawg said. "He's a mean SOB, just like we heard."

"Yeah, no question. Safe to go in?"

"Let's dance. We're ready, right, Smitty?" Dawg gave a short laugh. "Yeah, for sure. You ready? Lookin' good from here."

"Lieutenant, are we in place?" Slade questioned Stoddard.

"Ready," Stoddard replied, confidence in his voice.

Slade spoke into his earwig. "It's party time, gang. Let's hit it."

Suddenly, the entire dock area was covered in bright light. The lights were blinding. Dimitri and the remaining Central American guy covered their eyes while Redman and the other men reached for their guns. But it was too late. A volley of firepower from the Richmond police quickly took down Redman, the Central American, and the other two men from the trawler. Dimitri held up his hands in surrender. Richmond police officers moved in to secure the scene as Stoddard hailed an ambulance for the badly beaten American women in the white van. Within seconds, Richmond police secured the trawler and pulled nine additional women out of the hole. The woman appeared malnourished, bruised, battered, and dazed.

Slade locked eyes with Dimitri before speaking. "I'd cut your throat right now if there weren't so many people around. What kind of an animal are you to beat up helpless women and steal their lives, you useless asshole?"

Dimitri winked and smiled at Slade and opened his arms wide to make his point. "I'm like you Americans. You capitalists. I'm a businessman. All of this is about business." A broad smirk sliced across his face and connected with the scar on the side of his jaw.

Slade's eyes bored into Dimitri's face as his Irish temper flared. He thought about Maria, Danielle, and Allison. He watched the paramedics load up the drugged, beaten women.

Dimitri continued to smirk at him.

Hell flew into Slade as his Irish temper flared. No one intervened when Slade knocked the powerful Russian mob boss to the ground. Dimitri lay in the snow and ice for several minutes as more police and emergency vehicles arrived at the scene.

Slade checked his watch and motioned for Lt. Stoddard. "Let's go. Mic knows where Allison Massie is. I've sent two units to the general location, but I think they may need some help."

"I knew somethin' was screwy with that guy," Stoddard said, staring down at the Redman's body. "Didn't like him at all and he turns out to be a damned Bratva soldier masquerading as FBI."

Slade growled, "Yeah, and he's responsible for Danielle's beating if he didn't do it himself."

Stoddard shouted for another officer to take command, and he and Slade hurried to their cruiser.

The entire takedown had taken less than three minutes.

Chapter 69

Allison woke from her sleep by the sound of a car door slamming outside the barn. She sat up and heard voices. Her heart jumped as she quickly moved deeper into the barn and climbed a wooden ladder used to service crates of chickens on the second and third levels of the hatching barn. She wedged her slim body behind several crates of chickens on the highest platform. Fortunately, the chickens didn't make any noise, and Allison breathed a sigh of relief as she lay crouched in her hiding place and peered at the barn below.

Allison lay quietly, her heart hammering in her chest, barely breathing and watched as the barn door opened. A tall, dark-haired woman with boots and a down vest entered the barn. She carried a large flashlight in one hand and a gun in the other. There was something about the woman that was familiar, but Allison couldn't place her in the low light. The woman walked up and down the aisles of chicken cages and talked quietly to herself.

Allison heard the barn door open again, and a beaten, bloody, and battered Dr. Smirkowitz came in calling softly for the woman. Allison couldn't hear much of what Dr. Smirkowitz said, but she thought he'd said something about other cars.

She was shocked when the woman ran at him cursing, "Shut up, Nicholas. Just shut up. I know what I'm doing." The woman took several long, angry strides toward the dentist and pushed him. Dr. Smirkowitz fell to the hard floor, screaming with pain as his injured shoulder slammed against the cold dirt.

It was then that Allison recognized the dark-haired woman. It was Tilda, the office manager, from Dr. Smirkowitz's office. The woman who'd interviewed her before Smirkowitz. The woman who'd sent her crying from

Judith Lucci

the office after her interview on Wednesday. The woman who'd told her she "wasn't qualified" to work for Smirkowitz. Allison was terrified as Tilda walked recklessly up and down the barn, disturbing the roosting chickens and cursing to herself.

Nicholas Smirkowitz dragged his body and stood with the help of a center barn post. He walked with great difficulty toward the crazed woman. "Tilda, my love. We must go. I think there're other cars and trucks out looking for us... or at least for Allison."

Allison's heart leapt in hope when she heard him. She wanted to stand and scream from the rafters but stayed hidden behind the chicken coop, as her heart beat a little less erratically.

Tilda tossed her dark hair and spoke so quietly, Allison had to strain to hear, "Nicholas, we have to find her. If she's alive, she can point the finger at us. We have no choice but to hunt her down and kill her."

"Yes, we do have a choice," Nicholas argued weakly. "Let's leave now. If we don't, we'll be caught."

Tilda glared at him but remained silent.

"Come, Tilda, I demand it," he persisted as his voice grew louder and angrier.

Tilda whipped her head around, took three long strides to where the brutally injured dentist stood, grabbed him by the collar, shook him savagely. "Shut up, just shut up," she snarled. "You're useless to me."

Nicholas grimaced with pain but stood patiently and repeated quietly, "We must go, Tilda, we've very little time. I beg you."

Tilda was enraged, her face suffused with anger; her voice caustic and cruel. She screamed at him, her lips curled

313

in an angry, sardonic snarl. "CAN YOU NOT HEAR ME? Look at you, Nicholas Smirkowitz. You're pathetic. Go over there and sit on that bale of hay, and I'll leave when I'm done here and damned ready to go." The words penetrated Nicholas's senses like sharp metal bullets. He sat quietly on the hay and looked around for a weapon.

Suddenly, and without provocation, Tilda screamed. She covered her ears with her hands and screeched, "Shut up, shut up" repeatedly until she sank to the floor. She curled into a fetal position screaming and crying until Nicholas stood and moved beside her and gently helped her to her feet.

Tilda glowered at him and hissed in a hoarse voice. "Nicholas, get out of my way, get out of my way or I'll kill you." She waved her gun in front on his face, a wild, demented look in her eyes.

Nicholas looked at her and said in a calm voice, his face gray with pain. "Let's go, Tilda. I'll get you some help. We need to get out of here while we have time."

Tilda laughed at him as an ugly smile spread across her face. "You're gonna get me help? Now that's a laugh."

She clasped her arms across her chest as the sound of her maniacal laughter pierced the barn. The chickens started to squawk and cackle with fear. They rustled their wings and mayhem broke out in the hatching barn. The noise was one of dissonance and disharmony.

KuuUUkuKuu, KuuUUkuKuu sounded repeatedly as the chickens clucked among themselves. The sound was horrific, eerie, and it seemed as though hundreds of musical instruments were being tuned incorrectly. Allison broke into a sweat. Chill bumps popped up all over her. She was in hell. She hugged herself to warm her extremities. The odor of the chickens' fear permeated the barn as they rustled about in their cages. Their squawks rose to a frenetic level.

314

Tilda's demented laughter lasted several seconds longer, then ceased abruptly as a look of hatred distorted her face while violence glowed in her eyes.

Nicholas's mouth gaped open as he watched the flashes of rage and insanity flicker over Tilda's features. Her face twisted into a snarl, and she looked like a monster as she paced around the barn and grabbed the chickens, yanking them off their nests, pulling their nests apart and slamming eggs to the floor. The stench of hay, fear, and feathers permeated the barn. The chickens were terrified. Their squawks became louder and deafening. Allison watched in horror as the mad woman created chaos below.

Nicholas stood to stop her. "Leave the chickens alone. No one is hiding in here," he insisted. "Let's go, now."

Tilda pushed him away. "Shut up, Nicholas. Leave me alone. I'm doing this for us." She continued to walk up and down the aisles of the barn searching for Allison.

Suddenly, out of nowhere, a large, black rooster with a bright red comb swooped down on Tilda and attacked her. He spurred her on her arm and attacked her face, pecking her eyes and nose. Tilda screamed in surprise. The rooster's wings spread over her face and made it impossible for her to see or breathe. Tilda pulled at him and yanked him away. She grabbed at his neck, but the big bird slipped away. Feathers and down flew everywhere as Tilda screamed, cursed, and chased the bird around the barn. The laying hens went crazy, and the flutter of a thousand wings created a horrific sound like a small plane landing. The black rooster swooped again and laid open Tilda's skull with its beak, creating a large head wound, that poured blood down her neck.

Tilda screamed in agony, but the rooster attacked her from behind sinking his spurs and claws into her back and biting her neck from behind. Tilda screamed a long piercing cry, and the barn went even wilder. The scene was frenetic as blood poured from Tilda's neck, face, and arms. The rooster made one more attack to her face, leaving several puncture wounds on her cheek that dripped blood. A final spur broke open and tore her lip leaving her a gaping hole in her mouth.

Nicholas watched, fixated on the bloody scene but unable to intervene. It happened so quickly. Allison looked down from her perch, unable to comprehend the awfulness of the scene below.

Tilda grabbed an axe learning against a support timber and swung it at the rooster, but the bird was too fast. He escaped and flew up to a rafter at the top of the barn and glared at Tilda through his beady little eyes. Tilda went crazy from anger and pulled more chicken coops off their platforms and threw them in the floor one after another until the rooster came at her again and bit her neck not once, but several times.

Allison watched her from behind the chicken coops in her third-level hiding place. Tilda was moving closer and closer to her. She was only about thirty feet away as she yanked roosting hens out of their cages, initially from the first and second platforms.   The crated crashed to the floor releasing the terrified chickens who flew to safety. Metal cages bounced off the floor as eggs crashed and cracked all over the barn floor. The floor was slimy with yellow yokes.

Total fear consumed Allison as she crumpled her body as tight as she could behind the chicken coops and awaited her fate. She'd be discovered in a few moments. Her heart screamed in fear and her head spun with dizziness. She prayed the black rooster would attack again.

Bedlam described the roosting barn. Chickens were flying around, screeching and squawking angrily... a scene from the deepest, darkest depths of hell. The noise, chaos, broken eggs, and blood dripping from Tilda was horrific. Reality crippled Nicholas Smirkowitz as he sat and cried like a baby while he sat on a bale of hay.

Allison's time had come. She closed her eyes as Tilda uncovered her hiding place and snarled at her.

"There you are, you little bitch," she hissed as blood dripped from her face and her torn lip displayed her lower teeth. She had a huge gash on her right cheek and part of her left ear was missing. She grabbed Allison's arm and yanked her from the wooden platform onto the barn floor where she stared down at the helpless young woman, gloating, with blood dripping from her face on to Allison.

The fall knocked the wind out of Allison, and she lay helplessly on the floor trying to catch her breath. Tilda watched her closely, a gleam of triumph in her eyes as she wiped blood from her face.

"Oh, too bad, you can't breathe," Tilda's voice dripped with sarcasm. "Let me see if I can't fix that." Tilda spat the words as she kicked the young woman in the chest and again knocked the wind out of her. Allison lay helpless on the ground and looked up at Tilda, her eyes wide with fear. She was unable to speak. She watched as Tilda raised her gun and prepared to shoot her in the head. Allison turned her head to the side.

"Oh no, you don't, you little fool," Tilda growled as she kicked Allison in the head until she was looking straight up into the crazed eyes of her killer. The barn was quieter now, and the silence was deafening until a clear voice shattered the silence.

Chapter 70

"Drop that gun. Drop it right now," Michaela demanded.

Tilda turned her head and stared wild-eyed at Mic, the hated woman from yesterday with the huge dog. Mic stood in the doorway of the barn, her Glock pointed at Tilda's head.

Tilda threw her head back and laughed again. "Never, I will never drop this gun." She fired just as Mic stepped forward, slipped on a piece of ice in the doorway, and fell on the barn floor. Tilda's bullet missed Mic's head by inches and smashed into the barn siding.

"Oh, tut-tut did the famous Michaela McPherson fall down and lose her gun?," she sang, walking toward Mic, her gun in her hand. "You know, you really need to get a grip," she said as she laughed at her own joke.

Mic stared at Tilda from the floor and their eyes locked. A moment later, the black rooster left his perch and moved closer.

Smirkowitz stood and walked slowly toward Tilda. He looked at her and said, "Stop, stop this, Tilda. This is wrong. This is insane."

Tilda cursed and scowled at him, fresh blood dripping from her face, her eyes crazed. "Shut up, Nicholas. You're a weakling. You were never worth my love, and I spent my entire life giving it to you, while I did everything you said." She cried angrily as tears spilled down her face and mingled with the blood and dirt on her clothes, "You're not worth it."

Smirkowitz took a couple of steps closer and reached out to Tilda. "Please, we've shared so much. Please don't kill anyone else."

319

Tilda gave him an innocent, beguiling smile and pushed him to the floor. Nicholas screamed as his broken body once again hit the hard ground. Tilda laughed at him and turned her attention back to Michaela who attempted to stand on a badly broken leg.

"Oh, what a shame," Tilda scoffed. "You've broken your leg."

Mic's eyes searched for her Glock, but it was too far for her to reach. She held on to a wooden beam for support and attempted to pull herself up. She locked eyes with Allison who remained on the floor, paralyzed with fear.

"Hang in there, Allison," Mic said softly. "Help is coming. Hang in there a few more minutes and this'll be over."

Allison blinked her eyes twice to show understanding.

Tilda was angered, incensed by the soft words Michaela offered as comfort to Allison. "Shut up, bitch. No help is coming, do you get it?" She again took aim at Michaela's head.

An instant later, the rooster swooped again and sunk his spurs into Tilda's white silk blouse, his body obscuring her view. He squawked loudly and bit her on the ear, and then took off again to the safety of his perch high in the rafters.

Tilda took her eyes off Mic for an instant, sighted the rooster and aimed. Before she could pull the trigger, her chest exploded and blood poured from her wound as she sank to the floor.

The noise was deafening and again, the barn was bedlam with the chickens squawking and screeching.

Michaela clung to the timber and looked toward the barn door as Dottie and Angel entered the barn. Dottie held her shotgun in her right hand. Angel ran to Mic and whimpered as he looked at her leg.

320

Mic patted him. "It's okay, boy, I'm gonna get it fixed."

Angel licked her hand non-stop and gave her anxious looks as she continued to scratch his ears.

"Thanks, old girl," Mic said, smiling up at Dottie. "You just saved my life."

Dottie put on her best countess smile and beamed from ear to ear. For a moment, Mic thought she saw the young Dottie, perhaps Dottie at the age of thirty. The way Dottie looked in the picture with the Count Borghase that hung over the fireplace in her living room. Mic was confused for a second.

"I may be old, but I'm not useless yet right, Mic?"

Mic nodded, overcome with relief. "Nope, that was a pretty good shot, particularly for an old girl." She winked at Dottie and continued. "But I was basically saved by a chicken, so don't let this go to your head."

Dottie shook her head and said, "Chicken, hell. That was no damned chicken. That rooster is huge, probably at least ten to twelve pounds."

Mic nodded and smiled as Dottie stood beside her and attempted to assist her to walk.

Neither of the women saw Dr. Dude move quietly and pick up the axe that lay close to Tilda's body. He secured it up behind his back with his good arm and started toward Dottie, his face a mask of hatred. Angel charged Dude, knocking him to the floor as the axe fell from his hand. Angel pinned Dude down to the ground as the man winced in pain and gasped for breath. The heavy, powerful dog sat on his chest, his eyes never leaving Dude's face. Angel had saved Dottie's life.

Dude writhed in fear as Angel remained on his chest, growling at him.

Mic laughed, "Thank God for great friends and hero dogs."

At that moment the police burst into the barn.

Mic ordered Angel off Dude's chest. She used her Glock to cover him.

Mic watched as Dottie walked over to Allison. She helped her up and said, "Come on, my dear, I'm taking you home to your mother and grandmother." Dottie enveloped her in a bear hug.

Tears streamed down Allison face as she murmured, "Oh, Countess Borghase, I thought I was going to die."

"Oh no, my dear, I'm glad you kept the faith. You knew Mic and I would save you."

Allison clung to her, still sobbing as Dottie led her towards the ambulance into the care of the paramedics. "I'll ride with you in the ambulance and your parents will meet us at the hospital, how's that?"

Allison smiled up from the stretcher. "Thank you, Countess, and you too, Michaela. Y'all saved my life."

Mic waved at her. "You're a brave young woman, Allison. Really brave."

Slade entered and ran to her side, a pained look on his face. "Mic, are you okay? Your leg looks pretty bad."

Mic had noticed the pain in her leg as the adrenalin rush faded. She felt sick and weak. "Yeah, it hurts," she said as she began to sink to the floor.

Slade assisted her and motioned for a paramedic with a stretcher. He watched as they cut away Mic's fleece-lined jeans. It was painful to look at her broken leg. It was a serious fracture with the bone exposed. Slade averted his eyes.

"Bad, isn't it," Michaela squeaked as they started an IV in her left arm and pushed in some morphine.

"Yeah, but we can fix it up just fine," the paramedic assured her.

Mic squinted her eyes, "Don't I know you?" She paused, flickering through the images in her mind. "You look familiar."

The paramedic smiled and nodded, "Yeah, I saw you last night when we found the young woman in downtown Richmond."

Mic nodded. "Yeah. Of course. You get around, don't you? Long night for you, right?"

The man smiled and said, "Apparently, it was a long night for both of us, and it seems we both get around."

Mic nodded and closed her eyes and as the pain medicine flowed through her veins. She opened them and looked at Slade.

"Don't let Dottie tell you she saved my life… A chicken saved my life. It wasn't her playing with her shotgun."

Dottie leaned down and said, "Bullshit, Michaela McPherson. I saved your life and you damned well know it. So, 'fess up, and we'll leave it at that," she promised. "And it was a rooster, not a chicken that helped."

Mic shook her head. "I'll never admit to that. I'm sticking to my story about the big black chicken, and that's it," she said stubbornly as she closed her eyes again and drifted off.

Slade laughed. "I hate to tell you, Mic. Dottie's right. That wasn't a chicken. That's the biggest rooster I've ever seen in my entire life." He paused for a minute and added, "And the meanest too, based on the damage on Tilda's body," he added as he glanced over at Tilda's corpse.

Mic nodded her head as she drifted off again. Her eyes popped open and she said, "No, she didn't," in a weak voice.

"Now, ladies, there's plenty of time for us to argue this one," Slade said. "Let's get Michaela and Allison to the hospital, and you, Countess Dorothy Borghase, home to bed. NOW," he added as she started to protest.

Dottie shook her head and said, "Nope, I don't take orders from you either, Detective. I'm riding in the ambulance with Allison and then you all can take me home."

Slade shook his head. "Okay, Countess, you're the boss."

Three Weeks Later

The thirty-six light Baccarat chandelier in Dottie's enormous dining room reflected her priceless Venetian and Capo di Monti glass collections and her Renaissance art. Her table was adorned with an eighteen-inch arrangement of spring flowers and sixteen scented candles of varying heights that reflected in the twelve-foot gold mirror over the long buffet. The guests had been well fed, and the libations were plentiful.

Dinner guests included the happy faces of Michaela, Allison and her parents, Danielle Alvarez, Margaret and Beau Massie, Cookie, Henry, and Slade McKane. The meal had been excellent and included a standing rib roast cooked to perfection by Slade McKane, a potato casserole with Gruyere, fresh broccoli with Hollandaise, and hot curried fruit. The collection of timeless, favorite recipes prepared by the guests had satisfied every appetite in the room. Mic had lost count of the number of bottles of wine that had been consumed, and Henry had just served after-dinner drinks to each of the guests to accompany their fruit truffle. The conversation was warm and joyful as each of the dinner guests remembered how terrifying life was a few weeks before.

"Okay, Slade. We know the police reports are in. Can you tell us what we don't know?" asked Michaela, who sat at the head of the table in a wheelchair she abhorred, her leg in a cast from the ankle to the thigh. Her surgery had gone perfectly, but it would be weeks before she could begin physical therapy.

Dottie echoed Mic's request and all heads turned expectantly to the ruggedly handsome Irishman seated to Michaela's left.

"Yeah, sure. What'd you want to know?" he asked as he looked around the room. "Basically, Dr. Dude remains hospitalized, and when he's discharged, he'll go to prison for the rest of his life. Dimitri's been handed over to the feds for trial and sentencing. The Russians are trying to extradite him to Moscow, but that's the same as putting him back in business, so I don't think that'll be happening."

"What about Redman? Was he really FBI and mafia?" asked Dottie. "Did you all ever figure that out?"

Slade nodded. "Yeah, he was. He and Nicholas Smirkowitz were both from mob families planted by the Russians in America shortly after their births. Unbelievable, isn't it?"

Beau Massie glared at Slade. "Why the hell don't you all know about these people? What's wrong is that the RPD doesn't have a handle on this stuff."

Mic smiled as Margaret touched his hand and chided him for his outburst.

"Beau, really," she said. "This man saved our granddaughter's life. Behave yourself." Then she gave Slade an apologetic smile.

Slade smiled back. "That's a good question, Mr. Massie. We do know how grave the human trafficking problem is, but honestly, most of our time now is spent on preparing and fighting terrorists from the Middle East. However, we've uncovered a few other bad guys we're watching on suspicion of human trafficking based on Redman and Dude. And, I can assure you the port of Richmond is now under our watchful eye.

Beau Massie stared at Slade but said nothing.

"We're doing our best, I promise you, Beau." He flashed him the official RPD professional Slade McKane smile.

326

"Beau, perhaps a large donation for RPD can become part of our charitable organization. Perhaps we can fund some officers to specialize in human trafficking and raise community awareness," Margaret suggested.

Beau's face lit up. "An excellent idea! We'll do it immediately. I'll talk with the commissioner."

Slade smiled at the Massie family members. "That would be a wonderful gift. Thank you."

Mic looked at Danielle. "Did you guys in Baltimore have any idea Redman was part of the Russian mob? Were you shocked?"

Danielle toyed with her wine glass. "Yeah, we were surprised. No one had any idea. We just thought he was a cocky jerk who had a problem with authority. We never knew," she assured them. "I frankly didn't like him and never trusted him," she added.

"Good judgment, Danielle," Mic said. "You're on your way to becoming a great cop."

Danielle nodded her thanks and then looked at Slade.

"What about the tattoo guy who tried to kill me? Did you figure out who he was," Danielle asked Slade.

Slade shook his head. "No. That's the only loose end in this case. We don't know who Snake Man is. We don't think he's with the Russian mob. He's nowhere on facial rec, and we couldn't get any fingerprints from the syringe he used to inject Danielle. He's still out there. Still a mystery, unfortunately... most likely hired muscle."

"You think he's a mercenary for hire?" Mic asked.

"Maybe, but we don't know for sure, but it's very possible," Slade replied. "For sure, he's a dangerous killer, but we just don't have anything on him. I'm sorry." He gave Danielle a short smile.

Danielle nodded. "Thanks, Slade. And thank all of you," she said as she looked around the table. "Thank you, Michaela, for saving my life, and you, Dottie, for having me to dinner. You all are the best."

Allison spoke for the first time. "I want to thank you all as well… for not giving up on me and for not forgetting me and for saving my life." Her eyes were full of tears. Her dad stood and went over to her chair and hugged her.

Dottie looked around the table. "I want to propose a toast...To great friends, great times, and new beginnings." She lifted her silver goblet in the air.

Everyone stood except for Mic, smiled, and clicked glasses. "And," Dottie added as she looked around the table, her eyes sparking dark blue, "in case you all hadn't heard, this eighty-two-year-old lady saved Michaela's McPherson's life just a few weeks ago."

Dottie gave Mic a huge smile. "Right, Mic?" she goaded.

Mic rolled her eyes and looked around the table. "No, she didn't, folks. It was a chicken… oops… a rooster that saved my life. Never believe otherwise."

Everyone cheered as Dottie shot Mic a happy, but haughty look. In her heart, she knew Thelma and Louise would ride again.

Judith Lucci

Favorite Recipes from Biddy McPherson's Irish Pub
Biddy McPherson's Traditional Cottage Pie

(OUR Friday night SPECIAL)

900g / 2 lb. peeled potatoes, quartered

6 tbsp. milk

110g / 4 oz. butter, cubed + 1 tbsp. for the sauce

Salt and ground black pepper

1/2 tbsp. lard or dripping

115g / 1 cup chopped onion

115g / 1 cup chopped carrot

1 clove garlic, minced

450g / 2 cups ground/ minced beef** see note

600 ml / 1 pint beef stock

115g / 1 cup chopped white mushrooms (optional)

2 tbsp. finely chopped flat leaf parsley

1 tbsp. all-purpose flour

115g / 1 cup grated Cheddar Cheese

PREPARATION

(Serves 6)

Heat the oven to 190°C/375°F/Gas 5

329

Place the potatoes into a pan and cover with boiling water. Boil gently until soft (about 15 minutes) then drain. Add the milk and butter to the pan, heat through until the butter melts, and add the potatoes and mash. Season with salt to taste.

Melt the lard or dripping in a large deep pan, ovenproof pan. Add the onion and carrot and fry for 5 minutes. Add the garlic and cook for another minute making sure you do not burn the garlic.

Add the minced beef and roughly one quarter of the beef stock, cook, stirring constantly until all the meat is browned. Add the remaining stock, the parsley and the mushrooms (if using) season with salt and pepper. Cover with a tight fitting lid and cook for 15 minutes.

Mash the flour into the remaining butter to form a paste. Add small pieces of the paste to the ground meat sauce, stirring until all the flour has dissolved, then repeat until all the paste is used up. The sauce should have thickened slightly.

Place the meat sauce into a 20cm deep glass, ceramic or cast iron ovenproof dish. Cover with mashed potatoes and then sprinkle with the grated cheese and bake in the heated oven for 30 - 35 mins until the surface is crisp and browned. Serve immediately with fresh seasonal vegetables.

Biddy McPherson's Warm Potato Salad with Beer

Salad

3lbs red potatoes

½cup finely chopped red onion

¼cup thinly sliced green onion

¼cup finely chopped celery

¼cup chopped fresh parsley

¼cup finely chopped sweet pickle

2tablespoons Guinness beer

2tablespoons cider vinegar

Dressing

¼cup olive oil, divided

¾cup finely chopped yellow onion

¾cup Guinness beer

¼cup cider vinegar

1teaspoon sugar

¾teaspoon salt

⅛teaspoon fresh ground black pepper

2tablespoons Dijon mustard

Directions

To prepare salad, place potatoes in a large saucepan; cover with water. Bring to a boil. Reduce heat, and simmer 25 minutes or until tender. Drain; cool. Cut potatoes into

1/4-inch slices. Combine potatoes, red onion, and next 6 ingredients (through 2 tablespoons vinegar); toss gently.

To prepare dressing, heat 2 tablespoons oil in a small skillet over medium-high heat. Add 3/4 cup yellow onion to pan; sauté 3 minutes or until tender. Add 3/4 cup beer and next 4 ingredients (through pepper); bring to a boil. Cook until reduced to 1/2 cup (about 6 minutes).

Place mixture in a food processor. Add mustard to food processor; process until smooth. With processor on, slowly pour remaining 2 tablespoons olive oil through food chute, processing until smooth.

Pour dressing over potato mixture; toss gently.

Serve immediately.

Judith Lucci

Biddy McPherson's Home Made Irish Cream

A Pub Favorite (My Mom's Favorite Irish Cream Recipe.)

"Irish whiskey mixed with cream and sugar with hints of coffee, chocolate, vanilla. Will keep for 2 months if refrigerated." Biddy says.

Cream, whiskey, vanilla, and coffee combine with sweetened condensed milk for a silky-smooth alternative to store-bought Irish cream. We love it added to coffee, used to sweeten cake frosting, or just on its own, enjoyed over a little ice.

MAKES 3 CUPS

Ingredients

1 cup heavy cream

1 tsp. instant coffee powder

½ tsp. cocoa powder

¾ cup Irish whiskey (We use Jameson but any will do)

1 tsp. vanilla extract

1 (14-oz.) can sweetened condensed milk

Instructions

Combine 1 tbsp. cream and the coffee and cocoa powders to make a smooth paste. Slowly add remaining cream, whisking until smooth. Add whiskey, vanilla extract, and sweetened condensed milk; stir to combine. Pour into a 24-

oz. jar and keep refrigerated until ready to serve, up to 2 weeks. To serve, pour into a tumbler filled with ice.

Biddy's Irish Shepherd's Pie with Guinness (Mic's family recipe from the old Country)

Ingredients

1 ½ pounds ground beef 80/20
1 (1lb) bag frozen mixed vegetables, thawed
2 packets of dry Brown Gravy Mix
1 medium onion
Olive Oil
2 bottles Guinness Beer
2 Tablespoons Tomato Paste
2 cups Sharp Cheddar Cheese
3 pounds baking potatoes
¼- ½ cup milk
1 stick butter
Salt and pepper

Preheat oven to 375

To make Potato filling...
Boil the potatoes in salted water until fork tender. Drain completely and place back in pot so all of the water evaporates.
In a medium mixing bowl, add butter and potatoes. Mash until smooth, while adding the milk for a medium consistency. Add salt and pepper.

Meat filling...
Cook and drain ground beef.
Place drained beef back in skillet and add 1 bottle of Guinness. Cook until beer has almost cooked out.

Add tomato paste to meat
In a medium sauce pan, prepare the brown gravy according to package directions,
however, use beer for half the liquid called for (1 cup water, 1 cup beer)
Pour gravy into meat mixture. And cook all together until you get a nice thick gravy.

In medium skillet with olive oil sauté onions until soft and translucent.
Add mixed vegetables to the onions and cook until warm throughout.

In a 2 quart baking dish, add meat as bottom layer, the add vegetables, and then add the mashed potatoes. Top with Shredded cheese.

Cook at 375 for about 20 minutes or until cheese in nice and bubbly

Dear reader

Thank you so much for reading **The Case of Dr. Dude,** the first book in the Michaela McPherson Mystery Series. I hope you enjoyed it. Since reviews are very important to Indie authors. I would be delighted if you would go to Amazon.com to review my book.

I always want to hear from and connect with my readers. Please feel free to contact me at any time with questions, ideas for new books, or just plain anything. I am happy to answer any questions. Feel free to email me at judithlucciwrites@gmail.com or use my contact form on my website, www.judithlucci.com.

Once again, many thanks for reading my book! You can continue the series with the next book in this series, The Case of the Dead Dowager.

Judith

Made in the USA
Columbia, SC
03 September 2019